PAWNS TO PLAYERS

A MATCH FOR THE WHITE HOUSE

A NOVEL BY JACK RANDOM

CROW DOG PRESS
TURLOCK CA USA

Pawns to Players:

A Match for The White House

A Novel by Jack Random

The Chess Series, Part II

Published by
Crow Dog Press
1241 Windsor Court
Turlock CA 95380

Cover artwork by Ray Miller.

ISBN-13: 978-0692701294
ISBN-10: 069270219X

PAWNS TO PLAYERS

A Match for The White House

*To the greatest form of government
the world has ever known:
Democracy.*

PLAYERS

Solana Rothschild, Heir to the Rothschild Fortune
William Bates, American Entrepreneur

WHITE PIECES

King: Shelby Duran, Democratic Presidential Candidate
Queen: Winfred Holmes, Campaign Manager
Castle: Lawrence McClure, Fundraiser/Entrepreneur
Castle: Sophia Cantu, Fundraiser/CEO
Knight: Dorothea Vargas, DNC Chair
Knight: Julia Sand, Political Operative
Bishop: Llewyn Davis, Fundraiser
Bishop: Chauncey Davis, Regional Campaign Manager
Pawn: Richard Dawson, Pollster
Pawn: Moses Dunn, Private Investigator
Pawn: Cato Mackay, Reporter
Pawn: Cassidy James, Campaign Volunteer
Pawn: Lorena Moreno, Aide to Chauncey Davis
Pawn: Jorge Ramos, Operative
Pawn: Jose Velasquez, Operative

BLACK PIECES

King: Daniel J. Wynn, Republican Presidential Candidate
Queen: Jacoby Morris, Campaign Manager
Castle: Jim Duke, Director Americans for America First
Castle: Rudolf McCall, Media Mogul Freedom Network
Knight: Charles Rogan, Political Operative
Knight: Ralph Peterson, RNC Chair
Bishop: Robert Joseph Lee, Fundraiser
Bishop: Nolan Gray, Operative
Pawn: Rowan Darby, Operative
Pawn: Jolene Dixon, Operative
Pawn: Sandy Merrill, Operative
Pawn: Jimmy Hill, Operative
Pawn: Darren McGhee: Operative
Pawn: Jed Parson, Operative
Pawn: Mary Jo Perez, Operative

Knights and bishops, queens and castles, they are all pawns to players, subject to sacrifice and eminently replaceable.

Sebastian Rothschild

1

PLAYERS

Selecting the Board

The world is a beautiful place, particularly to those who can choose to be anywhere at any time for as long as they desire. William, who loved city life with its hustle of humanity, its art museums and historical sites, cafes and restaurants, had already been everywhere he could imagine wanting to be but Solana, younger and more adventurous, had a great many destinations still on her wish list. Solana loved the great cities as well but she yearned to see and breathe and taste the natural wonders of the world. She wanted to scale the heights of Mount Everest, explore the ruins of Machu Picchu and ancient Rome, bathe in waves of the northern lights in Iceland, tour the Taj Mahal and the Great Pyramids of Egypt, camp at Victoria Falls in Africa and absorb the splendor of Australia's Great Barrier Reef.

In time they would do all this and more but for now they had business, the kind of business that was to them pleasurable, pure intellectual pursuit. They had a problem to solve or rather a complex puzzle, a multi-variant equation to pull apart, examine and reassemble. They required focus more than inspiration. They needed a place where distractions could be minimized. They needed isolation.

So Solana booked a cabin in the Alps, fully stocked with supplies that would allow them a week without interruption. The view was breathtaking; it could not be denied. But it was nothing new to either Solana or Willy and neither wished to be surrounded by the mundane. After a day or two the aesthetic grandeur would fade into the background and they would be able to concentrate on the game at hand.

They had already enacted the grandest experiment in the history of human intellectual pursuit. They had created history. They had transferred a chess match to a real world board. They had carried the match to its logical conclusion, its end game, a resignation under threat of imminent mate, and that accomplishment had suffused their souls with profound gratification. But there were flaws in the match, something lost or distorted in translation, and it haunted them.

Fundamentally, they had neglected the role of emotional attachment, an attachment that does not exist in the game itself. No matter how intricate the design, a black king is just a king, identical to its opposing piece in white. The game's resolution rests on the king's continued existence combined with the submission or destruction of the opposing king but there is nothing in the piece itself that elicits a sense of empathy or belonging. It is an inanimate object without values, character, principles, charm or moral compass.

They had made the mistake of choosing their own kings without considering the possibility that the opposing king might be an individual the player admired. That element of attachment or empathy, no matter how irrational, might subconsciously alter a player's strategy. For example, he or she might play for the draw or the resignation rather than attacking for the kill. The inner workings of the human mind are as unknowable as the deepest mystery.

As it happened Solana had admired her opposing king, the first Hispanic President of the United States, Jaime Marquez. Had it altered her play? She could not say for sure but the very fact that it entered her thoughts suggested that it might have. They had gone over every move to see if she might have chosen another path but they could come to no certain conclusion. It would forever remain in doubt.

They corrected the problem for a prospective future match by resolving to choose opposing kings subject to mutual consent. While emotions could not be eliminated entirely the revised procedure would be a significant improvement.

But there were other flaws that concerned them as well. For one, Solana had had to deal with a rogue queen in the desperate hours before resignation. In the game of chess, even a queen moved according to strict rules and only at the command of a player. Desperate humans acted irrationally and unpredictably. Solana had acted quickly to mitigate the infraction but it left a shadow. Had she failed to act the Secretary of State and over two hundred fellow passengers on a commercial flight would likely be dead and the entire match nullified. She had no choice.

They both understood that as long as they continued the experiment, using real world characters in real world situations, the possibility of rogue characters and unauthorized moves would exist. They could only anticipate and act without delay to correct such transgressions as Solana had done. Like emotional engagement, it was a flaw that could only be mitigated, not eliminated.

Finally, there was the problem of pawn variability. Having decided early on the necessity of allowing a variety of persons to serve as individual pawns they nevertheless recognized the practice as a flaw to be avoided if possible. They believed they could limit variability by selecting a more limited playing board. Their inaugural board had encompassed the American political establishment, the intelligence community and European finance. The possibilities extended across both Europe and America. They were determined to narrow the field in their next match.

Perched on a teak balcony, looking out at the mystic snow-covered peaks, the lush green valley looming far below, Solana sighed.

"It's exhausting."

Willy knew exactly how she felt. For three days they had thrown themselves into the process of analysis, synthesis, deconstruction and problem solving so it did not seem so ironic that two individuals who had not engaged in more than an hour of physical labor in their lives were now spent. If you are someone who has worked double shifts waiting tables, pounded a hammer ten hours a day at a construction site or clocked time on the line in a cannery or production plant, you can be forgiven for not feeling sympathetic but they were in fact physically depleted. Mental exhaustion is manifest in every facet of the physical body, often centering in the lower back or shoulders.

Willy embraced her from behind and massaged her neck and shoulders.

"I know it is, dear. But it is gratifying."

"Is it?" she replied. "I wonder."

He turned her so that he could gaze into the deep reservoir of her dark brown eyes, eyes that held the power to both possess and inspire him.

"In all of recorded history, few have altered the chain of events more profoundly in such a brief period of time than we have. No one has achieved what we have achieved, transferring the world's most perfect game into a living, breathing reality."

"How would we know?"

Solana's mind invariably cut to the core. How would they know? How would anyone know? That being the case, what difference did it make? Why would they spend so much time and effort, expending vast resources, if no one would ever know what they had done?

It reminded Willy of former president Bill Clinton's explanation as to why he had allowed himself to become enmeshed in the Monica Lewinsky affair. His answer: Because I could. Translation: Because it did not occur to him that he might be caught. It begged the question: What else did you do because you could? It was an absurd answer really. It hardly scratched the surface but it would have to stand. The public accepted it and the former president moved on.

He knew that Solana would never be satisfied with such an answer though it came close to the truth within his own psyche: He did it because he enjoyed manipulating powerful individuals who in turn enjoyed manipulating other less powerful individuals. He did it for his love of the game. Solana's motivations ran much deeper than his or her father's. He knew and accepted it.

"There may come a time to tell the story, my dear, but that time is far, far away."

"Do you think so?"

He could not be sure if she referred to the telling or the timeline but he assumed the former. They had kept meticulous records of the inaugural match with the idea of preserving the story for posterity. Perhaps in time they would contract a writer to chronicle the events in narrative form. It would be published as fiction but with such detail that inquiring minds could not but wonder.

"Of course," he replied.

She pressed her lips to his and held his embrace. She could not imagine her life without him or without the game.

They enjoyed an excellent dinner (delivered from a nearby resort) and indulged in a flash match, thirty seconds per move, less a test of strategy than an exercise to keep their minds tuned to the rhythm and tenor of chess. Then they sat down with a bottle of Beaujolais before a warm fire and began a discussion of the critical issue yet to be decided: the field of play or as they termed it, the chessboard.

The possibilities were not endless but many and varied. Each had its advantages and disadvantages. Each had a distinct set of variables. They wanted something of importance (after all, their first match had been sweeping) and yet not so broad that they risked losing control. It had to be a subject area with clear sides, good versus evil, pro versus con, black versus white; it was the nature of the game. The realm of underworld crime intrigued them. If they could pit one crime lord against another (perhaps in Mexico or Eastern Europe) they would have no sympathy for the fallen. On the other hand violence would be a given and Solana still balked at the notion of blood on her hands. Still, the idea that they could put a major drug lord or human trafficking cartel out of business attracted them both. Then again, the victor would absorb the vanquished and the world would move on as if nothing had changed.

They discussed international corporate finance, wars in the Middle East, terrorist organizations, even sporting events but in the end the realm most suited to their needs was presidential politics. They were particularly intrigued by the race for the American presidency.

President Jaime Marquez was in the final years of his second term and candidates were aligning themselves within the party structure for a run through the primaries to the general election. By most accounts it was wide open and, therefore, ideal for a game of chess. It would present unique challenges in that other players (party bosses, political operatives and billionaire sponsors) would be engaged. For the match to work properly their chosen kings would have to survive the primaries and secure their party's nomination. If all went well, Solana and Willy would, in effect, choose the next American president.

Solana smiled in sweet anticipation and Willy reciprocated. They never felt so alive or impassioned as when the board was set and all possibilities opened to them. For one of them there would come an even more intense experience, the moment before mate, but that emotion would not be shared.

Solana's skin tingled and Willy felt his desire rising from deep within. They had one more bit of business before the first move. They had to identify the kings to mutual satisfaction. Then they would engage a single match for the

16

White House.

Willy filled their glasses and proposed a toast:

"Here's to the next President of the United States of America!"

2

KING'S PAWN TO FOUR

Political campaigns attract a variety of volunteers. Some are nameless worker bees that make calls, answer phones, walk precincts, run errands and put up signs on lawns and fences. They are loyal to the party and its chosen candidates. They receive the vicarious pleasure of being allowed in the company of movers and shakers.

Others solicit contributions and design websites, field test ideas and issues, and are sometimes invited to policy and strategy sessions. They are skilled workers with greater ambitions. They tend to float between campaigns and candidates, seeking winners and seizing opportunities to rise in the chain of command. They are managers, pundits and politicos in training. They know it is better to serve at the periphery of a winning campaign than in the center of a losing campaign.

Cassie James was among the latter. Still in her twenties, she had graduated with a Bachelor's in political science and completed her advanced degree at George Washington University while working on two successful congressional campaigns. She had offers for paid positions but she set her sights on a presidential campaign. Until recently word on the street said Secretary of State Shelby Duran would not run. She had no experience in electoral politics, had never run for office, and had no desire to do so now. So they said. In the last few weeks something had changed dramatically. An exploratory committee was formed without the secretary's blessings. What it discovered was almost unprecedented in modern politics: She had a strong current of support from the ground to the penthouse.

The grassroots, the base, the activists and idealists, loved her for what she had accomplished at the State Department: She had help keep the world at peace while advancing the cause of human rights around the globe and she played a key role in thwarting an effort by the intelligence community to establish its own power base, circumventing the authority of government. She fought for fair trade, equal pay, fair wages, social justice and environmental responsibility. Of course the base loved her and wanted her to run. The surprise came in the astounding level of support for a Duran presidency from the economic elite. Given her policies and positions, the elite stood to lose a great deal if she took the Oval Office and yet all indications were she would attract greater contributions than any other candidate.

Cassie was not alone in wondering why? Was it possible Duran was not what she seemed? She would not be the first candidate to be converted to the corporate cause once elected but she was not even a candidate. She came from a business background, international banking and commerce, but she had always espoused a progressive economic philosophy. The Republican side would not hesitate to label her a socialist. How and why she would attract big money at this early stage was the mystery of the moment and Cassie wanted an answer.

She received an invitation from the exploratory committee to join them in New Hampshire as a paid political consultant. Her instinct said yes, this was the opportunity she desired, but she had responsibilities. She had an overpriced apartment in Washington and a desk job at the Smithsonian. Others of her type would kill for such a position. She was blessed to have an employer who understood her interests and ambitions. Her supervisor knew she might leave on short notice if the right opportunity came along. But this opportunity seemed altogether too sketchy. The New Hampshire primary was nearly two years away and the position depended not only on continued funding but also on the candidate actually becoming a candidate.

She hesitated and lingered on the edge declining the position when her supervisor summoned her to a meeting in his office. Mr. Thomson, a pleasant man who had long lost the battle for hair supremacy to balding gray, welcomed her with a smile.

"Ms. James, please sit."

She did, still trying figure out the reason for this meeting, taking some comfort in his manner but knowing he would be pleasant regardless of its purpose.

"How long have you been with us, Ms. James?"

"Almost three months."

"Are you enjoying your time with us?"

Okay, she thought, this is getting weird.

"Yes."

"Let me put your mind at ease. We're very satisfied with your work. We'd like you to stay as long as you'd like."

If he's coming on to me, she thought, I'd have to quit. And then I'll file a complaint.

"It's come to my attention," he continued, "that you've received an offer of employment in your area of interest. I simply want you to know: If you accept that position and it doesn't work out, your job here will be waiting."

She was stunned. How in the world would he know? And why would he care? He smiled like Mr. Rogers, an impossible kindness, and she recoiled. She didn't trust him and yet she knew her best play was to go along.

"I do have had an offer," she replied. "It's a very interesting offer but I was considering turning it down because I value my job here and I didn't want to lose it."

He nodded as if he understood all along.

"That's what I wanted to tell you, Ms. James. You won't lose your job. You're free to pursue your dream. We understand."

Cassie stood and extended her hand.

"Thank you, Mr. Thompson. I will take the position and I appreciate your support and understanding."

"Very good. I'll file the paper work."

She went home and packed a suitcase. She accepted the position by email and boarded a plane for New Hampshire the following day.

QUEEN'S PAWN TO SIX

Every campaign of substance has its moles, spies and saboteurs. The bigger the campaign, the more likely an infestation of lowlife becomes. Some spies hide in plain sight, attending rallies and events large and small, recording everything, hoping to capture some morsel of inappropriate language or betrayal of principle or a moment behind the curtains when the candidate speaks his honest thoughts (as in Mitt Romney's 47% are freeloaders comment to a group of privileged contributors circa 2012).

Rowan Darby had worked as a stalwart operative for the Grand Old Party since the elder Bush captured the White House in another time and place that no one really remembers. There were no cell phones then, no twitter accounts, no button sized cameras (except in British spy movies) and no worldwide web. CNN was the only 24-hour news program then and the New York Times stood as the ultimate arbiter of what qualified as newsworthy.

By all that squares old Darby should have retired to Florida long ago but too many party bosses liked keeping him around if only for his occasional witticisms and stories about the good old days. Still, he was among the most closely watched individuals in the political world because where he went money invariably followed. Darby was a leading indicator of party loyalty and corporate sponsorship.

So when Darby signed on as a senior consultant to the exploratory committee of Manhattan billionaire Daniel J. Wynn, aka Danny Diamond, it attracted the attention of every operative in both parties. Wynn was anything but a party favorite and he had no need of corporate sponsorship. He had never held office and though he had threatened a run for the White House on more than one occasion no one really took him seriously until now. Hiring Darby was a smart move if you wanted to capture attention and it signaled that Wynn had someone knowledgeable behind his candidacy.

Rated one of the nation's fifty richest individuals, Wynn made his name and reputation on a reality TV show that inevitably ended with Danny Diamond lowering his hammer on the career of some wanabe entrepreneur. America loved him once a week. He appealed to the working class despite business practices that capitalized on job exportation and exacerbated the divide between the elite and the rest of us by gutting labor unions. His hardcore style and New Yorker attitude appealed to the common man like few in the political establishment could. He was tall and thick, a big man, with an artificial tan and a bizarre yellow comb-over that made you think he was trying in vain to recapture his youth.

He welcomed Darby to Team Wynn with a firm handshake and a thirty-minute round table on his strategy for the primary season.

"The way I see it," said the big man, his hands clutched behind his head, "we soft-pedal Iowa and hit 'em hard in New Hampshire. We win there and run the table. What do you think, Darby?"

Darby looked around the table, three average looking men and two very attractive women ranging from late twenties to early forties, none with experience beyond the city of New York, and tried to determine whether or not Wynn was serious. It seemed apparent he was.

"Well, that's one strategy."

Wynn cocked his head and leaned in.

"I take it you have another?"

The old man had been around too long to care. People still valued his input because he didn't parse words or bow down to authority. He hadn't kowtowed to presidents and

America's favorite billionaire celebrity would not intimidate him now.

"I knew a big city mayor who made quite a name for himself. Trouble is he started taking his press clippings seriously. He figured he was the exception. He'd all but skip Iowa, place third in New Hampshire and stage a miraculous comeback in the great state of Florida. By the time he left Des Moines he was yesterday's news. You don't skip Iowa, Mr. Wynn, and you don't soft-pedal anywhere. You're in or you're out. If you're in, you're all in."

Wynn waited and looked at each of his advisors as they avoided direct eye contact.

"And you told me Rowan Darby was over the hill! By God, I like you, Darby! You're the man who's going to take me from the penthouse to the White House! Just Wynn, baby! Just Wynn! Welcome aboard!"

Darby nodded, realizing he'd alienating everyone at the table except the big man. He'd have to correct that over the next week or so if he was going to make his mark. What they didn't know and didn't suspect was that Darby was working for a rival candidate. At least he assumed it was a rival. Someone had contacted him by hand-delivered message. He had encountered some financial problems, one bad investment after another, so when presented an opportunity to climb out of the hole he took it. An unknown party deposited a large sum in his bank account with the promise of more for useable information.

He finished the round table making it a point to agree with whatever ideas, good or bad, the billionaire's advisors offered. When they wrapped it up, making plans for another session in the evening over drinks, Darby smiled. He had his place in the circle. The big man valued his input and the others felt he was someone they could work with. It was only a matter of time before they gave him the information he needed.

WHITE PAWN TO QUEEN FOUR

One of the many peculiarities of the American system for choosing a president is the disproportionate importance given to the states of Iowa and New Hampshire. For reasons no functioning human being wants to recall, Iowa is the first major event on the road to the White House. It is the reason corn production is heavily subsidized and ethanol still exists. (Whoever sold the idea of growing tons of inedible corn for the purpose of converting it into a burning liquid in a process that requires more energy than it produces should either win the Nobel or a lifetime of free lodging at Guantanamo Bay.)

The Iowa caucus is where candidates go to prove they can stand on bales of hay, eat mass quantities of county fair cuisine, attend rodeos, listen to country music with a tap of the toe, cheer NASCAR drivers as if they cared, and generally appear as though there is no other place on earth they would rather be until the last vote is counted and the last campaign bus has left the state. In other words, it's where candidates must prove they are real people by pretending to be what they are not.

The caucus is less an election and more a series of town meetings, gathered in churches and schools and civic centers across the state, that end up selecting the frontrunners and also-rans for the presidency. A more absurd process for anointing the next leader of the western world cannot be imagined, yet anyone who aspires to the highest office must yield to this solemn reality: If it don't play in Iowa, it won't make it to Super Tuesday.

A veteran of two campaigns, pollster and consultant

Richard Dawson knew all about Iowa. He grew up in Indiana, which is a lot like Iowa but with more letters. He knew that the best way to win in Iowa was not through television advertising and definitely not through traditional campaign stops and stump speeches. You won in Iowa by getting the pulse of the people and stepping to the same beat. You never rush and you never shuffle. Iowans walk with a purpose and very little rhythm. They want to know that you worry about the same problems, that you're angry with the same villains, that you love the warriors even if you hate the war and that your family is more important than all the oil in Saudi Arabia.

Dawson liked Secretary of State Shelby Duran. Having watched her navigate the impregnable mazes of foreign policy and domestic politics, he admired her as much for her skill as for her principles. She stood alone in her mastery of global economics and foreign relations. Among the field of viable prospective candidates for president, she alone had not already sold her soul. He wanted her to run and he wanted her to win. The problem, of course, was that she was not a politician. Running for president was not a learn-as-you-go proposition. She had to hit the ground on a dead run and she could not afford to trip. Iowa would be her first test and it would be less comprehensible than the foreign minister of Azerbaijan. In short, she would need a translator (or rather, an interpreter) and Dawson had all the essential qualifications for the job.

So he looked up her support group online to volunteer his services. They welcomed his inquiry with a great deal of enthusiasm and absolutely no moxy. Moxy is what people have when they walk into a biker bar knowing what to expect and how to respond when it happens. They didn't have it. So he tried again and again until he contacted a staffer in New Hampshire by the name of Cassidy James.

"You made that up, didn't you?" he said on the phone.

"What's that?"

"Your name: Cassidy James."

"Afraid not. You can call me Cass."

"Look Cass, I don't know how much experience you have but I hope it's more than some of your colleagues."

"I assure you, I know what I'm doing."

"Good. Then you can appreciate what I have to offer."

"What do you have to offer, Mr. Dawson?"

"I'm an experienced pollster and strategist and I've worked Iowa before."

There was a moment when she realized that the person she was talking to was in fact someone she had encountered before. They had both been in Iowa during the last presidential run. She was working for the president's re-election, he for an upstart libertarian on the Republican side. It did not inspire confidence.

"I remember you. You were working for the enemy."

"Gregory was hardly the enemy. He had about as much chance at becoming president as the village librarian."

"His prospects have improved."

Indeed they had. Ryan Gregory had parlayed his unsuccessful presidential run into a successful campaign for the United States Senate. That alone qualified him for a second run for the presidency.

"And you worked for him."

"I wanted the Republican Party to listen to a libertarian voice. In that sense we made an impact."

"He'll run again."

"Not with my help."

She sympathized with his position and knew he was right. Gregory had forced the GOP to acknowledge its libertarian roots even though its policies, especially in regard to civil liberties, remained antithetical. That he would run again was all but certain. She had to consider the possibility that Dawson was still loyal to him.

"So now you want to work for Duran. That's a little surprising, Mr. Dawson. Do you mind if I ask why?"

"I worked for Marquez in his first run. He didn't need my help in the second. I haven't changed, Ms. James. I'm as progressive as you are and I like Duran."

It made sense. However much campaigns like to pretend everything is at stake, Marquez had a clear road to re-election. He certainly didn't need any help in the primaries.

"I'm not in charge here, Mr. Dawson, but I know how much we need your services. I'll do what I can."

"Who is in charge?"

"That's a little hard to say right now. I'll get back to you."

"Good enough. When your people get your act together, I'll be on the ground in Iowa."

"I appreciate that, Mr. Dawson, and I thank you."

"One last question: Is she running?"

"That's the question of the day. The answer is: I don't know. As far as I'm aware, nobody knows just yet. Not even Duran."

BLACK KNIGHT TO KING'S BISHOP SIX

When Charles Rogan showed up at the annual Fall Firefighters Fundraiser, a combination bake sale and social in Concord, New Hampshire, the political world took note. Rogan had no political allegiance and specialized in sabotage. There are a number of ways to win a campaign but a thousand ways to lose one. Rogan generally found one of the latter, exploited it and moved on to his next client. Rogan and his ilk usually came into the game at a later stage when the field had already been narrowed. His services did not come cheap. What was the point of eliminating a candidate if the natural process of attrition achieved the same result without the cost? That Rogan showed up this early in the season meant that someone was extremely worried about a particular candidate and felt it would be easier or wiser to strike early before anyone saw it coming.

The smart money said the target was Shelby Duran. Despite her expressed lack of interest or perhaps because of it she continued to lead the early polling by a sizable margin. That would change of course as soon as she announced (if she announced) but someone was clearly worried enough to hire the noted saboteur. The question was who?

All of the prospective contenders had professionals scouting the field. All except Shelby Duran. Her exploratory campaign consisted of a hodgepodge of volunteers with a surplus of enthusiasm but a distinct lack of experience. If Rogan had his sights set on disrupting the Duran campaign he could expect little resistance.

He knew all the players in both parties and moved easily

in their circles. He made a point of sharing enough useful information that everyone wanted a word with him. At the Firefighters Fundraiser he made inquiries about the various campaigns, including Duran's. The consensus seemed to be that Duran's people were in constant chaos, a hopelessly idealistic gathering of neophytes who didn't have a clue, with the notable exception of Cassidy James.

Rogan spotted her enjoying a chat with a Democratic Party official and gradually moved in for a word. Cass recognized him at once.

"Well, I was wondering how long it would take you to get to me."

He smiled and took her hand, pleased that she had heard of him. He was older but pleasant in appearance with his neatly parted black hair and stylish gray suit standing in contrast to the Dark Knight he was reputed to be.

"It is a pleasure to make your acquaintance, Ms. James. I've heard good things."

"Word on the street is you're after my candidate."

"I wasn't aware you had a candidate. Do you really think she'll run?"

Cass took a breath. She had answered the question countless times since her arrival in New Hampshire but she still didn't know how to respond. She could only be honest.

"I wish I knew, Mr. Rogan. We're operating on the Field of Dreams theory: If we build it, she will come."

"An interesting theory for a Hollywood movie, less so for a political campaign."

"Just the same she leads the polls."

"It's easy to be popular when you're above the fray."

"Granted."

She tried to read his intent, knowing – like a master poker player – that he could not be read. Would he offer any clue to his purpose here? She saw no downside in making a direct inquiry.

"So what brings you to New Hampshire, Mr. Rogan?"

"Aside from your personal charm?"

She almost blushed, finding his charm surprising. She realized any further inquiry was pointless but she continued for the pleasure of it.

"Aside from that."

"My employer has business here."

"Who is your employer?"

"That is confidential."

"What is your employer's business?"

"It is multi-faceted. For one, I'm scouting talent."

"Have you found any?"

He nodded and let his eyes rove around the hall. He noted that more than a few interested eyes were observing them. It pleased him.

"Let me offer you a hypothetical, Ms. James. Let us assume that the unlikely does not come to pass, that Secretary Duran does not choose to run. Would you be open to working for another candidate?"

"Are you tempting me, Mr. Rogan?"

"We're just dancing, Ms. James, but I can't help thinking: Working for an imaginary candidate can't pay very well."

"It's not about the money. It's about the cause."

"When one cause falls, another rises."

He was nothing if not relentless. It reminded her of a child at a certain age when the last word had to be spoken by her. She did not wish to be that child.

"I'll let you go, Mr. Rogan. I'm sure you have less imaginary candidates to worry about."

He smiled. He understood and admired her. If he tried hard enough he could remember a time when even he had a code of conduct and a vision of a better world. Those days had slipped into the hidden recesses of his psyche where he did not dare glimpse. He liked Cassidy James but, however he felt, it would not prevent him from taking her out if that's what his job required.

WHITE KNIGHT TO QUEEN'S BISHOP THREE

Rumors across the beltway are the life force of politics. Media pundits feed on them like scavengers on a dead horse and political operatives count on them. The rumor that Secretary of State Shelby Duran would announce her intention to run for president had made the rounds, gathering the interest and support that Winfred Holmes relied on. Her position in the polls remained strong and the ad hoc committee promoting her candidacy enjoyed an acceleration of small contributions from individual supporters.

But as the deadline for inclusion in the first round of debates neared, rumors were not sufficient to nail down the support of major contributors. The players in American politics would not be content to remain on the sidelines for long once the process began. Those who secured initial investments would hold a decisive advantage. Without a major contributor no candidacy (with the exception of the independently wealthy Daniel J. Wynn) could survive.

Holmes dispatched Julia Sands, one of his very best and most persuasive operatives, to Silicon Valley with the objective of convincing one or more of the nation's new rich to sign on with Shelby Duran. Her first stop was a meeting with visionary Lawrence McClure who had financed half a dozen startups that turned into multi-billion dollar companies. Holding a seat on the board of each, his net worth landed him a place on the Forbes list of the wealthiest individuals on the planet. If McClure committed to Duran, others would surely follow. The trouble of course was that it was difficult to commit to a candidate who had not yet declared her intention to run. It was like betting on a horse that had never run a race or a company that did not yet exist. McClure was rich and famous for doing both.

Ms. Sands arrived at Gonzo.com, a modest two-story building in Santa Clara, in the early evening. McClure kept odd hours and Gonzo was his odd duck baby. Rumor had it he spent a million dollars to buy out the name from a porn site in honor of the late Hunter S. Thompson, the notorious inventor of gonzo journalism. The rumor was true except for the amount. It had cost only three hundred grand, not a significant amount for McClure although he considered it ironic that Thompson would not have objected to the term and concept he invented being usurped by a porn site. He would have loved it.

She walked through the newsroom where some twenty Gonzo journalists and a handful of photographers engaged each other in conversation while manning their computer terminals. Gonzo journalism required reporters to become a part of the story they were reporting. Rejecting the objective standard of traditional media, they engaged, they took sides and exposed themselves to risk. Gonzo journalists had been assaulted, jailed, kidnapped and shot at while covering protests, riots and wars. They accepted the risk as a part of the job.

Few in the business world considered Gonzo a viable investment but the numbers revealed a different story. As the established news organizations, pressured by profit motivated international corporate megaliths, reduced costs by releasing correspondents and ground crews, the consuming public looked elsewhere for the real story. More and more turned to Gonzo and a handful of grassroots media organizations.

McClure descended a wooden staircase just as Ms. Sands approached the receptionist desk. Tall and well built, a rough beard and medium-length shaggy hair, he didn't fit the mold people wanted to apply to men in his position. He marked his own path and held to it like a man on a spiritual journey.

He stopped halfway down and waved.

"Julia Sands! Come on up!"

She climbed the stairs and followed him into his cluttered enclave, most of it a tribute to Hunter S. Thompson. Gazing at the walls she found it a little overwhelming, the books, magazines, photographs featuring Johnny Depp and the Gonzo himself, movie posters of *Fear and Loathing in Las Vegas*, and blown up copies of the Doonesbury comic strip with the Duke, an unscrupulous character based loosely on Thompson. It belonged in a museum, a piece of America's underappreciated culture.

"Are you a fan?" he smiled.

"I am. He was one of the most insightful political writers of his time."

"Not the first thing that comes to mind for most people but I agree. I loved his writings in the Rolling Stone on the Nixon campaign in 72."

"Fear and Loathing in Tampa."

"You are a fan. Now I know why Holmes sent you."

"He sent me to take some of your money."

"Please!" He held his hand up as if to say: Not now! "Have you had dinner?"

"No, I just got off the plane."

"Where are you staying?"

"The Hilton at Union Square."

"Excellent! I've made reservations at the Café de la Presse."

He escorted her out of his office, down the stairs and through the pressroom, acknowledging his reporters with a smile and a wave as he called someone to bring his car, a Toyota Prius, to the front of the building.

He handed the parking attendant a twenty and drove like a video game madman down Highway 101 into the city. Along the way he peppered her with questions concerning her wine and food preferences, cinema, art, theater, books and sports preferences, anything but politics. She took it in stride, answering as honestly as she could and wondering if her journey would be feckless. Holmes warned her McClure was eccentric but also fascinating and politically engaged. She had seen profound evidence of the former yet little of the latter.

They arrived at Union Square where tourists gathered and shoppers swarmed like crazed ants to the many swanky shops in the neighborhood. He parked at the Hilton, allowing Ms. Sands to check in, and they walked among the throng to the bistro. Seated in the outdoor pavilion she felt immediately at home. Animated conversations concerning the politics of the day rang out from all corners. Disagreement centered on whether the president was too moderate or too timid to do what needed to be done, countered by claims of an obstructionist congress that thwarted every effort.

They ordered a bottle of Merlot and settled in to enjoy the banter.

"This is my kind of place," said Ms. Sands.

"I thought it might be."

She took a moment to drill into his thoughts through the gateway of his eyes. A universe of wonder and intrigue lay hidden there.

"I was beginning to think you were retreating from politics."

He laughed in a knowing, subtle manner. "Gonzo? Apolitical? I don't think so. I just wanted to watch you, get to know you a little before we engaged."

"Foreplay?"

"An apt analogy."

"Fred told me you were with us. Was he wrong?"

"I love Shelby Duran. Not many know the full extent of what she's done for this country. I do. At least I think I do. As far as business goes, she's a fierce defender of intellectual rights. That's blood. No question she has my support. The real question and the reason my colleagues are not willing to throw down is: Is she running?"

She hesitated. Fred had instructed her to state emphatically that she was running. He didn't intend for her to deceive McClure; he believed it. But she still had doubts and the very fact that she hesitated conveyed those doubts.

"Fred is certain that she is."

"But you're not so sure."

"Winfred Holmes is never wrong."

McClure took measure of the people around him and the discussions that captivated both him and them. Things were much better now than they were when Marquez was first elected but there was so much more to do. Even in San Francisco, one of the most affluent communities in America, the prevalent mood was discontent. People were angry at the one percent. People were angry at corporate domination of the political process. People were angry at the still unfathomable discrepancy between the elite and the working class. People were angry at the cost of medical care, police misconduct and the painfully slow process of reducing carbon emissions and protecting the water supply.

He knew a president could not change everything overnight. Marquez had proven as much. But he also knew how much harm a single president could do. Everything he believed and stood up for told him the nation needed Shelby Duran as the next president. His job as he perceived it was to make sure that she ran and to provide the resources she needed to win.

"Let me offer you a scenario," he said. "Tomorrow there's a terrorist attack by some foreign entity. Chicago, Boston, San Francisco, it doesn't matter. We know who did it and we know what nation they came from. Under those circumstances, how could the Secretary of State resign to run for president?"

Ms. Sands took a breath, knowing he was right, knowing that there would always be some crisis in foreign affairs that could prevent Secretary Duran from running. The more she delayed the less likely her candidacy became.

36

"For what it's worth, I agree with you."

"I though you might. You're a smart woman, Ms. Sands. Fred is a smart man. But if *we* know this, Duran's enemies know it as well. With so much at stake, don't think they wouldn't resort to something nefarious. They would."

"I'll talk to Fred. He'll talk to the Secretary. That's how it works for now."

They enjoyed dinner almost as much as they enjoyed each other. With their pressing business out of the way, they talked without editing on every issue, controversy and concern they could think of, always finding a common ground. By the time they walked back to the hotel both felt they had establish the beginnings of an enduring friendship, the kind of friendship that could develop into something more interesting. That possibility, confined to their minds and exchanged in their eyes, would have to wait for a more opportune time, a time when neither had expectations of the other beyond personal affection. As they hugged and said goodbye in the lobby, McClure delivered the promise she had hoped to bring back to Washington.

"I've set up an account earmarked: Duran for President. I guarantee you she will not lose the nomination or the White House for lack of financing. But she needs to resign now and announce her candidacy. If she doesn't, the opportunity will slip away like a brilliant idea lost in mitigation."

7

BLACK PAWN TO KING'S KNIGHT SIX

Someone has to occupy the bottom of the food chain, the expendable foot soldier, the entry-level errand runner, the girl or gal Friday, the first to run down to Starbucks for coffee and a tart. Jimmy Hill filled that role for the Alonzo campaign, where everyone knew him as an amiable, quiet young man who never hesitated to fulfill menial needs without hesitation. If anyone had bothered to engage him in conversation they might have found him interesting, politically knowledgeable and eager to advance in the political world. No one had.

When the people in charge of the campaign thought of him at all, they wondered why he showed up every day. They shuffled him some pocket money now and again but he was not on the payroll. They figured he was a political groupie who enjoyed being around the men and women who made history. How he made a living did not concern them. If all went well and he was still around when the chill of winter gave way to the fresh warmth of spring, maybe they would find the money to hire him. Until then he was on his own.

With nearly eight months to go before the Iowa Straw Poll, the first test of a campaign's ground game, politicking was a backroom affair consisting of organizational meetings, polling, canvassing, soliciting contributions, collecting volunteer lists and the occasional private dinner where major contributors and players could share a room with the actual candidate.

Marco Alonzo had not been to Iowa since the midterm

election where he made public appearances with Republican candidates for statewide office and claimed success for having done so. In truth it was a typical midterm landslide in which his participation may have bolstered his image locally but had no impact on the outcome.

Alonzo came back to Iowa for a private fundraiser in which his primary audience were representatives of the agricultural behemoth Monsanto, the world's leading creator and purveyor of genetically modified foods, including soy, rice, wheat and corn. Alonzo had one purpose: To assure Monsanto that he fully supported genetically modified foods in all forms. He embraced the message with every particle of his being.

He opened his remarks in pure pandering style.

"Hello Iowa! I know you're all busy eating your $500 dinners and don't let me interrupt you. I hear the three-headed salmon is particularly delicious this season."

A subdued guffaw surrendered to laughter all around.

"The rice pilaf has that special radiant glow."

Again, laughter.

"Seriously, I know that some of my opponents on the other side of the aisle, the wrong side, say that genetic modification of the food supply is the most dangerous experiment ever conducted on the human species. I say no, that would be democracy."

They nearly choked on their rice pilaf, they laughed so hard. It seemed clear to everyone in the room that Alonzo was their kind of candidate. He was one of them. He could make them laugh at themselves. He could eat their food and take a slap on the back. He could watch football or NASCAR and not have to pretend to be interested.

At the rear of the hall, unnoticed and unassuming, Jimmy Hill pretended to be interested. He was actually but not for the reasons the Alonzo campaign assumed. They were wrong about him. He was on the payroll. It just wasn't their payroll. He worked for a private consulting firm that had yet to declare its allegiance. His job was to collect uncomfortable and embarrassing moments, anything that could be used against a candidate, and deliver them to his employer.

Jimmy delivered lattes to the candidate and his staff shortly after the speech. He had recorded the speech and would record what followed. One of the staffers complimented the candidate on his presentation, noting that it seemed to go over exceptionally well. Another commented:

"So I take it we're all for genetically modified foods."

Alonzo smiled sarcastically and said: "You walk into a den of vipers, you tell them exactly what they want to hear."

A week later the tape would hit the web. The campaign would deny its authenticity and threaten a lawsuit for defamation. The site took the ad down but the damage was done. Alonzo would learn what more seasoned candidates already knew: You're never off record.

8

PLAYERS

Selecting the Kings

The tradition began at the Cannes Film Festival where Solana's father Sebastian Rothschild met and befriended the younger William Bates. By the end of the week they formed a deep, almost familial bond based on their mutual love of film and chess that would endure until the elder Rothschild's tragic demise when his private jet hit a random wind current over the Swiss Alps. The tragedy played out in Solana's mind too many times to count. It was one reason why she had chosen the Alps for their prior meeting.

Solana met Willy at her father's funeral where they formed their own bond and resolved to continue the tradition with her in her father's stead. Cannes remained a part of that tradition and there they returned for this critical final stage of preparation.

Unlike their contemplative week in the majestic Alps, here they welcomed a full array of distractions, most especially the films. It was the golden age of television. Production values had risen to the extent that a series on HBO, Netflix or Showtime could not be distinguished in quality from the most elaborate Hollywood film. The monopoly on innovation, acting-directing talent and technology had vanished leading Solana to believe that the entire film industry had entered its final days.

William acknowledged the ascent of television but he believed that film would endure by developing three-dimensional technology on a scale that television could not readily duplicate. He foresaw a time when the characters of a film would inhabit the same space as their audience, a sort of theater in the round for film. He also believed that actors would inevitably be replaced by holograms and that phenomenon would enable film to thrive for another generation.

Solana concurred but she saw no inherent reason that television could not develop the same technology in a relatively short time frame. They both agreed that eventually film would be confined to art spaces with a severely limited audience and they would mourn when that day arrived.

"What will become of Cannes?" asked Solana.

"Or the Academy Awards? Or Grauman's?"

"Perhaps they'll survive on a smaller scale for the nostalgic hearts."

"Perhaps we could sponsor them."

Solana smiled that wry grin that Willy understood as an expression of genuine affection. When the time came, they would do exactly that.

They glided through days from one screening room or grand auditorium to another, enjoying the films but lamenting a general absence of true greatness. There had been only a couple of films in recent years that captured their imagination and gave testament to genius. One was or at least appeared to be the first seamless full-length film in history. Directed by Mexican filmmaker Alejandro Gonzalez Inarritu *Birdman* defied convention and created an engaging cinematic experience. French Director Jean-Luc Godard provided the other exception in the appropriately titled *Goodbye to Language*. Though its plot defied description it left them with the sense that they had experienced something too profound for words. They had screened it three times, gathering new clues and hidden meaning on each occasion, and would do so again.

While the days and much of their evenings belonged to

film, at a certain point each evening they turned their attention to chess. More specifically, they focused on their own imminent real-world match and the problem of identifying their kings. The ideal candidate would be one whom the player embraced and would not hesitate to sacrifice others in defense. At the same time the opposing player would not hesitate to take that king down.

Taking what he considered a more objective approach, William found a wide range of possibilities acceptable. Viability as a candidate was his primary consideration. For Solana, however, who had experienced conflicting emotions in their inaugural match, the selection presented a greater challenge.

As the festival drove to its final day, their discussions narrowed the field to the point where they felt prepared to render their decisions. Sitting on the terrace of Willy's coastal estate, sun setting on the Mediterranean, Solana dreaming of far away places, Willy admiring her, their thoughts converged on the game and the task at hand.

"There is one thing on which we can both agree."

"The beauty of a setting sun, the quality of the wine?"

Her sense of humor rarely failed to seize an opportunity.

"The White King, my love. Secretary Duran."

"She's not running."

"She will."

"She's never run for any office."

"She's leading the polls."

"The polls are misleading."

Willy leaned back to enjoy the view, the richness of his Beaujolais and the charms of his mistress. He knew her. She admired the Secretary of State, his queen in the previous match, as much as or more than she did the president. She loved the way her mind worked and the tenacity she displayed when engaged in a cause. Solana only wanted to be persuaded. She offered the impression that accepting Duran as her king required compromise, a sacrifice that could be bartered against her choice of his king.

"I'm certainly open to suggestions."

"Warner would be interesting."

"She would indeed."

"Black of Ohio, Duvall of Massachusetts, even Andrews or Gregory as dark horse candidates."

"All worthy selections and all acceptable."

Solana poured more wine and gave him a knowing look. He was being exceptionally gracious. She knew him certainly as well as he knew her. She knew where this was going and she knew how it would end.

"You're saying basically that I can have my choice."

"I suppose I am."

"Then let's move on to your selection."

He laughed and poured more wine. The game had already begun. Like the extensive preparations for a championship match, the city, the setting, the lighting, the board and set design, all was a part of the game. Some masters said the game was won or lost before the first move.

"Can I assume you will be selecting from the Democratic side?"

"You can," she smiled. "Ironic, isn't it? A child of unimaginable wealth and privilege embracing the principles of social democracy. I despise Tony Blair for cutting the heart out of the Labor Party. I was forced to become a Liberal Democrat."

"Blair only followed Clinton's example. I would argue that any difference between the major parties is less substantive than rhetorical."

"Voices more knowledgeable than mine or yours have said the same but even a rhetorical difference is a difference."

They fell into contemplation as sunlight spread in a display of dying glory on the placid waters of the Mediterranean. At moments like these the miracle of life warmed even the coldest heart. They allowed it to play out before they resumed negotiations. Solana spoke first.

"I'll accept Shelby Duran as my king on the condition that you do not select Ryan Gregory."

"Deal."

"You weren't going to in any case."

"True."

"Shall I guess or would you like the privilege of naming him?"

"You're certain it's a man."

"I am."

"Sad, isn't it? If the Republicans could only find a Margaret Thatcher they could march to the White House with little resistance."

"Your choice?"

"Daniel J. Wynn."

"Danny Diamond?"

"Dear God, I think I've managed to surprise you."

"You do like a challenge."

"It's true. I do. But don't think I would choose a king if I didn't believe I could win. I'm an American, my dear. I know how deeply my fellow citizens are disenchanted. They despise the political class. They're primed and ready for an outsider: Just Wynn, baby!"

Solana wondered if he was playing her a fool. She expected him to rescind his selection any moment and submit his real choice. But he made it clear he was not joking. He had only made his decision in the last 48 hours, leaning at times to either former Governor Ellis Pierce or Senator Marco Alonzo, the boys of Florida. He gave the fat man from Pennsylvania some consideration buy only Danny Diamond gave him the thrill of having produced a viable and original thought. The more he thought about it the more he liked it. He could win with Wynn.

"He carries his share of baggage," he said. "But he's tough, he appeals to the working man and he's not afraid to play hardball."

"Is that a baseball metaphor? I've never really

understood America's sports obsession."

"You're being modest. Americans have football. England has soccer. As for baseball, you can't understand our politics without understanding baseball. Football is war. Baseball is chess."

"We have cricket."

"Not the same."

"Granted. What baseball is to America, cricket is to England. So be it."

She poured wine into both glasses and proposed a toast.

"Businessman Daniel J. Wynn versus Secretary of State Shelby Duran! May the best player win!"

They drank and let the tension release from their bodies with the last glimmer of sunlight. The moon was almost full, casting a dark blue hue on all it touched. They would savor this moment for a very long time. The board was set, their chosen kings were in place and all God's children awaited the next move.

All other pieces (knights, bishops, rooks, pawns and the all-important queens) would only be revealed as they came into play. This was the moment Solana and Willy lived for and they hoped, perhaps irrationally, that Sebastian was watching from his castle in the clouds.

9

WHITE BISHOP TO KING THREE

There is no greater truth in modern American politics than this: A successful run for the presidency costs a great deal of money. Any politician who enters the fray enters it knowing that he or she will have to spend in excess of a billion dollars before the last ballot is counted. That kind of money doesn't come from small contributions. It doesn't come from labor unions, teachers and nurses. It doesn't come from lawyers. It doesn't come from Hollywood. It comes from industry; it comes from Wall Street; it comes from pharmacology and technology. It comes from Monsanto and the food monopolies. It comes from multi-national corporations or extraordinarily wealthy individuals. There is no other way.

As a Democratic fundraiser Llewyn Davis faced the difficult task of finding a way to build a financial base that could compete with a party whose policies could have been written by the big money interests and often were. The leverage his party possessed was their prospects for success. These were businessmen after all and they were acutely aware that there is no return on their investment if the candidate lost. Shifting demographics made the Democrats viable in a national election even in the face of vast financial disadvantage. Davis' job would be to transform that leverage into an increased corporate hedge fund (translation: insurance against loss).

At this stage, however, he only wanted to scout the field, to get a feel for how Wall Street in particular would respond to different candidates on the Democratic ticket. He booked a table for dinner at Le Bernardin on Seventh Avenue with Lloyd Blankenship, the Chief Executive Officer of Goldman-Sachs, and flew to New York.

The chef greeted them at a private table and announced that he had prepared something special. They left everything to the chef's taste with the understanding that Davis would personally foot the bill. It was the price of Blankenship's time.

In keeping with the Chief Executive's protocol, they did not speak of the business at hand until the last bite of desert had been consumed. During the course of an exquisite meal they exchanged thoughts on recent books, films, Broadway plays, economic trends, the Yankees and the weather. It had been another brutal winter. They spoke of everything across a broad horizon of topics except politics.

At long last, after Davis laid his card on the table and Blankenship summoned his finest adjectives to describe a memorable meal for the chef's pleasure, Davis presented the Democratic field and Blankenship addressed their prospects with Wall Street.

"You know how it goes," said Blankenship. "Money follows success. There may be exceptions but I can think of none and if I could they would only prove the rule. Success is what we crave and influence is what we expect on our investment."

Davis considered the message, knowing it was not that simple. Money created success and more money followed. No one could succeed on the grand scale of presidential politics without an early infusion of cash in ample amounts.

"That said," he replied, "there may be candidates you are more or less inclined to support. For example, it is difficult to imagine Wall Street supporting Senator Warner under any circumstances."

Senator Bethany Warner of Massachusetts had championed Wall Street reform after a catastrophic collapse in the markets nearly triggered a great depression.

"You may have found the exception to the rule and yet my gut tells me even she would enjoy substantial support if her path to the nomination became clear. Until then, however, a large percentage of my colleagues would invest liberally to insure that does not become necessary. In short, Senator Warner's path is treacherous indeed. The same can be said of Ohio's Senator Black. His unyielding stance on trade policy combined with his unwavering support of organized labor may endear him to the masses but it is toxic in the financial world."

Davis swallowed hard. He liked both senators but he knew they would face nearly impossible odds. As long as both remained in the race, they would split a relatively small pot of individual and union contributions. They would eliminate each other before spring. Anyone who says money doesn't choose a president cannot deny the stone cold fact that money winnows the field.

"You might find both senators more flexible than you assume."

"Highly unlikely."

"I guess there's no point in bringing up Senator Andrews?"

Blankenship laughed and waved his hand in a circular motion as if to suggest: Move on. Senator Andrews, affectionately known as Uncle Barney, was a democratic socialist – an idea the common voter continued to believe was something akin to a serial bomber or an enemy of state. Throughout Europe a social democrat or democratic socialist is indistinguishable from a mainstream liberal, a believer in progress and the role of government. Not so in America. So a distinguished senator becomes a joke, a fool, like the fool in King Lear, the wisest and most honest voice on the stage. Such is the state of American politics.

"How do you feel about Governor Howard?"

"He had his shot. It's not going to happen."

"Governor Duvall?"

"Great campaigner. Not this cycle. Maybe next time."

"Senator Webber?"

"He won't play on a national stage."

It was stunning how quickly Blankenship dismissed serious, qualified candidates and yet Davis had a similar assessment. So much of the presidential sweepstakes was about timing. You either had it or you didn't. The time was right or it was not.

"Let's talk about Governor Molinari."

Blankenship smiled. Molinari had a reputation of working with Republicans often to the detriment of his own party in Albany.

"We love Molinari," said Blankenship. "Sadly, few believe he can gain traction in the primaries. But if he does, he will find considerable support."

Davis nodded his assent. Up to now the esteemed voice of Wall Street had said nothing he had not already known or at least suspected. They both knew that only one prospective candidate remained and she was the reason for this visit.

"That leaves Secretary Duran."

His smile deepened. At length they had arrived at the heart of the matter. What did Wall Street think of America's political rock star?

"Of course. Everyone's favorite non-candidate: Do you think she'll run?"

"We've no more information than you. Honestly, I don't think she wants to run but there's an awful lot of pressure."

"No one is more appealing than the reluctant candidate," Blankenship reflected. He sipped his coffee and leaned back, offering the appearance of deep thought. He continued.

"I like her. All my colleagues like her. She is the one potential candidate with an accomplished resume in finance and foreign policy. She has the skill set that could make her a phenomenal president. Ironically, the one skill she has not demonstrated is the most important to her election: She has never run for office."

Davis continued to nod his agreement point by point. He then asked the critical question.

"If she ran, would she attract support from Wall Street?"

"Absolutely. The consensus is: She is someone we can work with. As long as that perception endures, she will attract a great deal of support."

Having paid the bill with a generous tip, Davis thanked Blankenship for his time and candor. He had collected the information he needed and the answer he had hoped for.

10

BLACK BISHOP TO KING'S KNIGHT SEVEN

In the game of politics there is always a hidden agenda. The art of politics is disguising that agenda. As a fundraiser for the Republican Party, Robert Joseph Lee was supposed to be unbiased. Until the field is trimmed to a single nominee, the party would not favor any candidate over any other. Of course, even that presumption is more myth than reality, a matter of maintaining the appearance of neutrality. In fact, the party wants to win. The National Committee would shape the process to favor those candidates it considered most likely to succeed in the general election.

The man his colleagues knew as Bobby Jay had a different agenda. He had accepted a large payment from an anonymous source to shape the process in favor of Daniel J. Wynn. He assumed the money came from someone in the Wynn campaign but there was no way to prove it. The offer arrived in his mailbox without return address from somewhere in the DC area. The unsigned, computer-generated message offered instructions for accessing an offshore account. If he accessed the account, it would signal his acceptance of their terms. Additional funds would be deposited in the account contingent on his success in securing backers for the Wynn campaign.

Ironically, Wynn didn't need backers. He had his own money and one of his primary selling points was that he didn't need contributions from anyone. But his rivals desperately needed funding and every source of contributions Wynn gained, someone else lost.

Bobby Jay considered turning the matter over to the RNC

but he thought twice before acting on that impulse. He could use the extra money. The cost of living in his modest but safe neighborhood had outpaced his annual salary. His request for a raise had been on hold for months. He knew that many of his colleagues enjoyed a standard of living that could not be supported by their salaries. The time had come for Bobby Jay to receive his fair share. Besides, he liked Danny Diamond. He liked his television personality. He liked the way he carried his power, like a lion among sheep. He rationalized that he probably would have favored the billionaire in any case. Why not take a little profit for doing what he would have done? It was after all the American way or at least the American way through capitalist eyes. Besides, no one figured Wynn had any chance of surviving the first round. Why not take advantage while he could?

He greeted James Delacroix, a representative of the Koch brothers, at the door of his K Street office, invited him to sit and offered his choice of beverage and a fine Cuban cigar. Mr. Delacroix chose Scotch and pocketed the cigar. Koch Industries reliably contributed enormous amounts to Republican candidates nationwide with the understanding that those candidates would support Koch policies, particularly policies involving energy, safety, regulation and environmental standards. They expected a promise that the Environmental Protection Agency would either be eliminated or defunded. They expected continued tax breaks for energy producers and liberal grants for research and development of clean coal technology – whose mythological existence persisted thanks largely to their efforts.

Both Delacroix and Bobby Jay knew that clean coal was a practical myth and that if a technology for clean coal was ever developed it would make coal the most expensive fuel on the planet. In fact, if energy producers were forced to pay for the damage they did to the air, the water and the land, solar, wind and other renewable sources would become an economic mandate. Neither Delacroix nor the Koch brothers were concerned with these realities as long as they could exert their influence on the political process.

Delacroix's job was to reiterate and emphasize the policies favored by his boss and to establish standards for political contributions. Bobby Jay's job was to steer Koch brothers' money away from anyone not named Daniel Wynn.

"How's the field?" opened Delacroix.

"Strong. I think we have some viable candidates. The more pertinent question is: How do your bosses feel about them?"

"We like some better than others."

"Of course. Can we narrow it down?"

Delacroix sipped his scotch and wondered why he was wasting his time. This clown couldn't add anything they didn't already know. But the Kochs gave the orders and he followed them. It paid well so he didn't ask questions.

"Well, we can eliminate the Texas boys. I think America's had enough of Texas to last a hundred years."

"I'm not so sure. You may be underestimating Rivera but let that pass. What do you think of Pierce?"

"Is he running?"

"Of course he is. There's never been a Pierce who didn't want the White House."

"We like him but he's a little too mainstream. He has a reputation for moderation, working across the aisle, making deals. You never know what kind of compromise he might make under pressure."

The assessment surprised Bobby Jay. By his own analysis, Ellis Pierce might be the strongest candidate in the field if he could get past the primaries. That the Koch brothers already had doubts made his job much easier.

"We think he'll stand strong on the central issues but I hear your concerns. I hear similar concerns about Gregory, that he might abandon energy subsidies. You never know with ideologues. I'm sure it's just a rumor. Nothing to worry about."

This was how rumors were born on the beltway. An offhand remark, a toxic seed passed from one camp to another, gaining credibility as it traveled. Delacroix knew as much but he would pass the rumor on just the same. He had to cover all the bases to protect his own interests. If his bosses heard the rumor from someone else first it would reflect poorly on him.

"What about the fat man?"

"Sampson? If the election was held today, he couldn't carry his own state!"

His job became easier still with every doubt Delacroix voiced. They were suddenly down to two: Alonzo and Wynn.

It was time for Bobby Jay to back off. He could not be seen as promoting a single candidate at this stage in the process and he'd already compromised his neutrality a little too much.

"I like Alonzo and the fact that he's from Florida doesn't hurt," he opined.

Delacroix consumed some time along with his scotch, letting Bobby Jay know he was beginning to smell a rat. Alonzo had well-known problems with consistency. Bobby Jay had not hesitated to criticize the others. Why hold back on Alonzo?

"What do you think about Wynn?"

"A good candidate. He appeals to the working class – even though he wouldn't stand downwind from them. And if he can win New York as a Republican we would stand an excellent chance of taking the White House."

"You're not worried about his scandals?"

"He's shown the ability to turn them around. He'll take a few blows and come back swinging. In the end, he's still standing, stronger than ever."

Delacroix nodded. He didn't know what to make of Bobby Jay but what he said made sense. It helped shape his thinking. He would take the message back to his bosses. In his judgment and the probable judgment of the RNC, it came down to Alonzo and Wynn. It remained to be seen if the party elite could work with Wynn. He had an awkward reputation for going his own way. If they could control him or, better yet, if he didn't need to be controlled, so much the better. It would cost them a lot less. That would free up funding for congressional and statewide races.

The more they looked at it, the more they liked the idea. If one billionaire businessman could take the nation's highest office, why not another and another? Why not give up this notion of a people's democracy and hand the reigns to the individuals who really ran things. Like the Koch brothers. Why not?

11

WHITE QUEEN TO QUEEN TWO

Winfred Holmes is the man who made Jaime Marquez the first Hispanic President of the United States of America. He took a little known Arizona congressman and catapulted him to the White House, a feat unprecedented in modern American politics. After the president won re-election Holmes wanted nothing more to do with politics. He wanted to retire to his Arlington estate, write his memoirs under quite skies, enjoy the company of his life partner, watch his grandchildren grow up, perhaps travel to distant lands, seeking the sights, sounds, smells and tastes that only other cultures can provide.

The president's legacy seemed secure. After decades of constant war, he had managed to keep the peace as much as any president could. He had improved the lot of working people, advanced civil rights for all minorities and oppressed communities, and kept the economy marching along while reducing carbon emissions by transforming the energy sector to cleaner, renewable sources. He had survived an attempted coup by the intelligence community and exploited that victory by restoring a good measure of civil liberties. Some would argue he had accomplished more than any president since Franklin Roosevelt and yet, nothing he had done could not be undone by the next president.

Winfred Holmes could not rest easy and he believed the president probably felt very much the same. He arranged a meeting at the White House to discuss what needed to be done to secure the future. For the first time in months, when they both were in crisis mode, he entered the Oval Office, closing the door behind him as the president rose from behind his mammoth desk to greet him with a firm handshake.

"Fred! It's been too long, my friend."

"Yes, it has, Mr. President."

There was no one in the world the president trusted or valued more than Winfred Holmes. He could have taken any position in the cabinet, he could have been appointed to the Supreme Court, but he declined. He always said his place was behind the curtain, a footnote on the pages of history.

"I know you too well to believe this is a casual visit. What's on your mind, Fred?"

They sat on opposite sofas, divided by a coffee table, and tried to relax, knowing that the Oval Office was hardly a place conducive to relaxation.

"I've been thinking about your successor."

"Are we there yet?"

"To be honest, Mr. President, we've been there since the moment you won re-election."

"Now that is a dismal reality."

"But no less true. It's been quite an experience, hasn't it?"

The president sighed. No one knows the pressures a president feels but those who have sat behind his desk.

"That it has, Fred."

"Any regrets?"

"Many. But becoming president is not one of them."

"I'm glad to hear it. You've done a great deal of good for the people of this country. Even if many of them haven't a clue."

"I've done what I could."

"Given the current political climate, what you have been able to accomplish is a near miracle. We should apply for sainthood."

The president laughed. He could always count on Fred to relieve the tension. In this case it was the calm before the storm.

"Unfortunately, Mr. President, I fear that everything you've accomplished could be undone if the people in their infinite wisdom make the wrong choice in the next cycle. That's what I've come to talk to you about."

"You have someone in mind?"

"I do."

"Let me guess: Shelby Duran."

Holmes smiled. He and Secretary Duran led the effort to fight back the CIA and save the Marquez presidency.

"You were always more insightful than anyone gave you credit."

"We have some good options."

"Yes but it's the same old dilemma: Those who should be president can't be elected and those who can be elected shouldn't be president."

"You have a way with words, my friend."

"Thank you. It is nevertheless true. I like Warner, Black, Andrews and Duvall. I think they'd make fine presidents. I also think their odds of winning this time around are about as good as a backyard nag winning the Kentucky Derby, which is to say negligible."

The president leaned back and frowned. He found his friends dismissal of the leading Democratic contenders harsh but he had never known Holmes to be wrong.

"I'm not sure I agree with you but I hear you. You think Duran would win?"

"It's always a fight but she's our best option."

"You know she's never run for office."

"I consider it a virtue. Do you remember what they said about you? He's never even run statewide! You can't jump from congress to the White House! It's impossible."

"But you didn't believe that."

"No. And I don't believe the secretary's lack of political experience is a handicap. She's proven she can take care of business in the private sector and the government, in business and in foreign affairs. No one is better qualified than Shelby Duran."

The president began nodding halfway through his rant. That he liked the idea of a Duran presidency could not be doubted.

"If it was anyone but you, Fred, I'd say you were crazy. With you, however, I know you're crazy: Crazy like a fox. What would you like me to do?"

"Talk to her, Mr. President. Talk to her like I first talked to you. The first part of any campaign is convincing the candidate to run."

The president seemed to look inward where he found the seed of sorrow.

"You know, old Joe still has ambitions."

He referred to the vice president. For six years he had been a loyal servant but recently he had begun to diverge from the president's policies, a sure sign that he wanted to run for the top spot. Holmes empathized.

"Not long ago I would have thought he'd make a decent president but with the noises he's made lately, he scares me. He seems to have yielded to the old school notion that the way to the White House is war. What he doesn't seem to understand is that by playing to the right, he's eroded whatever support he had among Democrats."

"It concerns me as well," said the president. "I'll talk to her, Fred. But this has to stay out of the press. I owe Joe that much."

"Understood, Mr. President. You have to maintain public neutrality."

They shook hands as friends and comrades, the kind of friendship that is earned with sweat and tears, the kind that has been to battle and survived. Holmes took his leave with a pensive glance back, reflecting that it might be his last visit to this most solemn office where he had helped to make history – at least during the Marquez presidency.

12

PAWN EXCHANGE

Black Pawn to Queen's Bishop Six
White Pawn to King's Bishop Three
Black Pawn to Queen's Knight Five

In any endeavor the most common, interchangeable and expendable individuals are the pawns: The line workers in a factory, foot soldiers in an army, janitors, clerks, office workers, interns and baristas. Anyone who can be replaced overnight is a pawn in the game of life. The difference between the game of chess and the game of life is that chess pieces have no families, no loved ones, no brothers and sisters, no friends to mark their passing.

The first lesson of any battlefield commander, franchise owner, CEO or industrial supervisor is not to overvalue the pawns. Hesitation is weakness and weakness will be exploited. A pawn's basic function is sacrifice. Their collective power lies in sacrifice. There will be blood and the pawn is eminently replaceable.

As the season shifted from late spring to early summer attention focused on the first presidential primary debates. More and more the candidates retired from retail campaigning, the handshake and kiss-a-baby routine, seeking seclusion behind closed doors where they could absorb information, take briefings and answer hard questions in preparation for the all-important first debate.

It may be cliché but it is no less true that the first

impression before a national audience is critical. Numerous candidates thought to be forerunners fell on the sword of the first debate. Campaigns take every precaution not to let that happen, hiring swarms of policy wonks, debate experts and media advisors. Day after day, night after night, they stage rehearsals and discuss the results until the candidates throw up their hands in exhaustion.

Spies and moles are rare among the inner debate circles. It's a good gig. The jobs pay well and for the lucky winners they go on and on. Anyone caught or even suspected of passing information would not only lose his job, he would lose any chance of being employed for future debates and future campaigns. Consequently, the spies generally inhabit the periphery of the inner circle: lovers, companions, confidants and business partners.

Jolene Dixon frequented the bars of hotels where members of the inner circle stayed. Possessing a classic beauty, dark stylish hair, a shapely athletic figure and inviting green eyes, she looked like an actress cast as a professional in an HBO series. She in fact was an actress who used gigs like this to cover costs while she waited for a break. Not the first woman you noticed as you walked into the room, you came around to her after a drink or two, especially when she seemed to welcome your inquiring glance.

Moses Dunn admired her from his table across the room. He had little doubt that she would one day find the success she desired on stage or screen. She had a quality of sincerity that is difficult to fake. Like an expert hunter or fisherman she did not seek out her prey but waited for the prey to come to her. He watched the scene unfold as if under the guidance of a skilled director. She caught the eye of her mark, a policy wonk from the Alonzo campaign and allowed him to buy her a drink before he joined her at the bar. A half hour later they left the bar together and Dunn entered what he had witnessed in his log. It would be up to his employer to determine what it meant. Like that of a private security guard, his job ended at observe and report.

Across the dimly lit room, Darren McGhee made his own notes. He took some small measure of satisfaction in a job that offered little in knowing that he alone had not been identified by his fellow operatives.

That all this happened at the bar in the lobby of the Watergate Hotel, where the most famous burglars in history swapped stories over scotch and bourbon during their nefarious operation, is an irony that escaped none.

13

WHITE KNIGHT TO KING TWO

The nation's capitol is like a small-town rumor mill. Moreover, when a butterfly lands in New Hampshire it sends ripples that become tremors by the time they reach the beltway. When the earth moves in Washington among the first to feel the impact are the chairs of the Republican and Democratic National Committees.

Dorothea Vargas heard about Charles Rogan's surprise appearance at the Firefighters Fundraiser as it happened. It alarmed her. Among her primary responsibilities as chair of the Democratic National Committee was to maintain party unity for the general election. Nobody knew who employed Rogan but the fact that he spent an inordinate amount of time with Cassidy James of the Duran camp suggested it could be a Democratic rival. Given the dynamics of multi-variable polling and past practices, she concluded that if it was one of their own the most likely candidate was Francis Molinari, Governor of New York.

Molinari badly wanted to be America's first president of Italian ancestry. It galled him that an African American and a Latino American had made it to the White House before the descendants of Columbus. It galled him that Columbus is no longer considered a bonafide American hero or indeed the man who discovered America. It bothered him that he had to downplay his own heritage to win elections even in New York where so many Italian Americans had thrived in both the political and business worlds. He was proud to be an Italian American and he wanted his people properly respected in history.

Dorothea Vargas had read the polls and the analysis that went with them: The leading barrier to a successful Molinari run for the presidency was the potential candidacy of Secretary of State Shelby Duran. She almost expected Molinari to be the first to step out of line. He suffered an acute case of Caesar's fatal flaw.

She called Ralph Peterson, her counterpart with the Republican National Committee, to sound out the possibility that someone on his side hired the saboteur. It seemed improbable at this early stage that anyone on the other side would expend their resources sabotaging a Democrat but illogical actions are not uncommon in politics. Peterson assured her it was not one of theirs. He found it amusing that the Democrats had found a way to divide their ranks so soon in the game. Vargas was not amused.

She arranged a roundtable in a conference room at the Mayflower Hotel with representatives of all the Democratic campaigns in operation. Some sent campaign managers, others assistants, but all were represented when she opened the meeting with a few candid remarks.

"Greetings, ladies and gentlemen. I'll be brief. We all know you can't win a campaign in January but you can certainly lose one. I spoke with Mr. Peterson of the RNC yesterday and he was overjoyed that we had found a way to engage in the practice of self-destruction before we've even had a primary. It's like stubbing your toe getting out of bed."

She quashed the muffled laughter with a stern voice and an expression of scorn.

"I won't have it. I was appointed to this position to win elections, most importantly the presidential election. Some of you may think you can do a better job and that's fine. But as long as I'm Chair of the Democratic National Committee, no one on our side will be hiring a saboteur to derail someone else's campaign without consequences."

She looked around the table before zeroing in on Vincent Gallegos, Molinari's campaign manager, who stared at his hands before raising his eyes to meet hers. She left no doubt she knew and Molinari would know she knew it.

"Everyone here knows what I'm talking about (if you don't you're in the wrong business) so I won't bore you with the details. I will tell you this: No one wins the nomination of this party without first winning the respect of this committee. And no one wins the general election with a divided base. It's my job to see that that does not happen."

The room went silent. They were not accustomed to this kind of scolding and some didn't quite know how to respond. The chair continued.

"Look folks, I'm no Pollyanna. I know there's a time for hardball. I know there's a time for a little dirt and a little smear. I get it. But for the time being we play by the rules. We play on a level field. If you have any questions about what that entails, don't hesitate to ask. In the meantime, if you are the guilty party my message is simple: Back off! If you're not the guilty party then this has nothing to do with you. Carry on and may the best candidate win."

She folded her papers into her briefcase and left them to ponder her words. Molinari's representative waited a judicious few minutes so he wouldn't have to share an elevator ride with the chair and followed her out. The others discussed what had happened with a variety of derisive smiles and what it meant to the future of their campaigns.

14

BLACK KNIGHT TO QUEEN SEVEN

RNC Chair Ralph Peterson got off the phone with Charles Rogan of the Wynn campaign knowing he had a problem. Rogan claimed to have knowledge that at least two rival candidates were planning to ambush his candidate at the first nationally televised debate. Eight months prior Wynn had survived a scandal in which several members of his staff were caught bribing elected officials and engaging in petty revenge schemes against individuals who refused to do their bidding on a development project. The project was proposed for the Chelsea district in Manhattan and famously threatened to evict an elderly woman from her home. Known as the Chelsea scandal, it was only the latest in a long series of scandals that the billionaire considered a part of doing business.

Largely through bribery, petty revenge and arm-twisting, Wynn was eventually exonerated by the state attorney general's office but it left a stain and a stench. Rogan had information that the campaigns of Senator Gene Rivera of Texas and Governor Sam Sampson of Pennsylvania intended to bring it up at the first opportunity just to watch the big man squirm. It was a calculated risk: the candidate who attacks first may be perceived as mean spirited. But as the outliers in the race they had to take risks, they had to bring the frontrunners back to the field before they could establish momentum. In collaboration, the Rivera and Sampson camps both agreed the newcomer was the most vulnerable target.

Without saying how they learned of the plot (a potential scandal in itself) the Wynn campaign was incensed. It violated what came to be known as Reagan's rule: Thou shalt not attack other Republicans. The rule would be discarded once they had narrowed the field but even then those who leveled personal attacks would pay a price.

Danny Wynn was not the only candidate with skeletons in his closet. Ryan Gregory had his father's inexplicable connections to white supremacists. Ellis Pierce had been neck deep in an infamous Florida disenfranchisement scheme. Alonzo had altered facts to make his campaign biography more appealing to Florida's Cuban community. Sampson had a well-publicized bridge scandal involving political revenge and Rivera had his own share of double-dealing if anyone bothered to look. If they started slinging mud at this early stage they'd be buried in it by Independence Day.

Beyond political pragmatism Ralph Peterson owed Danny Wynn. As a major contributor to his congressional campaign fund, Wynn wielded great power within the party. More than any other individual, Wynn had helped Peterson secure his position as the head of the RNC. He had no choice but to act if he wanted to retain his position. Moreover, if Wynn by any chance were to take the presidency he would be in line for a cabinet post, perhaps White House Chief of Staff. He liked the sound of it. He liked the respect and prestige and social status that went along with it. It was a long shot but it was the best shot he had.

He called a teleconference with representatives of all leading candidates. Sitting behind his desk with an American flag and a leather-bound edition of the Federalist Papers in the background, he opened the meeting and came straight to the point.

"As you all know, the first debate is just around the corner. For those of you who might be new to the process, I just want to establish the ground rules. For the rest of you (and looking around that would be all of you) this will serve as a reminder.

"First and foremost, Republicans don't stab Republicans in the back. We do it up front or we don't do it at all. Is that understood?"

Nods around the monitors, set up in a semicircle around Peterson's desk so that they were visible to all, suggested that they understood and agreed in principle, but their expressions told a different story. While Jacoby "call me Jack" Morris and Adam Davis, campaign managers for the Wynn and Gregory camps, remained stoic, Mary Jo Perez of the Pierce camp and Cliff Harris of the Alonzo camp looked quizzical as if someone forgot to brief them. John Kagan of the Rivera campaign wore an expression of controlled rage and his cohort Rick Johnson of the Sam Sampson campaign glared off camera as if looking for blame.

In an instant everyone had the lowdown on what was happening. The Rivera campaign was out of line and no one was surprised. The Wynn and Gregory people were in the know and Wynn put the stop on it. With all the cards on the table, little more needed to be said so Peterson wrapped it up.

"Look, there will come a time for hard ball. We Republicans are not pansies. We can take the shot and fire back. But we play by the rules and the rule is: We play nice, we fight on the issues, until that time comes. Understood?"

Adam Davis raised his hand, requesting permission to speak.

"Adam?"

"Yes. Can we assume you'll let us know when the gloves come off?"

"You can."

"Any other questions?"

All parties stood silent.

"Good. Just to make things clear, I want it on the record that we all agree on this: A level playing field, nothing personal, until the time comes. Rick?"

Johnson still looked dazed but threw up his hands:

"Agreed."

"Cliff?"

"Agreed."

Around the circle of monitors they went until all concurred. The only person more pleased than Peterson was the big man himself.

WHITE BISHOP TO KING'S CASTLE SIX

Greed is the seed that unlights the brightest star. Once Llewyn Davis said yes when he should have said no the seed took root and grew, infecting him with the gambler's disease, the need, the yearning for more. For fifteen years he had been among the most reliable, most trustworthy and most effective servants of the Democratic Party. Now he was compromised and it ate at his soul.

Because his payments were contingent on and proportionate to his service to the Duran campaign, he looked in directions he had no business looking. The more he looked the more he perceived double-dealing and corruption. Transactions and casual meetings that he would never have given a second glance suddenly looked suspicious. Was this the way of the world revealed to him only when he joined the ranks of the corrupted? He deeply regretted his decision but having made it he could see no way out without irreparable harm to his career, his financial stability, his marriage and his children's future. He understood now how pernicious corruption was, how it led from one small step to another and another until you betrayed everything you believed in and everyone who believed in you.

When someone claiming to represent the still unofficial Duran campaign left a message in his box asking for a face-to-face meeting it left him in a bind. This was explicitly not a part of the deal. They were never to meet. He would never have a name or a face connected to the deal. Then again, how could he know this was the Duran campaign? He couldn't even be sure the Duran campaign had made the deal.

He assumed as much because the arrangement benefited Duran. Now it seemed possible it benefited someone else as well.

The unsigned message called for a meeting the following day in an out of the mainstream diner after lunch hour. He hesitated, vacillated, deliberated and decided on another course of action. He would contact the Duran campaign directly. Whatever this was and whatever it would become it had to stop now.

He called the Washington office of Duran headquarters and asked for a meeting with Winfred Holmes before the day expired, explaining it was a matter of immediate importance. Holmes called back within the hour and instructed him to meet in the lobby of the Smithsonian Art Museum as soon as he could manage. He hung up the phone, walked out to the street and hailed a cab. Holmes spotted him the moment he walked through the doors.

"Well, Mr. Davis, so good to see you."

As they shook hands, Holmes leaned in and whispered, "Were you followed?"

He looked over his shoulder. That possibility hadn't occurred to him.

"I don't believe so."

After a moment, Holmes whispered, "Do you think you might be?"

He thought it through in an instant and concluded his unknown adversaries would have no reason to believe he would do anything but what he was instructed to do.

"No," he answered.

"Follow me."

He followed Holmes through a side door to an outdoor café where they ordered coffee and talked baseball until Holmes was relatively sure no one was watching them or monitoring their conversation.

"What's going on, Mr. Davis?"

He recounted the entire story from his acceptance of the

arrangement months prior to the message received this morning.

"It's got to stop, Mr. Holmes. I can't go on like this. Who knows what they'll want me to do next?"

Holmes ordered more coffee and admired the gardens with their rich splashes of color punctuated by modern American sculpture, abstract configurations of light and shadow changing seamlessly from one moment to the next.

"If you want my help you'll have to give back the money."

"How? I don't even know who gave it to me."

"How do you feel about Doctors without Borders?"

"A sound organization as far as I know."

"You will pay the exact sum of the money you received to them, not all at once but gradually so as not to attract the attention of the IRS."

"Agreed."

"You know you'll have to retire from the DNC."

"Of course."

He didn't know and his face showed it. Events were moving more rapidly than he imagined they would. Somehow he hoped he could save his position by coming clean and making amends. He knew now and accepted it: Once you betray the trust you can never get it back. Holmes watched his struggle and decided to help.

"It's one of the great ironies that the man you can trust most is the one who has faltered and come back to the fold. You'll have to take a break from politics but I know some people in charities that could use an excellent fundraiser. You'll be fine. Meantime, I want you to take the meeting."

"Wear a wire?"

Holmes shook his head.

"We don't need to know what's said. We only need to know who you're meeting with and to whom he or she reports. As you know, in politics you're guilty upon first doubt. When you resign whoever set you up will be forced to do the same."

He cursed the day he agreed to take the money. It had all seemed so innocent: money for doing what you were inclined to do anyway. What was so wrong?

"What do you want me to do?"

"Simple. Agree to anything they request. Anything. Tomorrow you hand in your resignation and go home."

"Won't they come after me?"

Holmes shook his head.

"Once you resign you're out of the game. You're no longer of any interest. I'll give you a reference to your new job. You walk away."

"You're sure."

"I am."

He sighed and nodded. In the end, he had no choice. He had placed his fate in the hands of a man he knew and respected rather than those who entrapped him and wanted to own him. His career in politics at least for the foreseeable future had come to a close. He could only hope that Holmes would make good on his promise.

16

BLACK BISHOP TO KING'S CASTLE SIX

First Blood: Bishop Takes Bishop

Past the rush of lunch hour on a Wednesday afternoon only a scattering of customers remained in the Jukebox Diner in Arlington. Bobby Jay sat by the window consuming fries, a cheeseburger and a chocolate malt, anticipating the arrival of his Democratic nemesis for a negotiation he would thoroughly enjoy. He bobbed his head up and down to the tune of Elvis, Bobby Vinton, The Four Seasons and The Supremes as he waited. He was a fifties kind of guy and this was his kind of joint.

Outside in the parking lot Nick Dunn felt a little exposed as he sat in his GMC van snapping photos of the Republican fundraiser. No one paid him any attention so he relaxed and did his job.

Looking like a business leader compelled to testify before a congressional committee, Llewyn Davis rolled up in his bronze Nissan Pathfinder right on cue. Bobby Jay waved him over with a broad smile and asked him if he wanted a malt. Davis declined and ordered coffee.

"Too bad," offered Bobby Jay. "These are delicious."

"I'm glad you're enjoying yourself."

"I am! I am! However, you don't look too happy, my friend."

Davis thought: You won't be once this is over. He said: "You lied to me."

Bobby Jay swiped a fry through a mound of catsup and

consumed it.

"Are you wearing a wire?"

"Why would I?"

Bobby Jay's bountiful cheer returned as he took a gulp of his chocolate malt.

"Good point."

"Look," said Davis, "I'll stipulate that you've got me by the balls. I'll stipulate that it's my own fault and I'm not too happy about it. Let's just get on with it. What do you want me to do?"

"You're a man who gets down to business. I like that. Here's the thing: Your old assignment ends today and a new assignment begins. Yesterday you worked in behalf of the Duran campaign. Today you work for me. Give me your phone."

He plugged in a number, entered another in his own and handed it back.

"You can contact me at that number and I can contact you. Don't worry. We only want information. Who's collecting how much from whom and where it's going. That sort of thing. Not much really. You should be pleased. Any questions?"

He finished up his cheeseburger, threw a couple of bills on the table and stood.

"Just one," Davis replied. "Who do you work for?"

Bobby Jay winked. "You really should try the malt. Delicious!"

He walked out. Davis waited for him to pull away before he followed. He drove home and drafted his resignation. Nick Dunn followed Bobby Jay at a safe distance to the headquarters of the Republican National Committee.

17

WHITE QUEEN TO KING'S CASTLE SIX

Retribution: Queen Takes Bishop

Winfred Holmes thanked Nick Dunn for his service and called the State Department to confirm his meeting with Secretary Duran. He knew the secretary like no one else outside her immediate family. He also knew politics. No one knew or played the game better than he did. His knowledge of politics informed him she could no longer wait. If she was going to run for president she needed to announce now. His knowledge of the secretary told him she didn't like to be pushed. Something had to give.

Files and folders, piles of paper everywhere, it was a wonder she could find a pen no less an archived brief on the Foreign Minister of Bahrain. She leaned back in her chair when her old friend clamored in, shutting the door behind him. She knew why he was visiting, why it couldn't wait and why it couldn't be handled over the phone. She didn't know which way she would turn.

"Fred! What brings a man of your character back to this sordid neighborhood?"

"I like the food," he smiled. "Always have."

He handed her the cell phone displaying pictures of Llewyn Davis meeting with Robert Lee aka Bobby Jay at the Jukebox Diner.

"By the end of the day," he said, "those two men, up to now considered pillars of their respective parties, will have lost their jobs. We've got dozens of people walking the precincts, manning the phones, priming the pump, from Iowa to New Hampshire to Washington DC, all for a campaign without a candidate. Please tell me and more importantly tell them, Madam Secretary, that we're not fighting for nothing."

"You're not fighting for nothing."

She was not being glib. It was not in her nature. She knew that any campaign was about ideas and policies. Duran for President fought for a continuation of the Marquez presidency and the first woman in the nation's highest office. The people had elected a man of African descent and another of Hispanic descent but it had not yet elected a woman.

"You know how I feel about you, Shelby. You're like a daughter to me. I know how difficult this is for you. Unlike every other candidate in the field, you don't want it. It's not in your blood to run. You have no thirst for power. That's what's makes you the perfect candidate and that is what would make you a great president."

"I'm flattered, Fred, but not convinced. We have some excellent candidates with essentially the same policies that I would bring and they happen to be politicians. They know how to run and win. They've done it."

He listened intently to her though he was familiar with all the arguments. He'd been through them all and always he arrived at the same conclusion.

"It gives me no great pleasure to say this, Shelby, but I wouldn't be here if we had a viable option. I like Warner as much as you do or nearly so. She'd make a fine vice president. But Wall Street hates her. Industry hates her. She has no following in the high tech world. Where does the money come from?"

"It comes from people like you and me," replied the secretary.

"The days when contributions from people like you and me could finance a presidential campaign are long gone. I'm not sure they ever existed. It would take a miracle for Warner to make it past New Hampshire. If she did, she'd run out of money before Super Tuesday. I wish it wasn't reality but it is and I'm in the business of acknowledging reality."

"Assuming your analysis is correct, what distinguishes me from Warner? I have no backers on Wall Street, in industry or in high tech. Where would my backing come from if not from small contributors?"

"You've always underestimated your appeal, Madam Secretary. I can tell you categorically, you have major backers. Wall Street believes they can work with you and it would be wise to keep it that way. As for high tech, your strong defense of intellectual rights has won you a lot of admirers. One of them is Lawrence McClure who has pledged his support. All you have to do is run."

Secretary Duran recalibrated her thoughts. The campaign had progressed farther than she imagined. Only Winfred Holmes could organize a campaign without a candidate.

"It is unfortunate Warner doesn't have you working for her. McClure might have pledged to back her campaign."

Holmes knew he would have to push hard. More than anything else, Shelby Duran wanted to reclaim her private life. She stood as a startling exception to the dictum that you had to enjoy the limelight to succeed in politics. At least, he believed in his soul that she would succeed if only she would enter the fray.

"I wish I could tell you that was true. Four years from now it might become true but for now every candidate on the Democratic side has an Achilles heel, a fatal flaw that will surely doom his or her run for the presidency. Black has the unions but the business leaders hate him. Andrews and Howard lack a broad base of support. Duvall needs experience, especially in foreign policy. Bolton has made too many gaffes to survive another campaign. That leaves Molinari and if we're willing to go there we might as well elect a Republican.

"If we really want to keep the White House and advance the policies of the president, it comes down to you, Madam

Secretary. I know the president has talked to you and told you the same thing. What he didn't tell you and what I couldn't tell you until we had the backing of Lawrence McClure is this: You can win. It won't be easy. You'll have to fight and scratch and claw like you've never fought before. You'll get knocked down a dozen times and you'll have to get back up swinging. But if you commit, if your heart is in the fight, by God we can win."

Secretary Duran had to take a breath. With the debates approaching she knew time was running out. She knew Holmes would push for a decision. But knowing is not the same as experiencing. Instinctively she wanted to push back but she was running out of arguments.

"I'm not prepared to jump in the race. I haven't run for office since high school. I haven't debated since college. How can you expect me to do this?"

Holmes would not back down. He had anticipated every argument and every objection. If she decided not to run it would not be for peripheral issues. It would be because the process repulsed her at a level that went to her core.

"We can use your lack of debate experience to your advantage. Debates are a game of expectations. You're the most knowledgeable person on the planet. There is no way you can embarrass yourself. You'll set your own bar and you'll rise to the occasion."

She rose and walked to the windows of her office. On a clear day she could see the Washington Monument. She could sense the history of the nation's capitol and the part she had played in it. She was comfortable in her role. She had thrived as Secretary of State. Running for office, any office would put her in a place that was anything but comfortable. Could she do it? Could she devote her life to it? Could she ask her family, her husband, her son and daughter, to sacrifice what remained of their personal lives?

She had broached the subject and each of them had given his and her approval but not without misgivings. They would not pretend for her sake that it was an easy decision or that they were somehow obliged to yield to her ambitions. But they understood as she did that circumstance and events sometimes come together in a way that makes things possible that would never be possible otherwise. Each of them separately had come to the same conclusion Winfred Holmes and President Marquez had: That she was her party's best chance at a critical time in history.

"I'll do it," she said, "on one condition."

"Name it."

"That if thing's don't work as you expect them to, if I fall flat on my face and I'm eliminated on the trail, you'll turn all of your resources and all of your efforts to nominating and electing Bethany Warner."

"Done."

Holmes felt palpable relief and oddly enough Secretary Duran did too. She would announce her resignation to seek the presidency by week's end and immediately hit the campaign trail. Holmes would be with her every step of the way.

Meantime, after the resignation of Llewyn Davis, he forwarded a set of photographs to the Republican National Committee, triggering a cycle of doubt and suspicion that Bobby Jay would not survive. He turned in his resignation before the RNC could fire him.

The first real casualties in the war for the White House were on the books. Holmes took care of Davis as he promised. He always kept his word.

BLACK BISHOP TO QUEEN'S KNIGHT SEVEN

Like every organizational structure in the modern era, contemporary politics is highly compartmentalized. There are specialists for every facet of a campaign. There are operatives for strategy, specialists in polling, operatives for the ground game, consultants for messaging, fundraisers, bundlers and handlers. But the latest and greatest development in political warfare, forming a complete second layer of organizational structure, is the independent attack dog.

Made possible by a corporate Supreme Court, the independent attack dogs are known by their IRS designation: the 501's. Under federal statute a political organization qualifies for tax-exempt status as long as it does not coordinate its activities with any candidate's campaign. Contributions to 501's are unlimited and may be anonymous, a combination that makes them the most powerful, most influential and most subversive organizations in electoral politics.

Nolan Gray worked for a powerful rightwing 501. Founded and directed by notorious conservative operative Jim Duke, Americans for America First was dedicated to eliminating moderates from the Republican Party. Duke sought a philosophical purity unheard of since the days of fascism. His critics claimed with some foundation that corporate fascism is in fact what drove him. In private Duke held little back in his criticism of the masses and the flaws of democratic government. He believed that some people, the financial elite among them, were inherently superior and that any reasonable system of government would find a way to allow the elite to rule without the interference of lesser beings. With the Supreme Court's assistance they were very close to achieving that goal.

Nolan Gray could not have cared less about Jim Duke's philosophy. He paid well and he expected results. The organization had already decided that Daniel Wynn was their man. The goal at this stage was to cull the field. Some candidates could be counted on to implode on their own accord. Some candidates were not considered a viable threat and so Americans for America First would not target them. They were considered potential allies.

Among the viable candidates the one they feared most was Ellis Pierce of Florida. Beltway wisdom held that Pierce's weakness in the primaries was his moderate stance on immigration but Gray believed it was his ambiguity on foreign policy. His spy in the Pierce camp said the candidate answered immigration questions with confidence but his replies to inquiries about the war on terror lacked conviction and consistency. He was stuck at "knowing what we know now" as in "knowing what we know now it's easy to second guess." If you pressed him his answers became even more muddled.

In other words, he waffled. Nothing kills a Republican candidate quicker than the perception of waffling. The problem Nolan Gray faced was that he had to persuade his boss that he was right and the beltway was wrong. With only three days to the first debate a decision had to be made. The only way of assuring that the right questions would be asked was to plant a story in popular media. It had to be done now.

He marched into Jim Duke's office to present his case.

"Mr. Gray! I understand you wish to file a dissenting opinion."

"I want to do more than that, Mr. Duke. I want to convince you that I'm right and everyone else is wrong."

"Well, if you put it that way..." Duke grinned with a

display of the sarcasm for which he was well known. The fact is his candidate had already planted his staff on immigration, accusing Mexico of sending its criminals and miscreants north of the border just to be rid of them. It gave him the inside path on both the anti-immigrant vote and the white supremacist vote in the Deep South.

Gray continued unimpeded.

"I know you're about to plant the immigration article. It's a mistake. Pierce knows how to face down every angle on immigration. The fact is people's views are changing on immigration, softening, even the base."

It was true and the numbers revealed it. As more and more illegals stepped out of the shadows, attitudes changed. They were not just faceless farm workers, landscapers and menial workers, they were teachers and instructional aides, they were lawyers and medical professionals and journalists and mothers and fathers. As with any other oppressed minority in American history, the more they became human beings in the eyes of society, the greater their acceptance. The hardcore rightwing base lagged behind but even their opposition was losing its intensity.

"It's still a winning issue," replied Duke.

"Sure but it won't damage Pierce. Everyone knows his position on immigration. He'll compromise. He'll promise to protect the border, put up a wall, electronic surveillance, border patrol, and then he'll point to his own family and the crowd will eat it up."

Pierce's family was famously mestizo. His wife was mixed blood Puerto Rican and Mexican, brown in complexion, and his children reflected the mixture. His entire family was bilingual. Much of the early support for his candidacy rested on the promise that Pierce could attract a double-digit percentage of Latino votes in the general election, something Republicans had been notoriously unable to do.

"I take your point," said Duke. "I'm not blind to

changing demographics or polling trends. The real question is: Have you got something better? Nobody cares about foreign policy right now. We're not in a war. There's been no terrorist attack on American soil. There is no crisis and the news is crisis driven. So what makes you think it's a winning issue?"

Gray tried to hide his exasperation. He'd been making his argument for over a week, ever since he received inside information on the debate preparations, and no one wanted to hear it. Why would he listen now?

"It's not the issue. It's how it makes Pierce look. If you ask about the wars, Iraq, Syria and Afghanistan, he answers: Knowing what they knew then, I think it was the right decision. If you ask him if he still thinks it was the right decision knowing what we know now, he refuses to give a straight answer. He hems and haws and circles back to his original answer. He waffles, Mr. Duke. He doesn't know how to answer it."

"Your sources are sure on this?"

"Source. It's second hand. But I've gone back and looked at his record over the years. He's always been evasive. It's clear he doesn't like talking about it. My gut tells me he knows Iraq was a strategic blunder. He was probably against it from the beginning but he's a Republican. He's a Pierce. He couldn't oppose the war and stay in the party. So he muddies the water and hopes you don't press him."

Duke waited and then nodded slowly. He had also reviewed Pierce's statements on the wars and came to a similar conclusion.

"You've primed the pump?"

He was asking if he had a story ready to be published at a prominent website or newspaper. The idea was to have the story appear and then run up the interest to the point that the news organization running the debate (in this case Fox News) couldn't ignore it.

"Ready to roll," Gray replied.

"Have you got a hard copy?"

He handed over a five-page, double-spaced article titled, "Pierce Waffles on Foreign Policy." Authored by a freelance writer, Gray had assurances at the Counsel of Foreign Affairs that they would run it online if given the word.

Duke took a moment to glance through it.

"I like it," he declared. "Let's do it."

Gray tried not to look as pleased as he was. At long last, he thought, he was getting a chance to make his mark.

"But I've got to tell you, Mr. Gray," Duke continued. "This is on your desk. If it works you move up. If it doesn't you move out. Are we clear?"

"Yes, sir."

He left Duke's office walking on a cloud of confidence. Of course it would work. Or it wouldn't. In either case it was better than standing still.

19

WHITE PAWN TO QUEEN'S CASTLE THREE

The first rule of gonzo journalism is: There are no rules. In the tradition of Hunter S. Thompson, Cato Mackay embraced his assignment to cover the Democratic primaries from the first debate in South Carolina to the convention in Miami with all his bountiful energy. With stunning ease he wormed his way into the bosom of every camp. He drank with party operatives, passed joints with spies and on occasion dropped acid with his more adventurous media colleagues. As a result he knew every rumor and every new development before it happened.

The second rule of gonzo journalism is: Play it straight. If you like a candidate you say so. If you like what she stands for that's the story. If you appreciate the actions a campaign takes, you say so up front. If you don't like it you say that you don't. Cato knew his boss not only favored Shelby Duran, he also knew he had offered his financial support. It presented a classic journalistic dilemma, a conflict of interest, and one Mackay was eager to dispense.

He broke the story that Duran would run, that her people had applied for a last-minute entry in the debate, and that Lawrence McClure would finance her through the early primaries. He did so without consulting his boss before the fact. It was his declaration of independence and he felt confident that McClure would respect him for it.

The third rule of gonzo journalism is brutal honesty. Let the chips fall. He reported the discrepancy between what the campaigns reported and what was actually happening behind the curtains of debate simulation.

Everyone knows the debates are a game of expectations, especially the first debate. A debate is not won or lost on the merits but on the perception of who exceeded expectations. Thus George W. Bush was able to claim debate victory over John Kerry by demonstrating he was slightly better than a talking monkey. The Bush team managed to set the bar so low that their candidate soared over it by being able to formulate a cohesive thought.

While much has changed since the Bush-Kerry debates the campaigns still played the game of expectations, describing their candidate's rehearsal performances as rough and flawed, halting and uncertain. Mackay exploited his spy network to expose the duplicity. The Warner camp claimed to be worried about the candidate's depth of knowledge on foreign affairs but behind the curtain they were ecstatic. The Black campaign expressed concern about their man's ability to connect with the common people when in fact that was the candidate's strength. Molinari's people said he had trouble dumbing down his comments in a debate format when in fact he had difficulty ginning them up. On and on, every candidate faced a critical review from his or her own camp.

Shelby Duran, the latest entry in the presidential smack down, was said to have been so dismal in her only session the campaign had decided to abandon them altogether. Until the Senate confirmed her replacement she was still Secretary of State. They would claim she was too busy doing her job to prepare for a debate. If it cost her points, so be it.

The account was partially true. Duran had engaged in only one practice session. Mackay obtained an audio recording of that session. His assessment: The Secretary was so good and so well prepared that further rehearsals were deemed unnecessary.

It was not the assessment the Duran campaign wanted to leak but it was the truth and Mackay was bound by his oath to report it. And so he did.

20

BLACK PAWN TO KING FIVE

Pawn Gambit Declined

The first debate ended without a clear winner. The polls and pundits praised the performances of Bethany Warner, Jerrod Black, Pat Duvall and Shelby Duran. If anyone exceeded expectations it was Senator Barnard Andrews whose impassioned plea for social equity struck a chord with the viewing audience. The media nevertheless continued to regard him as something less than a serious candidate. If anyone failed to meet expectations it was Governor Francis Molinari who came off as arrogant without cause.

Attention turned to Iowa, site of the first caucus. Word on the street held that Senator Black of Ohio was running to gain name recognition, to advocate a pro-labor fair trade position, and possibly, if all went well and the cards fell in his favor, to be nominated for the vice presidency. Of course, the same could pretty much be said of every candidate with the exception of the sitting vice president Joe Bolton. Despite Bolton's lack of traction the vice presidency was still considered a stepping stone to the presidency.

Richard Dawson continued to build a ground game in support of Secretary Duran. He enjoyed a surge of interest when she announced and again after her performance in the first debate. He had helped establish campaign headquarters in Des Moines, Cedar Rapids and Davenport and the volunteers were lining up for assignments. He gathered opinions, compiled voting data, drew maps of likely voters and districts favoring Duran. It didn't take long for Winfred Holmes to notice his work and put him on the campaign payroll.

One of the advantages of having worked in Iowa before was that he knew many if not most of the players. Regardless of the candidates the same people tended to run the ground campaigns. For this reason Dawson was surprised to see Sandy Merrill of the Black campaign sitting down for an early dinner with Mario Macias of Americans for Fair Trade. They certainly had common cause. Americans for Fair Trade was a 501 group set up to support the primary issue of Jarrod Black. Black was their man. The trouble was it was a violation of campaign finance laws (as weak as they were) for a campaign to be associated in any way with such an organization. The campaign would be subject to substantial fines, damaging their candidate's image, and the organization could lose its tax-exempt status.

If they were going to engage in collusion why would they do so in a public place? True, Blake's Diner was not exactly a gathering place for politicos but still. It was a place that Dawson frequented every time he came to Waterloo. Could they have known that? Was this a test of his ethics or of his loyalty to the Duran campaign? He knew Sandy well enough to say hello but when he recognized Macias, he took a seat outside their view. Whatever was going on he wasn't ready to confront it head on.

He ordered his usual cheeseburger with fries and watched them finish their meals, noting that Macias paid the bill. He walked out and she lingered before following. He thought she caught a glimpse of him as she strolled by but she did not acknowledge his presence.

The whole thing stunk of dirty politics but Dawson could not figure out the angle. It seemed clear to him that she wanted him to witness the event. Maybe she didn't work for Black after all. Maybe she secretly worked for someone else (Molinari came to mind) who wanted to create a rift between the Black and Duran camps. He had not heard what they discussed so it was less than open and shut. Maybe they were friends or lovers, who knew? Maybe it was just an innocent romantic tryst.

Still it had the appearance of impropriety and in politics appearances count. Often they count more than reality.

The next time he got a chance he'd mention it to his boss, William Carmichael, the state campaign manager of Duran for President. Let him decide what to do about it.

It was probably nothing more than what it seemed: two veterans of the campaign trail sharing a meal. People still did that. Everyone knows everyone after a couple of campaigns. It didn't really matter who you worked for on a given campaign. It was a brotherhood-sisterhood thing. Like cops and Teamsters, there was a common ground. He told himself it was nothing to get excited about.

21

PLAYERS

The Trouble with Humans

Solana watched in amusement as her queen nearly slipped out of her control. Winfred Holmes had nearly driven her over the edge of madness. Attacking with the queen so early in the match was a bold move. She used all of her influence to push him into that decision and he had reluctantly done so, leaving her queen in a position of power with bishops on both sides eliminated.

Just when she thought the situation had been normalized, Holmes threatened to undo it all by allowing her bishop back in the game. It could not be allowed. She rallied her forces a second time to persuade him that politics could have no tolerance for betrayal. He should have known as much but his empathy for Llewyn Davis was inexplicably powerful. He believed in him. He believed that Davis would become his most trustworthy operative and perhaps he would have but that was decidedly beside the point. Others would perceive weakness. When the word made its way through the circuit, it would hurt contributions. It would affect recruitment. It would alter the course of the campaign.

In the end, Llewyn Davis himself made the case. When Holmes tried to bring him back on board, he refused and Holmes came to his senses.

Joining Willy for a few days in the nation's capitol, no one was more relieved than Solana. She was pleased with her progress in the match and Willy was impressed. She would have hated to wipe the board clean and start over. The match would have been a failure and the responsibility would have fallen on her shapely shoulders.

Sipping wine over Washington's finest Italian cuisine at Obelisk in Dupont Circle, Solana laughed and sighed. Willy shook his head and admired her strength and perseverance. While he certainly had moments of trepidation, he had not been so severely tested as she had. He surmised that his choice of primaries (bishops, knights et al) tended to think as he did, strategically and with far less emotional attachment. He believed it was to his advantage but he had to admit her play had far exceeded his expectations. She was playing at a level of which he had not suspected her capable. It both alarmed and delighted him.

"That's the trouble with humans," she said. "They tend to believe in free will."

"Humans do have free will," countered Willy. "Fortunately for us, some possess a great deal more of that precious commodity than others. You and I, for instance, have a great deal more than ordinary humans."

"Do you think that makes us better?"

He reflected on the question. He had given it some thought and debated the point with her father. In truth, he did believe in a qualitative difference between the elite and the rest of humankind but he was loath to admit it.

"I think it makes us...different."

Solana saw through him as no one else could. She did not always challenge him on his little deceptions but she did on this one.

"I know you, Willy. You believe in the ruling class. You believe that our elite status is more than the product of culture and education and good fortune. You believe it is in large part the product of genetic inheritance. Am I wrong?"

He hesitated. Was it time to reveal this fundamental truth? Would it alter her perception of him? Would it change their relationship? He decided it would not. She would not challenge his beliefs if she were not prepared for the truth.

"Not entirely. It is a question I have struggled with and I am well aware of the exceptions. Still, on balance, I do believe in a ruling class. I also believe it will emerge under any form of government."

"That's a dodge and you know it," replied Solana. "The exceptions you speak of are rather profound. The leading innovators of the technology era were college dropouts and members of the middle class. Then there are the artists. The greatest artists in all of recorded history: Shakespeare, Picasso, Monet, DaVinci, Rousseau, Sartre, Mozart, Beethoven, Rodin, Steinbeck, Marquez and McCarthy, all of them emerging from the vast sea of humanity. None of them from the elite."

"I note that you do not mention Rembrandt, Raphael, Michelangelo, Duchamp, on and on, individuals born of privilege and standing. There are many examples on both sides of the issue. I concede that art or the creative mind is by no means the sole domain of the elite. But we are talking about governance, are we not?"

"We are," she smiled. She did enjoy their repartee. It had been too long. One of the unintended effects of their chess matches was that they often disguised their true feelings as if revealing them would offer the keys to victory or defeat.

"Let it be," he concluded. "Let us enjoy our brief stay in this city of paradox, a city that combines dire poverty and crime with the culture and comforts befitting the cradle of political power for western civilization."

"I'll drink to that," she replied.

He looked at her with intense curiosity and wonder as he often did. No matter how well he thought he knew Solana she always managed to surprise him.

"There is one question that haunts me in the wake of this incident," he said. "If indeed Winfred Holmes or one of your primary pieces does act independent of your wishes, would you carry on or declare an end?"

"That, my dear Willy, is a very good question. Would it be unethical to carry on? Or could we negotiate an exception?"

Willy wrinkled his face as he contemplated the implications: the possibility that he or Solana could choose to hide a rogue move rather than end a winning match or the possibility that one of them could falsely claim such a move rather than proceed with a losing strategy. It came down to trust and that was something chess did not allow.

"It is quite a dilemma, is it not?"

"It is."

"Let us hope it does not occur but if does, we must declare and negotiate on our honor. Agreed?"

"Agreed."

They drank and enjoyed the ambiance, the exhilaration of the match, the pleasure of their company, the taste of their wine, the sensation of being at the heart of power and the mysteries of their special relationship.

"That does raise another interesting question," Solana added as an afterthought.

"What's that?"

"Is there honor in chess?"

It was a good question and one they were not prepared to answer at this time and place. That was the trouble with humans: We can only carry on and see what the future brings. We pretend we have free will but by and large the events that guide our conduct are beyond our comprehension and control.

22

QUEENSIDE CASTLE

Lawrence McClure liked to play poker. He once entered a World Poker Championship tournament in Las Vegas, finishing in the top fifty. Few things in life gave him more pleasure than the moment at the table when he could look his opponent in the eyes and declare: All in! It was a moment when all distractions peeled away like dust in the wind. A rare moment of clarity and purpose.

When McClure watched the first Democratic Party Presidential Primary Debate on television, he declared all in. Shelby Duran was everything he hoped she would be. She spoke with authority on all subjects, foreign and domestic, and did not hesitate to advance her position on controversial subjects. Most critically to the high tech community she condemned technology theft by China, India and other nations as one of the most significant threats to the security of the American people and the global economic system. While other candidates agreed with her only Duran had demonstrated her in-depth comprehension of the issue. Her understanding informed her position and gave it certitude. While other candidates might pay lip service, Duran would act accordingly.

McClure mobilized some of his best people to form a political unit within his company. He would take on the role of a bundler, actively recruiting others to contribute to the Duran for President campaign. He called Winfred Holmes to inform him of his decision and ask his advice. He had intended to call a meeting of the leading high tech minds in the country but Holmes advised him against it. It would be more effective to approach them individually. He should meet first with those he considered most likely to support the cause. The more contributors he enlisted to the cause, the more persuasive his case would be.

McClure had no illusions. The technology sector had been notoriously quiet in the political arena. Some wanted to avoid the appearance of bias. Others considered it a waste of time and money. Still others felt conflicted, their political views running contrary to their financial interests. For the most part, the players in the high tech industry came from progressive backgrounds, lived in progressive communities and enjoyed the blessings of being welcome in the dominant liberal culture of America's major cities. It was time past time for at least some of them to step forward.

He started with Sophia Cantu, CEO of Oracle. While Oracle's infamous founder leaned to the right, Sophia leaned hard in the opposite direction. She agreed readily to join the cause, pledging a contribution of fifty grand with a promise of fifty more if Duran made it to Super Tuesday. She expressed her conviction that the primary source of opposition to Duran and other Democrats among their colleagues was not so much trade policy (although that was certainly important) as it was offshore tax shelters.

"No one wants to pay their fair share," she said.

"As if we don't make enough money," he replied.

"It's incredible. We've created this idea that cheating the government is somehow smart and patriotic. We're the job creators and we deserve every penny we can get our hands on."

"It has to change sometime. Why not now?"

"I can think of a few billion reasons why but I wish you luck."

She advised him to go after Jaso at Amazon, Zimmerman and Sandberg at Facebook, with an outside chance at Meyer and Chang of Yahoo. They were worth a shot even though they preferred to remain on the sidelines. In her view, Apple was a lost cause because of its reliance on cheap labor in China. The executives at Google were hopelessly bipartisan despite its popularity among the liberal crowd. If they contributed at all, they would give to both sides according to the probability of success.

Every one of them knew they were indebted to Secretary Duran for her work on intellectual property. While an attack on tax shelters might hurt their balance sheets an erosion of intellectual property rights threatened their existence. He would remind them that a new president with a less informed view of free trade could easily reverse what Duran and the Marquez administration had accomplished.

McClure went down the list one by one and managed concessions from all, even Apple and Google. Only Microsoft refused outright. Some found his arguments persuasive. As expected, others hedged their bets. In the end, he amassed a sizable war chest for the Duran campaign. As they moved forward everything would depend on winning. Winners attract money and support; losers repel them. As least now the high tech industry was invested. They were in the game. They were players and every single one of them hated to lose.

23

BLACK QUEEN TO KING SEVEN

Jacoby Morris wanted to play some hardball. He lived for the down-and-dirty, nose-to-nose, face-to-the-floor battle. He had instructed his candidate to play the race card on day one, reminding Wynn that even Ronald Reagan had opened his 1980 campaign at the infamous Bob Jones University in South Carolina. When the time came, he would play the race card again before Super Tuesday when a string of Deep South states were in play. It would be key to winning the south from the evangelical Rivera campaign.

To Morris the hardest part of the game was the waiting. He had been waiting long enough. Known as the toughest operator in the business, he liked his candidates the same way. That's why he signed up with Danny Diamond to begin with; he was the man with the magic touch.

After a week of watching Wynn try to play the nice guy Morris calmly walked into a conference room where all the consultants and coaches and pollsters and image specialists were sharing their views on the candidate's performance in the latest rehearsal session. He listened with all the patience he could muster for about a half minute; then he ordered them all out and glared at his candidate.

"How you doing, big man?"

Wynn glared back. No one called him anything but Mr. Wynn to his face without receiving the pink slip. He liked Jack Morris. He held him in highest regard. That and that alone kept him from lowering the hammer. He was counting on him to lead his march to the White House but he'd be damned if he'd let Morris disrespect him.

"Fuck you, Jack off! Don't think you're so important that I can't fire you."

"Well, well, it's good to see you still have some fight left in you! Another week of this bullshit and I wouldn't even recognize you!"

"What the hell are you talking about?"

"I thought you might be tired of being a pussy, that's all."

"Excuse me but my impression is you were the one who arranged for this nice guy routine! Am I right or am I right? My understanding is it plays to my advantage."

Morris shook his head.

"The nice guy routine is for the suckers, Danny boy, not for you. You got to where you are because you're a tough guy, a bully, a guy who dishes it out and doesn't take it. You want to play nice you won't get any closer to the White House than you are today. Have I made myself clear? Am I getting through that thick skull of yours?"

Wynn squinted, letting it settle before he acknowledged the stone cold truth.

"It's all a setup," he said.

"That's right, big man. For the past few weeks every candidate on the Republican side has been practicing the soft shoe, just like you have. The day after tomorrow you'll go on stage and do what you were born to do: Attack! They'll never know what hit 'em."

Wynn smiled when he fully processed the implications. This was the reason he hired Morris. He was the only man less scrupled than he was.

"They're not going to like it."

"You're not out to make friends. You're out to kick some ass and plant the seed of fear deep in their psyches. Are we on the same page?"

"We are."

Wynn wondered why he hadn't seen through the façade. He also wondered why he'd been wasting his time playing nice in debate rehearsals when they had no intention of going through with it. Morris read his mind.

"Look, you don't need to practice what comes natural. I guarantee you there are one or two spies in that debate crew, if not them then their lovers or drinking buddies. What happens behind closed doors always comes out. It's inevitable. We don't want anyone knowing what we're planning. That stays between you and me."

"Got it."

"You've got one more session tomorrow. Go through the motions. Come Friday night the real Danny Diamond takes the country by storm. We'll tell everyone it just came out. A tiger can't deny his stripes. It'll piss 'em off and that's just fine. You'll have the lead and we won't look back until the convention. Got it?"

"Got it."

It was still possible word might get out. Wynn was known to knock a few down in the evening hours. He might say something to someone he trusted. That was why Morris waited this long to let him in on the joke. At this point, it almost didn't matter. They wouldn't know what to make of it and they wouldn't know how to respond. They weren't prepared.

"What about Peterson?" wondered Wynn. "The RNC could make it rough on us."

"Don't you worry about that," replied Morris. "It's all under control."

He winked and Wynn didn't ask. Some things were better left unspoken. After all that had transpired during his brief campaign, he understood. He thanked a god he didn't believe in that Jack Morris was on his side.

24

WHITE KING TO QUEEN'S KNIGHT ONE

Secretary Duran was in a position of power. After her showing in the first debate contributions flowed in, her numbers rose and momentum swung in her direction. One major obstacle that other candidates did not face still stood in her way: She remained Secretary of State. One international crisis would bring her campaign to a sudden halt and expose her to an allegation of negligence. They could manage to maintain momentum for a spell but the inevitable time would come when she had to abandon the campaign.

The secretary had strongly recommended Samantha Powell, her deputy secretary and former ambassador to the United Nations, as her successor. Powell had demonstrated a breadth and depth of knowledge in foreign affairs few in the world could rival and her performance under the constant flames of crisis had drawn both the secretary's and the president's admiration.

The president needed to nominate a new Secretary of State immediately. He could not hold his foreign policy initiatives in place indefinitely. He needed someone now to initiate the process of securing consent of the senate. He summoned Secretary Duran, Winfred Holmes, Senator John Winthrop and Samantha Powell to the Oval Office, vowing that the meeting would end with a nominee in place.

Accustomed to being the first to arrive it surprised her to find everyone assembled before her as she entered the room. The president greeted her with an expression of solemnity.

"Secretary Duran, please have a seat."

She did as the president requested. Glancing around she

had the distinct and uncomfortable feeling that everyone knew something she did not. Her instincts were rarely off on these matters. It was a quality that served her well in her role as the nation's lead negotiator. President Marquez broke an awkward silence.

"We've had a good discussion prior to your arrival and for that I apologize. The short of it is: I'd like you to meet the next Secretary of State."

He gestured toward Senator Winthrop who nodded in acknowledgement. The president continued.

"We all know that your choice to succeed you is Ms. Powell which is why we invited her here today. We wanted her to understand that the selection of Senator Winthrop is by no means a slight. I wanted the senator to know that in fact he was not my first choice. Ms. Powell has my full confidence and she's graciously agreed to continue her service as deputy secretary."

Ms. Powell nodded in a manner that managed to convey both disappointment and understanding.

"May I speak freely, Mr. President?"

"You always have. I'd hate to think that would end now that you're a candidate."

"With all due respect to Senator Winthrop, I'd hate to think that the cost of my running for president includes the career of my deputy director. Samantha Powell has put in the time, serving admirably under the most trying conditions. She deserves the appointment."

"I agree," replied the president. "And when you become chief executive I sincerely hope you'll be able to appoint anyone you like, including Samantha Powell as Secretary of State. Senator Winthrop understands that. It was not easy persuading him to give up one of the most powerful seats in the United States Senate to take a job that may only last two years."

The secretary took a step back. Senator Winthrop was a solid choice and an honest man. He had been an important ally in the upper chamber of congress. Many would consider his resigning from the senate to serve a lame duck president a step down.

"I apologize, Senator Winthrop. In no way did I mean to diminish your service or your capabilities in any way."

"I understand," replied the senator. "Loyalty is an admirable quality and Deputy Secretary Powell is a worthy choice. I also understand the United States Senate. We might be able to push her through the process but the Republicans hold the majority. It would be drawn out and you, Madam Secretary, would be the target of confirmation hearings."

Ms. Powell felt compelled to weigh in.

"I agree with the senator's assessment. We all do. The Republicans would use my nomination to attack you as a candidate for president. That's something we cannot and will not allow."

Secretary Duran looked around the table for a dissenting voice. The only head that was not nodding belonged to Winfred Holmes.

"Fred?"

He sighed deeply, leaned forward and spoke as if the two of them were alone in his study. How often they had done just that. Like the president, she trusted him above all others.

"I pushed you to run for president. I pushed hard. But I also warned you there would be times like this, times when you would regret your decision to run. It happens a lot in this business and a lot more in this office. If you want to be president, these are they kinds of decision you will have to make. Senator Winthrop is not your first choice but he is a viable option. He knows the senate. He knows senators on both sides of the aisle. He's built a lot of good will and collected his share of markers. They won't deny him the appointment and they won't use him to get at you."

"It's a political thing."

"Yes."

The president weighed in.

"Ms. Powell will have her day but this day belongs to Senator Winthrop and we'd like your approval before we announce it."

The secretary looked Samantha Powell straight in the eyes.

"You're okay with this?"

"I am."

"And if I took you aside and asked you to tell me the truth?"

"I would still be okay. In fact, I would insist."

The secretary stood and extended her hand to Senator Winthrop.

"Congratulations, senator."

25

BLACK PAWN TO QUEEN'S CASTLE SIX

There are many ways to diffuse a scandal and none of them have anything to do with whether or not the scandal is grounded on fact or fiction. Those whose specialty is to deal with scandals are well compensated and they all operate by the same rules.

First rule: Deny. If you're caught with your hand in the proverbial cookie jar, deny. If you're filmed taking a bribe, deny. If the police walk in to find you standing over a dead body with a smoking gun, deny, deny, deny and ask for a lawyer. Never admit guilt. Never.

Second rule: Accuse. Accuse your accusers of nefarious intent, dubious character and a history of wicked deeds. If the accuser is the pope, himself, accuse him of dark and ulterior motives. It is better if your accusations have a parcel of truth but it is decidedly not necessary. The accusations should be repeated and intensified until the accused is compelled to take defensive measures. The original scandal begins to fade and takes on a "he said, she said" nature.

Third rule: Evade. Deny the charges once, then defer. Explain that the people are tired of hearing the same old, trumped up accusations over and over again. The people want their representatives working to create jobs, solve problems and fix our crumbling infrastructure. Those in the media who fixate on such matters betray the public trust.

Fourth rule: Discredit the accuser. The accuser always has a conflict of interest. Find a history of inappropriate behavior, unsubstantiated charges, questionable financial transactions or sexual misadventures, anything that will force the observer to see the accuser in a different light.

Jed Parson's assignment fell under the jurisdiction of the fourth rule. The Wynn campaign had learned that the Pierce campaign was particularly upset in the wake of the first debate. While Pierce was still playing the nice guy, Wynn went on attack, raising accusations that the former governor had personally approved hiring a private firm to disenfranchise predominantly black voters. Hell-bent on vengeance, the Pierce machine went into overdrive, gathering incriminating data and testimonials for a counterattack.

Parson gave them what they most desired: Something new and damning, a virtual smoking gun. It not only had to seem authentic, it had to be authentic, and yet easily exposed as a fraud. Adept at deception, Parson had an I-phone, audio-only recording of Wynn bragging about hiring a full crew of foreign workers to undercut the local union. He went on to boast about bankrupting an official who crossed him on the project.

"I not only did it," he exclaimed, "I'd do it again! As a matter of fact, as soon as the smoke clears and we get past this damned election, I will do it again! Fuck 'em all! That's what happens when you mess with Danny Wynn!"

That was all there was to the recording. It was uncut and unaltered, a critical quality in the deception. It was actually part of a spoof at an office party in which Wynn bragged about committing every crime from bombing the twin towers to personally torturing a terrorist suspect at Guantanamo Bay. At the end he promised to unleash a wave of nuclear bombs on every town in America that didn't vote his way.

There was clearly nothing to it but out of context it seemed like the perfect weapon. Parson contacted Margarit Saldana of the Pierce campaign and offered the incriminating evidence in exchange for a job once the Wynn campaign imploded as it inevitably would. His reputation for double-dealing served his purpose.

Saldana believed him and she felt certain that her

candidate would believe him as well. She told him they'd be in touch if it all checked out. It did and she contacted him with a standing offer of a job at twice his current pay. He smiled, knowing that when it didn't work out as they intended, he would move to the top of their enemies list. Danny Diamond would be providing the pay raise.

26

WHITE KNIGHT TO QUEEN'S BISHOP ONE

Politics is dirty business. No one who rises up the ranks in party politics does so with clean hands. Democratic National Committee chairperson Dorothea Vargas was not an exception. Starting with her days as a local activist in Southern California politics she learned how to recognize dirty deeds and trace them to their source. She became a master at countering acts of sabotage and mud slinging with a deft hand, disguising her own double-dealings so that no one could hold her or her candidate accountable. The best dirty tricks are those the victim never sees coming and never finds out where they came from.

It was not a secret that Vargas held Secretary Duran in highest regard. Her enemies were constantly on watch to discover any decisions or activities that revealed favoritism. No one wanted to see her bumped from her position of power more than Governor Molinari and Vargas was acutely aware of his animosity. Any move she made had to have the appearance of neutrality.

The Iowa caucus was fast approaching and the numbers were coming in hard and fast. Senator Black of Ohio had a decided edge with Warner and Duran vying for runner up. All other candidates plodded along in the second and third tiers. The numbers behind the numbers clearly revealed that Warner and Duran were pulling from the same trough: the progressive wing of the party.

Vargas, like most analysts within and without the party, was convinced that Warner's campaign would fade for lack of funding but in the meantime her continued presence would hurt Duran. A number of party emissaries had asked Warner to pull out for that reason but she was on a mission. Only she could deliver her message of Wall Street greed and the unequal distribution of wealth with her passion and knowledge. She liked Duran and would support her but she would not withdraw until absolutely necessary.

Vargas feared it would be too late, that the damage done in the early going would enable other candidates, Duvall or Black or Molinari, to gain momentum. If that happened she was convinced they would lose the general election.

The DNC was an information-gathering machine. She had in her possession a video taped interview of Warner by an obscure web-based progressive organization in which she spoke honestly about farm subsidies and the need to get rid of them. It was an uncomfortable truth that everyone knows and accepts but no one who wishes to be president speaks aloud. The reason: it spells death in the Iowa caucus.

Warner had eased around the issue of farm subsidies during her campaign, never using the term "corporate welfare" as she had in the interview and never stating directly that they should be abolished.

Vargas had ways of releasing information so that it could not be traced back to her or her associates. She had her own operatives and her own team of hackers. She delivered the interview tape on flash drive to one of her hackers with instructions to release it anonymously through two websites that were well viewed by politicos. She told him to plant a seed of suspicion connecting the tape to the Duvall camp. The charge would never stick but it would blur the lines before anyone got around to accusing the Duran campaign.

Right on cue a 501 group loosely affiliated with the Molinari campaign fashioned the footage into an attack ad and ran it throughout Iowa. Local media picked it up and ran with it to the day of the caucus.

Bethany Warner never knew what hit her and would never learn who threw the punch. It cost her at least ten

110

percentage points in the caucus, a blow that reverberated across the country and directly to New Hampshire. Contributions fell off and allegiances shifted from Warner to Duran.

Three days after the New Hampshire primary Senator Warner would announce her withdrawal from the race and declare her full support for Shelby Duran.

27

QUEENSIDE CASTLE

Daniel J. Wynn did not create Americans for America First. It was created for him. Even before any of the candidates had announced their intentions to run, its founder decided to make America's favorite bully, the big man of the Big Apple, president of the United States. Jim Duke was a powerful man, a man of influence and a man who made kings.

Wynn possessed the essential qualities Duke looked for in a politician: He never wavered in his support of corporate supremacy. He supported coal, oil, fracking and nuclear power. He took the hard line on global warming, doubting the science and falling back to the position that humans could do nothing about it in any case. While others who took the same position looked like captains on a ship of fools, Wynn managed to look strong and almost logical. On foreign policy, he opposed stupid wars by stupid leaders but took the hard line against Islamic extremists, Iran and North Korea: Our enemies would rue the day they placed themselves in the path of America's interests. He made noise against free trade policies but everyone knew he was just playing games. Behind closed doors he gave the necessary assurances.

Overall, the campaign was going well. Nolan Gray's strategy of attacking Pierce's credibility on foreign policy issues had worked. Pierce fell back and Wynn surged ahead. He faced a surprising challenge in Iowa where the evangelic appeal of Texas Senator Gene Rivera threatened to steal the first contest of the presidential campaign. He needed a win in New Hampshire where his primary threat emerged in

Governor Paul Casey, a relative moderate with a country boy appeal.

Wynn managed a slim victory in the Iowa caucus while Casey finished in the bottom tier. If he could win in New Hampshire he would become the clear frontrunner. If he could win by a large margin his campaign would take on the air of an unstoppable force.

Knowing this and recognizing Casey as the man standing in his way, Jack Morris sent an emissary to pay a visit to Jim Duke, strictly off the record. Americans for America First remained fixated on destroying Ellis Pierce, running a barrage of attack ads in the New Hampshire market. Rowan Darby's job was to convince Duke that it was time to shift gears and level a new attack against Casey. Darby was not officially on the Wynn campaign payroll so it was technically not illegal for him to meet with Duke but if the word got out, it would raise questions and those questions could be used against their candidate.

They met in the lobby of the George Washington hotel, a few decades past its elegant days, and proceeded to the bar. These were the fabled dark, smoke-filled rooms where operatives decided the fate of the nation, without the smoke. No one smokes inside anymore. There are places where the only legal substance to smoke inside or out is marijuana. Such is the state of our progressive social engineering.

"I'm not actually here," opened Darby.

Duke gave a crooked grin. He knew the game.

"And if you were, this would be a prelude to a job interview. How would you like to work for Americans for America First?"

"How much docs it pay?"

"More than you're getting now."

"That's not saying a lot."

"Depends on what you're worth."

This was foreplay. They ordered drinks, Darby a brandy and Duke a single-malt scotch, glancing around to see if

anyone was curious. No one was. Darby got to the point.
"Pierce is down. He can't win in New Hampshire. The most he can hope for is to stay alive. Alonzo has no traction and the Rivera campaign doesn't even know the language in New England. The real threat to Wynn right now is Casey."

Duke listened carefully as if he was being pitched a new product or the opening of a new mall in Peoria. He appreciated Darby's forthright logic but he didn't necessarily agree.

"In my experience, when you've got a man down you step on him. You kick him in the gut. You make damned sure he doesn't get up. Pierce is the long-term threat, not Casey."

"Casey has built a career on being under-rated. Name an operative who thought he had a chance at winning the statehouse in Ohio. You can't. Everyone thinks he's a boring, slightly dim hayseed. He's a hell of a lot smarter than he looks. He's reshuffled the deck, moved to the center, found ways to reinvent his image with a broader appeal. They love that crap in New Hampshire. Even people who don't think he has a chance will vote for him because he's sincere and if he happens to pull it off he becomes a media darling: The little guy who stood up to the big bad bully. Don't kid yourself. He's a threat."

Duke sipped his scotch and fought back the urge to light up a cigar.

"I'll give you this much: You've honed your argument. You make a good case. What have you got on Casey?"

"Ohio libertarians hate him. He's staked his entire campaign on being perceived as the Honest Abe of this election. The libertarians in Ohio know better. His Secretary of State forced the Libertarian candidate for governor off the ballot with a highly suspect challenge of his signatures. He followed that up with a law to restrict the Ohio ballot to Republicans and Democrats. Honest Abe starts to look like Johnny Hayseed: just another politician who likes a fixed game. We just need to package it and force him to respond. Every day he spends defending himself is another day lost and another day losing ground in the polls."

Duke sipped, nodded and again fought back the urge to smoke. The fact that his dirty trick went against Libertarians would play exceptionally well in New Hampshire. It was an ingenious attack.

"Where do his votes go?"

"They split. Wynn will get more than his share."

"Unless he's perceived as the attacker."

"That's where you come in: Americans for America First."

"It could become a pretty thin cover."

"It'll hold through New Hampshire. Who knows? Maybe it holds all the way through Super Tuesday."

Darby caught sight of a woman across the room that held her gaze on their table a little too long for comfort.

"We may need to take this discussion somewhere more private," he whispered.

Duke took a subtle glance at the woman, an attractive woman in modest if stylish dress. "A woman captures your eye and you immediately think she's a spy. You've been in this business too long."

"Caution is why I've been in this business this long."

Duke laughed, finished his scotch, tossed a couple of bills on the table and stood.

"Very well. Let's step outside. I need a smoke."

Darby followed him out. The curious woman watched them leave but remained in her seat. He had the uncertain feeling that he knew her or at least had seen her somewhere.

"I'll tell you what," said Duke. "We've got the money. We go both ways and see how the numbers play out. Agreed?"

"Agreed."

They shook hands and Darby handed over a flash drive as Duke smoked his cigar. The drive contained all the materials he needed to take down Paul Casey. It was a thing of beauty. They'd never see it coming.

"This should do it."

"Nasty habit," said Duke, taking a puff. "And for the record, we take nothing for granted. We've got an extensive file on everyone, including you."

He winked and Darby hailed a cab.

28

WHITE KNIGHT TO QUEEN'S KNIGHT THREE

As chair of the DNC, Dorothea Vargas cultivated a close relationship with the government agencies that generated news and the media that disseminated it. She had friends on the Federal Election Commission and friends on staff. She had friends at the Internal Revenue Service. She had friends and allies among the reporters and editors at the Times, the Post and the Daily News.

When the FEC discovered violations in campaign financing law she was among the first to know. When the commission came across irregularities in the reported income of candidate Francis Molinari it landed on her desk only days before the New Hampshire primary. It did not surprise her that Molinari had exploited offshore accounts to avoid taxes. It did surprise her that he tried to hide that fact on his official campaign forms.

At first she thought it prudent to sit on the story until after the primary. It was no secret that she favored Duran but the perception of equanimity was critical to her job. She had already chastised his campaign for hiring an attack dog to go after Duran. She could not release damaging information on the eve of a critical primary without his campaign crying foul.

She had all but arrived at her decision when Megan Forsyth, a staffer relatively new to her office, reopened the discussion. Megan had spent most of her career in California politics, helping to bring the golden state securely back to the Democratic fold. She came with the reputation of being tough and smart and worked her way into the inner circle by displaying an uncanny ability to know what the chair was thinking. On those occasions when she took an opposing view she appealed to her boss's better half, her core sense, as she did now.

She had learned through her own sources about the problems with Molinari's financial filings and pressed the chair to release the information immediately.

"Look, it's a twisted media world. A scandal is not a scandal unless it hits the news cycle on the right day, the right hour, the right minute. A congressman from upstate New York was re-elected after being indicted on felony tax evasion. The story hit on a Saturday. Just his luck. You can take money from the Chinese government. You can run a Ponzi scheme on small investors. You can defraud the treasury and reveal state secrets. As long as it's not a slow news day during the week you can get away with anything short of posting your genitals on line. It's all in the timing. If we don't get this out before the primary, it dies a slow death. Nobody cares."

Megan was always energized and animated, moving her arms and pacing to accentuate her arguments, but now it seemed to Dorothea she was even more so. Why was this decision so critical in her mind?

"Duran can win New Hampshire on the merits," she responded. "She doesn't need a scandal to beat Molinari."

"Of course not. But it's not just a matter of winning. Molinari is well financed. If he does well in New Hampshire, he can hang on to Super Tuesday. We're talking millions of dollars that could otherwise be spent in the general election."

"I know how it works. The question is: Is it right?"

"Is it right to defraud the government you want to lead? Is it right to cheat the people who pay their fair share of taxes?"

Dorothea studied her employee and wondered if she'd underestimated her. She seemed destined to a higher position in the not too distant future. Was it possible she was playing her hand now?

"Is it right for the chair of the Democratic National Committee to deliberately sabotage the campaign of a Democratic candidate for the presidency?"

Megan took a moment to reframe her argument.

"It's politics, Dorothea. It's the politics of the greater good. The real question is: Would you expose any other candidate for the same offense? Would you release the same information if it were Warner or Duvall or Duran? The answer is: You wouldn't have to because none of those candidates would avoid paying their fair share of taxes. You know it. Molinari doesn't deserve to be president and he doesn't deserve to cost Duran her chance."

Once again Megan went to the heart of the matter. She was right. Anyone who would go to extreme measures to avoid paying taxes, legal or not, didn't belong in the White House. He had disqualified himself and in a very real sense betrayed both his party and his country. Democrats did not shirk their fundamental, patriotic duties, Republicans did. In this light it was her responsibility to do the right thing: That meant eliminating a flawed and unworthy candidate before he could do any further harm.

She called one of her connections in the press. It would be attributed to a knowledgeable source. Molinari would not suspect the chair of the DNC. He would look instead to his many political enemies. It no longer mattered. He would finish in the second tier in New Hampshire and that would be the death knell to his presidential ambitions.

29

BLACK PAWN TO QUEEN FOUR

Pawn Takes Pawn

Richard Dawson did a stellar job in Iowa, getting the word out and pumping up the turn out for Secretary Duran. Many attributed her strong showing to his efforts. It did not go unnoticed. He moved on to New Hampshire and took over the canvassing operation. He had a talent for talking to people as if he knew them, as if he was an old friend. Folks liked him and didn't mind spending a few minutes talking politics.

The New Hampshire campaign was outstanding. Duran surged as they neared Election Day. When the Molinari campaign imploded in the final days, struck by accusations of tax evasion, Duran pulled ahead for a clear and decisive victory. With Warner out of the race and Molinari struggling, the path to the nomination cleared. The race was hers to lose.

It should have been a great moment in Dawson's career but the celebration lasted less than twenty-four hours. He had already packed for South Carolina when Julia Sands called him into her office. The campaign had brought them together. He would have called her a friend and entertained ideas of a closer relationship down the road but the look on her face was anything but amiable. Something had changed. Something had altered their connection to its core.

"I'm sorry to call you in here. I really am," she said.

He thought: *Shit, if the next word out of her mouth is but*

I'm fired!

"But I don't have a choice. You know this campaign is founded on the principle that Duran is different. She doesn't play politics. She doesn't change her positions to please some pollster. She doesn't throw mud. She's fundamentally honest and operates on a plain above ordinary politics."

He didn't know what to think. Was she accusing him of dirty politics? Was she saying he'd taken a bribe or lied to someone to protect his interests? Had he violated the code of ethics? No, he had done none of these things. He took great pride in his ethical conduct. That was one of the main reasons he'd chosen to work for Duran. What then was this about?

"I understand all that. That's exactly why I wanted to work for Shelby Duran. I know she's different. I know she's honest and trustworthy and she expects the same of those who work for her. If I've done anything to compromise the campaign or betray her trust, I swear to you I don't know what it is."

Julia believed him. She needed to hear him say it but she already knew the truth. It didn't change anything except the way she felt. She still had a job to do.

"Have you heard of Gonzo.com?"

"Sure. I like it."

She handed him a hard copy of a recent column by Gonzo reporter Cato Mackay. Under the title "On the Campaign Trail" it chronicled a series of questionable meetings and double-dealings including the meeting at Blake's Diner in Waterloo, Iowa, between Mario Macias of Americans for Fair Trade and Sandy Merrill of the Black campaign.

"Shit," he said. "It was a setup."

Her shoulders and her entire persona seemed to droop.

"I was hoping you could deny it."

He shook his head and accepted his fate.

"I was there. It happened just as he says it happened."

"Why didn't you report it?"

He shrugged. "I meant to. I convinced myself it was nothing. Just a couple of veterans of the trail sharing a meal. I know these people. For what it's worth, I respect them. I have no idea what they were talking about."

"A representative of a 501 colluding with the campaign it supports. For god's sake, there's not much that's still illegal these days but collusion between a campaign and a 501 is. You know that."

"I do. I understand. I made a mistake and I have to pay the price."

"Look, I know you didn't do anything illegal or from my perspective unethical."

"But it's a distraction and it looks bad. I get it. I know how it works. I'll pack up and go home. The campaign is over for me."

Julia was having a harder time with this than she anticipated. She truly liked Dawson. She considered him a friend and she knew how hard he had worked and how effective he had been. The campaign would take a hit but they couldn't keep him.

"When this blows over," she said, "I'll see if I can get you back on the payroll."

"That's not going to happen and we both know it. It's a part of the game. We know it going in."

He stood and opened his arms for a last embrace. She held him a little longer than she should have and let him go. He was absolutely right. This was the nature of the game. You play by the rules no matter the consequences. Still, he was the first casualty on her watch and it hurt.

"When it's all over," she said, "I'll give you a call."

He smiled and gave a wink.

"I'll be waiting."

He turned and walked out. The campaign would go on without him. They would not see each other again until the nation had a new resident at 1600 Pennsylvania Avenue.

30

WHITE CASTLE TO QUEEN FOUR

When he heard the story of Dawson's firing, Lawrence McClure was enraged. He summoned Cato Mackay to Gonzo headquarters immediately. Mackay thought about what the Gonzo would do. Would he kowtow to his publisher and slink back to headquarters with his tail firmly tucked or would he carry on and sort out the consequences later? Thompson was famous for his insubordination, his independence, his defiance of rules and authority, but Cato Mackay was no Hunter S. Thompson. He needed his job and he had no doubt that defiance would put him out on the street. He slinked back to headquarters on the redeye and reported to his boss the next morning.

McClure tossed his reporter's column on the desk. Still operating on his first cup of coffee he was in no mood for bullshit.

"Do you have any clue what you accomplished with this story?"

Mackay muttered and stuttered and tried to formulate a response to cover the stone cold fact that he in fact did not have a clue. He finally managed a cohesive sentence.

"I reported what I observed."

"Bullshit! You reported what somebody wanted you to report! You think you're the Great Gonzo! You were played, Mackay! I'm surprised you don't have frets across your face, you damned idiot!"

McClure waited for his reporter to respond. When he did not he proceeded with his diatribe, his mantra, a lesson he hoped would last a lifetime with an imprint as indelible as

Indian ink and a wound as deep as a surgeon's scalpel.

"You think I don't know what you did? I know exactly what you did. Some guy comes up to you and says: Hey kid, you want a story? A campaign operative meets with a 501 rep at a diner in Waterloo and a Duran operative observes the whole thing. So you drive on down to Waterloo, find the diner and what-do-you-know there it is just like he said it would be. You report what he wanted you to report but you leave out the part about the dirty, double-dealing asshole that put you in that particular place at that particular time. You were used! You did his dirty work! You did damage to the Black campaign and knocked out a valuable asset in the Duran campaign! You want to know how many times Hunter S. Thompson allowed himself to be used by some political hack with an agenda? Never! Not one fucking time!"

Mackay was speechless and felt himself shrinking to the size of a rat. He wanted to get out before he disappeared into the woodwork. He was cooked, fried, exposed as a disgrace to his profession. He'd never get another job. Strangely enough, before he walked into his boss's office, he had no concept that he'd done anything wrong.

"I'm sorry."

"You bet you are!"

McClure paused to take assessment of the shrinking man before him. He concluded that his message had been delivered and received. Time to move on. He was standing and pacing, thinking ahead.

"Alright. Damage done. Water under the bridge. All that bullshit. Who was the asshole that gave you the story?"

"Rowan Darby. I think he works for Wynn."

"You think?"

"Yeah."

"Find the fuck out! What did he say to you?"

"He offered me the story if I didn't use his name."

"Lesson number one: We don't do deals. Promise

anything you want but don't hold to it. After a while, these assholes will learn. We don't do deals."

"Yes sir."

McClure stopped at his expansive windows, gazing into the distance, seeking his next move.

"Alright. I want you to revisit the story. No apologies, no retractions. Only this time you tell the whole story, featuring the asshole Rowan Darby. Find out everything you can, every dirty deal, every double cross, every waitress he didn't tip, every woman or man he left with a grudge, everything. By the time you're done I want this guy to rank somewhere between Karl Rove and Benedict Arnold. No, that's too fucking good. I want him tarred, feathered and shipped out of town in an unmarked freight car on a runaway train. Are we clear?"

"Yes sir."

McClure looked his reporter in the eyes. He didn't know if the kid had it in him but he deserved another chance. How do you train a gonzo reporter? How do teach irreverence? Obviously, they hadn't done a very good job. He was a work in progress. Aren't we all?

"One last thing," said McClure.

"Yes sir."

McClure shook his head and breathed in and out in exasperation.

"That is the very last time I want you to address me or anyone else as *Sir*."

Mackay almost said, "Yes sir" instinctively but he caught himself.

"Got it."

He stood and walked back to his job, feeling very lucky to still have one. He wrote the story and within three days they learned that Rowan Darby had lost his. He became a pariah, a toxic piece of shit that no one would touch. Message delivered and received: Mess with Duran and you will pay a price.

31

BLACK PAWN TO QUEEN'S BISHOP FIVE

If you've ever been to the bottom, sleeping with the ants, awakening in the gutter of forgotten souls, you have an idea of how Cato Mackay felt. By all rights he had failed to uphold the fundamental tenants of his profession and should have been fired. He should have been wallowing in his misfortune, living on pizza, wasting his hours on consumable television programming and Internet porn, waiting for the ball to drop and hoping he could get that job at the Stop-N-Shop. Instead, he was back on the campaign trail in North Carolina and he felt blessed, renewed and forgiven.

Under any other circumstance he would have sensed something amiss when Jolene Dixon, an attractive thirtyish woman and fellow traveler on the long road to the White House, sat down at his booth with a wink and an engaging conversation. It was early evening and they were at the Renaissance Hotel bar, an establishment frequented by political types. They talked about the weather, the trials of travel and the dirty underside of politics. Like everyone else, Jolene heard about what happened to Rowan Darby and applauded him for it. No one deserved to be kicked under the bus less than Richard Dawson or more than Rowan Darby.

"You did the right thing," she said with a wink.

Cato felt his face go flush with a tint of shame.

"I'm kind of responsible for both," he muttered.

"You were duped," replied Jolene. "You're not the first to fall for one of Darby's tricks but at least you'll be the last on this cycle."

He raised his beer mug sheepishly, like a feeble elder with a limp wrist.

"I'll drink to that!"

"I'll drink to almost anything," she replied.

They were having a good time and decided to step out for some dinner at a Thai restaurant nearby. Gradually the conversation turned to Gonzo.com and its enigmatic owner Lawrence McClure. He began to feel a little uneasy, a shifting in his shoes, doubt in his bones, suspicion in his eyes as he perceived an agenda in her manner. Any man would feel uncomfortable engaging an attractive woman in conversation about another man, especially his boss, his unmarried boss. She seemed to notice his reticence and backed off the subject a spell before bringing it up again.

"What exactly is your job, Ms. Dixon?"

"What do you mean?"

"It's not a complicated question. You're a spy. I know that. You dig for information that is useful to your employer. But who is your employer?"

It was Jolene's turn to squirm. She had thought he would be an easier mark; now she recalculated.

"Jeez, you sure know how to turn a girl off."

"Come on, I never turned you on. If you don't want to tell me who you're working for that's fine. Why are you so interested in Lawrence McClure?"

She took a breath and placed her chopsticks on the table.

"Alright. Here's how it works: I'll give you something and maybe, somewhere down the line, you can return the favor."

He nodded, remembering his boss's advice: Promise anything but by no means be bound by it. After a while they'll get the idea.

"I'm listening."

"Your boss is a major fundraiser for the Duran campaign. He's also the owner of a media organization. That's a conflict of interest. It could cost your standing as a reporter."

This was news to Cato. He had no real concept of the rules of traditional journalism. Gonzo was another kind of beast.

"You're kidding," he laughed. "I don't have any standing as a reporter now."

"You have a press pass, don't you?"

That much was true. His press pass got him through doors that would otherwise be closed to him. He valued it. He would have a hard time doing his job without it.

"I do."

"Your boss can't be seen as manipulating stories to favor his candidate. If he told you to write that last story, for example, it would violate the standards of journalism. Rupert Murdoch of Fox News can't be seen as favoring a single candidate, even though he may and obviously does, and neither can Lawrence McClure."

Cato thought it over. The ground was unfamiliar to him and it was probably unfamiliar to his boss as well.

"He doesn't tell me what to write."

"Doesn't he?"

How could she know? No one knew what he and McClure had talked about in his office. They might assume but they couldn't know.

"No."

"Alright, I believe you. But appearances matter. It matters to his enemies and now that he's backing Duran he has more enemies than ever."

"I get it. I'll relay the message."

Jolene stood and grabbed her coat.

"You're cute," she said with a wink. "I wouldn't mind if you wanted to finish this in my room."

"I'm gay," he replied.

He was not but it was as good a way to end their interaction as any he could think of on short notice. His sense of attraction abandoned him somewhere around the mention of Rupert Murdoch. He thought about calling or emailing McClure but he could not be sure his communications were secure. The spy game had begun and he was in the middle of it.

He booked a flight on the redeye to the West Coast. He would advise his boss in person. How seriously he would take it was up to him.

32

WHITE CASTLE TO QUEEN ONE

Cato arrived in the early morning hours and slept half the day before reporting to Gonzo headquarters. He found his boss in his office, working the phone and going through stories. He was more than a little surprised to see his cub reporter.

"Aren't you supposed to be in South Carolina?"

"North Carolina. Charlotte."

"The name is Lawrence and you're a long way from either Carolina."

"There was something I had to tell you."

"You couldn't call?"

Cato looked at his shoes. He honestly didn't know if he was being paranoid or cautious. The world of politics had a whole new feel to it now that he'd been on both sides of the sting. He didn't trust anyone.

"Is this place safe?"

McClure squeezed his eyes into a piercing glare.

"You think my office is bugged?"

Cato shrugged. "All I know is: You're a target. People are after you. Is there somewhere we can go?"

McClure called in his head security man and ordered him to sweep for bugs. The man nodded and placed a call as McClure and Cato walked out. The found a coffee shop and Cato told his boss what Jolene Dixon had told him: He had a conflict of interest. As the head of a media organization he could not be seen manipulating stories to favor one candidate. As a primary fundraiser for Duran he could not be involved in Gonzo at all. McClure seemed baffled. He tried to wrap his mind around the message he was receiving.

"Is this true? There's a law prohibiting political involvement of media owners? What about Fox?"

"I don't know what's true and what's not, boss, but Murdoch doesn't run the news operation as far as we know. He doesn't advocate one candidate and he spreads his contributions across the field."

McClure wondered what else he didn't know. Little wonder he had not been engaged in the political process before now. He was out of his comfort zone and beyond his expertise. He felt a sudden and powerful need for legal advice.

"Alright. I can see I'm out of my league here. I'll call in the lawyers. Have you any idea what this woman was after?"

"As far as I could tell, she wanted me to confirm that you ordered me to write the story that nailed Rowan Darby."

"Did I?"

Cato went silent. He couldn't recall the exact words his boss used but it felt like an order. If he were under oath that's what he would testify.

"You kind of did."

McClure reflected. That was his recollection as well. What he needed to know now was how much trouble he invited.

"What did you tell her?"

"Not a thing."

"You're sure."

"I am."

"Good. But you think she knows."

"Yes."

They walked back to the office. When they got there his security man had two small devices laid out on a table.

"Are these what I think they are?" asked McClure.

"Yes sir."

He thanked Cato for the information and told him to go back to Charlotte. Then he called in his legal team and consumed a few hours hashing it out. They all agreed: He had to give up his direct involvement in Gonzo.com. He would hire a managing editor and move to a new office in a building across the street. From this moment until the end of the campaign, he would devote all his efforts to fundraising and leave the reporting to others. It did not sit well but he had no choice. The technology game was peculiar enough; the political game was complex to the point of absurdity. Franz Kafka would have relished it.

33

BLACK KNIGHT TO QUEEN'S KNIGHT SIX

Just Wynn baby! Things were off to a rocking start for the Wynn campaign. Coming off victories in Iowa and New Hampshire his standing as the frontrunner made him the target of all other candidates. They came at him with everything they had. With the exception of Paul Casey, every other candidate in the Republican field had roots in the south, the foundation of the Grand Old Party's base of support ever since Lyndon Johnson championed the Civil Rights movement.

Ralph Peterson's RNC decree against personal attacks no longer applied after Wynn himself went on the offensive in the first debate. Peterson made a show of criticizing the big man for his attacks but qualified his critique with the standard excuse that every candidate had to be tested. The Democrats would not after all hold their punches in the general election.

Peterson offered the opinion on Fox News that Wynn had demonstrated the ability to appeal to voters outside the south, a quality that made him the single most likely candidate to win the general election. He made a point of saying that the others still had time to demonstrate their own electability outside the south but time was running short. His assessment enraged the other candidates who cried foul and accused the party chairman of playing favorites. Still, they knew his assessment was valid. Contributions *were* running short. Any candidate who could not manage a win soon would not survive to Super Tuesday except as a symbol of opposition. That might be enough for the libertarian Ryan Gregory, whose candidacy never got off the ground, but it was not enough for anyone whose goal was to win the White House.

The candidates with any realistic chance of overtaking Wynn were Rivera of Texas and the Florida contingent: Marco Alonzo and Ellis Pierce. Rivera was counting on winning the southern states on the back of evangelical voters. Jack Morris knew that only one thing could trump the evangelical vote in the south and that was the racist vote. He had a plan and it began with playing the old southern pride tune "Dixie" at his southern rallies. The rallies would also debut a new slogan, prominently displayed on signs and placards from Memphis to Atlanta: Wynn Dixie! They would have to pull back for the general but for the primaries it was brilliant and it would effectively derail the Rivera campaign.

The Florida boys considered the South Carolina primary their last stand and consequently were willing to empty their depleted war chests to win it. The only way to make up ground in the allotted time was television advertising. The difficulty they faced was that airtime had already been contracted to the various candidates of both parties, the 501 groups allied to them and the national party committees.

Pierce managed to buy some time at an inflated price from the Gregory, Rivera and Sampson campaigns. Alonzo did the same, bidding up the price. As primary day approached they inched up in the polls but it became clear it would not be enough. There were not enough days on the calendar. In a last ditch effort Pierce appealed to the RNC to release their airtime in the name of fairness.

Mary Jo Perez went to RNC headquarters in Washington to state their case.

"We're only asking for a level playing field. The Wynn campaign has bought more than their share of airtime. We all know that. We also know that it is in the party's interest to have a good and fair fight in the primaries. If we allow one candidate to essentially buy the South Carolina primary, for all practical purposes, this race is over. We go into Super Tuesday without a contest. We yield all public interest to the Democratic race."

Peterson spoke for the committee.

"Are you saying Pierce will concede the race if he fails to win in South Carolina?"

"No sir, I'm not saying that."

"Your candidate had the same opportunity to buy airtime in the Carolina market as Wynn did. Are you asking this committee to compensate for your mistake?"

Perez knew she would be up against stiff resistance. It was a hard case to make but it was her job to make it.

"With all due respect, Chairman Peterson, we didn't know our backs would be against the wall. We had to concentrate on Iowa and New Hampshire."

"Are you saying that it was somehow this committee's fault you didn't do well in Iowa and New Hampshire?"

Perez took a moment. It was exactly what she thought and she knew that some of the people on the committee shared her view.

"It was Wynn who violated your civility rule. His attacks caught us off guard. We've been playing catch-up ever since. And yet he faced no consequences."

"We were assured it was unintentional. Wynn being Wynn. He's not a politician."

"A tiger can't deny his stripes, so we've heard. We have our doubts."

The chairman felt his temperature rise. He had become sensitive to accusations of favoritism but he was not accustomed to hearing them in an official setting.

"Was it this committee that prepared your candidate on foreign policy?"

Perez went flush. They had made a huge blunder in assuming Pierce was well prepared on foreign policy matters. His poor performance on the subject wounded him in New Hampshire just as Wynn's attacks had in Iowa.

"No sir, it was not. I'm not saying we haven't made mistakes. I'm simply saying that this committee has the authority to restore some measure of equity in this race. You have a large chunk of time. We're not asking for a handout. We'll pay full price."

"We had intended to use that time to bolster the entire Republican field, your candidate included, and to attack the leading Democrat. We're looking long term."

"We understand that, Mr. Chairman. So are we."

Peterson took account of his underlings on the committee and decided to offer some concession as a show of good will. They would need it for the campaign ahead.

"I'm certain this committee can arrive at an equitable accommodation, Ms. Perez. You've stated your case well. We'll be in touch."

In the end, the committee sold a substantial portion of its airtime to the Pierce campaign, still only a fraction of what they wanted. It would not be enough. Wynn would claim a decisive victory in the South Carolina primary and head into Super Tuesday with all guns blazing.

Wynn, baby, Wynn!

34

WHITE PAWN TO KING'S BISHOP THREE

From the moment Senator Warner's campaign buckled Chauncey Davis needed a job. He had offers from half a dozen campaigns on both sides of the political divide but he held out for a job with the one candidate he not only believed in but also believed had a chance to win. He waited for the call but it hadn't yet come.

Results were in for the South Carolina primary. On the Republican side Daniel J. Wynn all but closed the deal. Barring a spectacular collapse, the big man from the Big Apple, the man the party establishment hated almost as much as fair trade Democrats, would be the nominee of the Grand Old Party. On the Democratic side results were less certain. Secretary Duran still had momentum but a surprise win by Massachusetts Governor Pat Duvall in South Carolina kept him very much alive and in the race. He had managed to rekindle the idea that he could duplicate what Barrack Obama did in 2008.

As an African American, Davis should have been excited by the prospect of a second black president but he knew the numbers. Obama had allied himself with Wall Street; Duvall had not. His reliance on small individual contributions was admirable but it had its limits. He had a funding problem that would soon catch up to him. Obama had pulled not only the black vote but also the Latino vote in record numbers. Duran was Caucasian but she was married to a Spaniard and her children were brown. She was fluent in Spanish as well as French, German and Russian, and she supported strong progressive immigration policies. In a contest between the black governor of Massachusetts and a white, Spanish speaking woman married to a Spaniard, Duran held a decisive edge. Moreover, if Duvall managed to become the nominee he did not match up well against Wynn. Duran did.

The best Duvall could hope for was to stay in the contest through Super Tuesday, to build his national reputation for a possible future run. He could also build his credentials for the vice presidency but he could not win the nomination.

The Democratic field was thinning. Andrews, Howard and Bolton had declared an end to their campaigns. Molinari hung on by an irrational thread, staking his all in Florida, leaving Black of Ohio and Duvall as the only realistic challengers.

Davis belonged to the school of thought that a good primary fight strengthened a candidate for the general election but there were limits. Aside from the money it cost, a particularly nasty campaign could leave scars. Black and Duvall were not inclined to dirty politics but Molinari was another matter. He was convinced that the next goal of the Duran campaign should be to eliminate Molinari with a decisive victory in Florida. It would also lay the groundwork for the general election against Danny "Diamond" Wynn.

He dispatched his leading aide Lorena Moreno to Miami for a meeting with Julia Sands of the Duran campaign. Her assignment was to spell out a comprehensive strategy for winning the Sunshine State and convincing Sands that they were the ones to implement it.

35

PLAYERS

Declaring a Truce

There are more possibilities in the game of chess than there are atoms in the known universe yet each match must find an end. Whether by mate, stalemate or draw, a chess match is a finite series of moves toward a certain end. Meeting in Madrid where the winter is mild, the people are comforting and time flows like a gentle breeze, Solana Rothschild and William Bates were worried. The match that they hoped would determine the leader of the western world was going extremely well. Their chosen candidates were well positioned to claim their respective party nominations.

The source of their concern was the number of moves the match had already required. The average chess match is approximately forty exchanges. They had completed sixteen, almost all of them fighting off rivals rather than confronting each other, attacking their opposing kings. With more than a month before Super Tuesday, more than six months to the nominating conventions and nearly a year to Election Day, they were worried that with so much ground still to cover they would run out of moves. They would complete their match before the designated pieces on the field of play could catch up to them. It would invalidate the experiment. It would be a massive waste of time and effort – not to mention substantial resources.

William proposed a suspension in play, a sort of truce that would last until the nominees were in place. While harboring the same concerns, Solana was less certain his proposal was equitable. After all, his king had all but secured his place as the nominee. Her king was still engaged in an ongoing battle.

They spent their days at the museums, most notably the Prado with its extensive collection of Goya, El Greco and Velasquez, and the Reina Sofia featuring the works of Picasso (including Guernica), Dali, Miro and Gris. They spent their evenings enjoying leisurely meals in the company of artists and musicians, discussing everything under the sun from art and economic theory to religion, war and terrorism. They enjoyed these evenings more than they could express. They seemed to bring a sense of youth and vigor to their souls and fire to their romance.

When alas they returned to their villa at Puerta del Sol, they returned to their negotiations, certain they would find a mutually satisfactory solution. Solana's confidence in her king, her chosen candidate, had grown with each passing day.

"It is of course your turn, Willy. You needn't win my approval. You could simply wait. You could delay the match as long as you wish. I would be powerless to act."

"That would hardly be fair. The World Chess Federation would never allow indefinite delay in any sanctioned match."

"Perhaps they should."

"I wouldn't think of it."

Sitting on a lush sofa surrounded by the beauty of the antiquities, they sipped wine and enjoyed classical music. They would never be closer or more alive than they were at this moment. They savored it as they would an extraordinary sunset or the masterwork of a master artist. They felt large and important, as if they belonged in the company of masters.

"Duran will win," said Solana.

"I'm certain she will do her best."

Solana gazed at her almost drunken lover and read his mind as a psychiatrist would read a familiar client.

"You doubt her?"

"She has exceptional strength of character, an almost religious adherence to principle. That is her weakness."

"And her strength."

They took sweet refuge in each other's arms and let their thoughts flow.

"Do you ever envy Picasso, Greco, Dali or Cervantes?" asked Solana.

"I do. Of course, we have our moments."

"Indeed we do."

"One wonders what carries greater importance in this world: the creators of art or the creators of history."

"Art, my dear. Leaders will fall, civilizations will crumble but great works of art will endure the ages. We are remembered for our art."

"Do you think?"

"I do."

"Then I envy Picasso."

"Would you cut off your ear for me?"

"That was Van Gogh, my dear."

"Still, would you?"

"Would you want me to?"

"No."

"Then let it go."

She did but only for a moment. The notion would not be left wanting.

"Would you?"

"I would."

"I thought so."

They let their thoughts rest until Solana at length arrived at a compromise solution that she believed they would both consider fair and practical.

"In my estimation, I may need one or two moves to secure the nomination. Allow me that much and I will agree to a truce until the conventions."

Willy considered the proposal with a generous smile. Of course it was fair. Solana would have it no other way. She wanted to win as much as he did but she would have no doubt to taint the results. More than anything else, they wanted the experiment to proceed to its conclusion.

So it was settled: One or two moves and then a truce. They would work out the details as they went along.

BLACK KING TO QUEEN'S KNIGHT EIGHT

Never content to sit still and watch the world go by, Danny Wynn wanted to go on attack. His rivals were like wild boars on a feeding frenzy and he wanted to join them. After reading his morning news, he stormed into the campaign war room fired up and eager to rally his forces. He carried with him a small stack of recent charges and attacks against his character, waving them like a red flag before an angry bull.

"Casey calls me a common playground bully! Alonzo says I'm not qualified to be a dog catcher no less president of the United States! Rivera says I have ethical challenges! Ethical challenges from a man who wouldn't know the truth if it smacked him across the face! The man has rigged more elections than Boss Tweed! Sampson says I should be facing a prison sentence instead of running for president! I say we let these sons of bitches know who they're up against! No one takes Wynn on without paying the price!"

He could see from the open mouths and slack jaws around the table that his diatribe did not exactly have the intended effect. Sensing the same dynamic, Jack Morris cleared his throat and asked for a moment alone with the candidate. The others packed their computers and briefcases and walked out, closing the door behind them.

"Why did you hire me?" asked Morris.

Wynn felt more than a little exasperated with his campaign manager at the moment. He didn't like rhetorical questions even if the came with a purpose.

"I hired you to run my goddamn campaign!"

"Why?"

"I was told you know what you're doing! I was told you're the best in the business! That's why I hired you. I always hire the best!"

Morris nodded and allowed his candidate a moment to think.

"You're a flawed candidate with sizable liabilities yet here you are: The clear frontrunner for the Republican nomination. Have I done anything that would lead you to believe I don't know what I'm doing?"

Wynn's enormous demeanor changed. No one but Morris could have this effect on him. He became the incredible shrinking man.

"I know you're the best. You're doing a great job! I know that. I just want to get out there and fight back! That's who I am! That's what people expect! A tiger can't deny his stripes, right? Tell me I'm wrong!"

"You're right," Morris shrugged. "That's exactly what people expect. That's what Rivera and Alonzo expect. That's what they want you to do and if you do it they'll pounce. They'll say: See, he's nothing but a bully who can dish it out but can't take criticism. Is that the kind of man you want for president?"

Wynn knew he was defeated. Without Morris guiding him, he would not have survived Ohio no less New Hampshire. His greatest virtue in this campaign was that he knew his own limitations. It's hard for a man who always gave the orders but he bit his lip and followed. He let Morris do the thinking. As long as it worked, he wouldn't challenge him.

"I get it. So what do you want me to do? Sit back and take this bullshit?"

"Yes. Look, you're the frontrunner. You act like the frontrunner. You've heard it all before. It's been litigated and re-litigated in the media. If there were anything there someone would already have found it. Your opponents are desperate. They'll say anything to take you down but it's beneath their dignity as candidates to engage in mudslinging and it's beneath your dignity to respond in kind. Got it?"

Wynn nodded. He looked like a bulldog waiting for his owner to give him a scratch on the neck and a bone of approval. Morris continued.

"Don't be surprised if you don't take Florida. The best that can happen is Rivera steals enough from Alonzo to give you a chance. If Rivera is smart and I think he is, he'll find a way to push Alonzo out of the race. If he does that it gives him a chance. The last thing you want to do is attack Alonzo. The other thing you explicitly don't want to do is bring up vote rigging because come November we'll be counting on the same game to win the general. Got it?"

"Got it."

Wynn had a sheepish look that told Morris he needed that bone of approval. The candidate searched for something to contribute to the campaign to restore his battered ego.

"Can we win without Florida?" he asked.

"Hell yes! The Florida primary falls on Super Tuesday. We can lose Florida and still wrap up the nomination by nightfall."

It seemed as though it all came as news to Wynn. They'd been through it a dozen times before: Be the nice guy. Nothing below the belt. Let the accusations glance off like pests on a summer day. Praise Alonzo to boost his chances. Never mention Ellis Pierce. Talk about immigration. Everyone knows immigration is Pierce's weakness. Study foreign policy. Follow every international story as if you were already president. Know the difference between AQAP, AQ Iraq and AQ Pakistan-Afghanistan. Know Boko Haram and the Islamic State. Reserve your passion for the terrorists and let it fly. In a Wynn presidency, we'll hunt them down like the rabid dogs they are. We'll never rest as long as any terrorist is alive to threaten the American people.

"The only man, woman or child who can keep Daniel J.

Wynn from becoming the Republican nominee now is Daniel J. Wynn. Don't be stupid and you win."

Wynn said he understood and agreed. He said he'd play it by the books. He said Morris had his full confidence. But Morris still wasn't convinced. They spent the next half hour going over it again: What to say, how and to whom. When Morris was certain he had his candidate under control, they went out and the hit the campaign trail.

37

WHITE KNIGHT TO QUEEN'S CASTLE FIVE

The one thing that can destroy a frontrunner faster than a brushfire on an open plain is over-confidence. In the hands of Jack Morris, the Wynn campaign had sufficient restraint but its affiliated Super Pac, the Koch brothers' Americans for America First, rushed ahead like a runaway train. Certain that their candidate had a firm grip on the nomination, they prepared a series of attack ads targeting the candidate they most feared on the Democratic side: Secretary of State Shelby Duran.

The ads highlighted Duran's privileged upbringing, her European background and what they perceived as socialistic tendencies and softness on terrorism. The charges were weak but the packaging was slick. It would carry sway with voters who never got beyond the headlines. They intended to run the ads in the week preceding Super Tuesday, hoping to derail or at least delay her run to the Democratic nomination.

They made the mistake of testing several of their ads in small markets where they thought no one would notice. They were wrong.

In the world of instantaneous communications and Internet access there are no secrets, certainly not for content released on any form of public media. Within thirty minutes of the attack ad debut it landed on the desk of Dorothea Vargas. Fortunately, she had anticipated such a development and immediately summoned James Delacroix of Koch Industries to her office at the DNC headquarters. Delacroix knew better than to ignore the invitation. If Vargas wanted to see a Koch brothers' representative, she had a deal, a threat or a warning. Ignore it at your peril.

He reported to her office mid-morning and was immediately escorted inside. He found Ms. Vargas, sworn enemy of his employer, leaning against her desk, watching a video on her computer. He knew at once what she was watching: the attacks against Duran.

"Mr. Delacroix, have a seat."

He sat in the designated chair in front of her desk as she spun her laptop around so he could observe.

"Have you seen these?" she asked.

"Some of them," he replied.

"What do you think?"

"My job," he said with a wry grin, "is not to think. I receive orders and I carry them out. That's all."

"That's why I asked for you. You're loyal and dutiful. You'll know at once the value of the information I'm about to give you and you'll relay it to your bosses without delay."

He did not particularly appreciate her summation of his character but she was precisely right. It was why the Kochs paid him so well. They could count on him to deliver important information in a timely manner. Anything the chair of the Democratic National Committee had to say would qualify.

"Are we reviewing attack ads?" he asked.

"We are," she replied. "We've had a look at yours. I'd like to give you a look at ours as a courtesy. By the way, did you really think you could keep it under the rug by playing it in Podunk?"

"Not really. It turns out Podunk is a pretty typical market."

"Really? I'll keep that in mind."

She cued up her counterpunch ad and let it play. It featured Daniel J. Wynn as a common playground bully, a man who tried to push an old lady out on the street to forward his business interests, a man who played both sides against the middle, a man who failed in business and was bailed out by his wealthy father, and a man whose depth of knowledge in foreign affairs and economic theory was as shallow as a mud puddle. It ended with this slogan:

Wynn: The Democrats' Choice for the Republican Nomination.

Production values were high and it seemed to Delacroix likely to make a mark on the electorate. He understood the implication: If Americans for America First ran their attack ads against Duran, the DNC would counter with this attack on Wynn.

"Has it been tested?"

"Not yet. We're in no hurry. We were planning to use some variation of it in the general, assuming Wynn is the Republican nominee."

"If you run that under the DNC banner, people will see through it. It'll backfire."

Vargas smiled.

"It's not ours."

"Of course not. People for the American Way?"

"I'm not at liberty to say."

Delacroix knew the deal. He knew they would have to accept it. It fell to him to convince the Koch brothers.

"Can we assume that if we do not run the anti-Duran ads, your group won't run the Wynn ad?"

"I think that's a safe assumption but I can guarantee this: If you run the Duran ads, the Wynn ads will follow."

Delacroix stood, hat in hand, extending his other. Vargas took hold. This was how deals were made.

"It's been a pleasure doing business with you, Mr. Delacroix."

"Oddly enough," he replied, "it has been a pleasure dealing with you as well."

38

BLACK BISHOP TO QUEEN'S CASTLE EIGHT

The notorious smoke-filled rooms where double-dealing, backstabbing and unsavory negotiations once went down with mythological infamy are largely gone now. The dark side of politics is carried out in the spacious, well-lit conference rooms of high-rise office buildings or the relative comfort of expansive living rooms of K Street lobbying centers. The well financed Americans for America First was one of the latter.

The Kochs were carefully insulated from their political operations. Low-level operatives like James Delacroix did not have direct access to the founders and financial base. He reported to Nolan Gray who in turn reported to Jim Duke, Executive Director of Americans for America First. Duke was their man in politics and had their explicit trust. Though they would review his actions at a monthly meeting, Duke had the power to decide the issue.

He called his staff together to run down the pros and cons. The seven chosen ones sat on sofas and easy chairs enjoying beverages and snacks, looking forward to a long lunch on a slow day in politics and the news. They were all news junkies. Duke began:

"We have a proposition from our enemies at the DNC. You might characterize it as a threat. You might call it an offer. In essence, they propose a truce. If we hold back our attack on Duran, they won't go after Wynn. My first instinct is to say fuck off. They wouldn't propose it if it didn't work to their advantage. Mr. Gray, however, has a different idea."

He gave the floor to Mr. Gray.

"The first rule of politics is: Don't shoot yourself in the foot. We're all confident that Wynn has a lead that can't be overcome but maybe we're a little too confident. Mr. Delacroix tells me he's seen their ad. It's a slick piece about Danny Wynn the bully. Typical stuff. But the tag line is: Wynn: The Democrats Choice for the Republican Nominee. It just might have an impact. It just might allow one or more of our rivals back in the contest. If that happens all bets are off. The money starts to flow to other options. We lose our advantage. We lose Big Mo."

The half dozen consultants and operatives in the room began to murmur. Duke called them back to order.

"We're paying you people to give us sound advice. So here's your opportunity. Do we protect our lead and hold back our Duran series or do we storm straight ahead and let the chips fall?"

Around the room they went drawing out the scenarios, parsing the possibilities, calculating the risks and rewards. The pollsters pulled out the numbers and concluded that any number of states might be vulnerable if the attack ads proved effective. They seemed to be coalescing around the conclusion that they should take the deal. A truce would all but guarantee Wynn would claim the party nomination.

Duke called for order and asked: "What if we call it what it is: A Democratic ploy?"

Gray responded: "Delacroix tells me they won't leave their prints on it."

"So what?" said Duke. "We tell the people what to think, not the other way around."

"That would put us on the defensive. We'd look bad."

Once again they went around the room in heated discussion until Delacroix finally spoke up.

"Look, with all due respect, it doesn't matter if it's a Democratic trick. If it works all the others will jump on the bandwagon. We're lucky Pierce didn't think of this or we might be looking at a different race."

Everyone sensed the argument had changed. They all knew he was right. There are times when the best option is doing nothing and this seemed to be one of them. Even Duke seemed to come around.

"Alright," said Duke. "We're going to put this thing on hold. The most important thing right now is to protect Wynn's lead. We'll revisit the issue after Super Tuesday. Does everyone agree?"

The silence spoke for them. No one wanted to go out on a limb. That's the trouble with political strategists: They are not by nature risk takers unless they have to be and they don't have to be unless their backs are pressed tight to the wall. As long as their man had a safe lead they would take no chances.

39

WHITE BISHOP TO KING'S CASTLE THREE

On the advice of Julia Sands, Winfred Holmes agreed to interview Chauncey Davis as a possible addition to the Duran campaign. He had scheduled a trip to Miami and the word was Davis wanted to run the Florida campaign so he sent him an invitation. The campaign had already named Miami congresswoman Frederica Clement statewide chair so Holmes would consider Davis for a regional position, chairman of the southeast campaign. He knew Davis by reputation only. Despite the unexpected collapse of the Warner campaign, he respected his work.

They met in the afternoon at the Miami headquarters of the Duran for President campaign. Like so many modern office spaces, the office was divided from the rest of the space by glass walls and doors. Holmes took measure of Davis as he walked in with an air of confidence and a sense of eagerness in his step. He met him with a handshake at the door and guided him inside.

"Mr. Davis, at last we meet."

"I had hoped we'd meet earlier."

Holmes questioned him with his eyes.

"We assumed you'd be going with Duvall after Warner withdrew. I'm surprised you didn't."

"Duvall can't win."

"And Warner could?"

"I thought she could, using the same formula you've used for Duran. Funding through technology. It's never been tried before. You beat us to it."

Holmes wondered if he was being flattered. He liked it in

any case. It showed the young man understood and could appreciate political stratagem.

"I know of at least two or three scenarios by which Duvall could win."

"I stand corrected. But it's a long shot. I know of a dozen by which Duran could win and she has the inside track. Look, I admire Duvall. He's a great candidate. But let's face it, Duran stands pretty much for the same things Duvall and Warner stand for and her time has come. It's like an alignment of the planet with heavenly bodies, like it was for Obama. She's destined to become the first woman president. I know I can help and I'd like to be a part of it."

Holmes thought and crossed his legs. He hit the intercom and asked for hot tea with lemon and a cube of sugar. He asked Davis if wanted anything and Davis declined.

"That's a nice speech. Have you ever considered going on the trail, making speeches in behalf of your candidate?"

"I could do that but I've never been asked."

Holmes took a moment to prepare his tea and decided to confront the young man head on.

"Why should I trust you? How do we know you're not a saboteur?"

Davis smiled.

"No one ever really knows, do they? But I'm not some new kid on the block. I have a history. I'm sure you've checked me out."

"I have. Of course I have. You're a highly skilled, highly principled operative. You'll have to forgive me if I have some difficulty accepting good fortune."

"You've been jaded by the process. I have too. I have to admit I thought of you when that footage of Warner came out before the Iowa caucus. It hurt us. We could never regain our momentum and we were always a long shot."

Holmes continued in his measured interrogation, allowing time between thoughts and statements to observe his prospective operative.

"How do you know it wasn't me?"

"Like you I have my connections. I knew it was Vargas. Everyone knows she favors Duran so she pulled one out of the hat to give her candidate a timely boost."

"I arrived at the same conclusion."

"We think alike," smiled Davis.

Holmes shifted in his chair and sipped his tea.

"Let me put it this way. If I worked for Warner and my second choice was Duvall, when Warner dropped out I'd consider sabotaging the frontrunner. Fair game. Wouldn't you?"

Davis had to think this one through.

"I would but I wouldn't use me as the saboteur. Much too obvious."

"And yet here we are."

"Yes, here we are. I guess you'll just have to go on instinct."

Holmes sipped his tea.

"Alright. What sort of strategy do you have for Super Tuesday?"

"I was thinking of Florida."

"Expand your thinking. We already have a campaign manager for Florida."

Once again Davis took a moment. He had given the question a great deal of thought but it was still a work in progress.

"How does Duran beat a black man in the south? That's the question, isn't it? We have to protect our frontrunner standing. Even blacks won't vote for a black man if he doesn't have a chance. Black women want a woman almost as much as a black.

"Duran has to be presidential. She's a good speaker. She should make a major speech on civil rights, emphasizing voting rights and discrimination against women and minorities. She should go to Selma and invite Duvall to join her. In Florida, she should stand strong for normalization with Cuba. She should align herself with the younger generation. She should make appearances with her family and address the people on Telemundo in Spanish. She should address the rights of immigrants. How am I doing?"

Holmes smiled. He had made up his mind. He wanted this man to be a part of the Duran campaign. He trusted him and he like how his mind worked. They were very much in tune with each other. He stood and extended his open hand.

"Welcome to the team. We'll have a press conference tomorrow. I'll get Duran to attend. You two can have a long discussion. I'll announce you as the campaign manager of the southeast district. How does that sound?"

"It sounds good," he replied.

"We'll work out the details as we go along."

They shook hands and sealed the deal.

40

BLACK PAWN TO QUEEN FIVE

Gambit Declined

It may be over-generalizing to say there are no secrets in politics but there are no secrets in politics. Sooner or later everyone on the inside knows everything there is to know though everything does not cross the threshold into public knowledge. People wonder how J. Edgar Hoover kept his secrets. He didn't. But he had the goods on everyone who mattered so he managed to keep it all behind the curtain until well after his death.

The truce almost held to Super Tuesday. As is so often the case in war, each side blamed the other for breaking the truce and the truth lay somewhere in the gray: specifically, Nolan Gray of Americans for America First. In a particularly sly bit of subterfuge Gray leaked the story that AAF had prepared a series of anti-Duran ads but withheld them in a backroom deal with the DNC to Sandy Merrill, who still managed to hold a spot in the Black campaign.

Never one to pass on an opportunity Merrill contacted Mario Macias of Americans for Fair Trade. After their last encounter Macias was highly skeptical. He ultimately agreed to meet with her but at a location of his choosing at a time of his determination. She agreed. They ending up meeting at a bar in Atlanta, where Senator Black was campaigning, in the early evening.

"How is it, Ms. Merrill," said Macias, "that we are still both employed?"

"Just lucky I guess."

By all that's right and reasonable they should have lost their jobs in the incident that ultimately cost Richard Dawson and Rowan Darby theirs. Because the content of their clandestine meeting remained unknown, their meeting was not illegal but it was suspect. Even in these days of lax electoral conduct laws, a 501 was not permitted to collude with a campaign. They had both been warned. Macias had been taken by surprise; Merrill was in on the sting.

"You'll forgive me if I don't trust you," he said as he kept one eye on the door.

"I forgive you. I wouldn't trust me either. But I have no reason to take you out. You're not the enemy."

"Who is the enemy this week?"

"Shelby Duran. Same as yours."

Macias could not hide his discomfort. Everything about Sandy Merrill made him uncomfortable. Still, she was the reason he'd kept his job. She made a living collecting dirt and she used it not only to protect herself but him as well.

"We both know Senator Black is not in it to win. It's an issue campaign. He wants to put fair trade on the table. A spot on the podium at the convention would be nice. A fair trade provision in the platform would be better. You know the senator. You work for him. He won't go after Duran."

"He doesn't have to attack Duran and neither do you. But the best way to get the message through, to accomplish our objectives, is to keep him in the race. The best way to do that is to weaken the frontrunner."

"I'm listening."

She told him about the deal the DNC had struck with Americans for America First. It came as no surprise to Macias that the DNC was looking out for Duran. That Dorothea Vargas favored Duran was by now common knowledge.

"Look," said Merrill, "all you have to do is come up with an ad with the punch line: Wynn: The Democratic Choice for the Republican Nominee. Make it all about trade policy. It doesn't really matter. If you use that line, Americans for America First will roll out a whole series of anti-Duran ads. It costs you nothing and Black lives beyond Super Tuesday."

Macias ordered a second whiskey straight up and mulled it over. Once again, Merrill had come up with a brilliant if diabolical tactic. Vargas and the DNC might not like it but what could they do? They had already overstepped the bounds of civil politics and everyone knew it.

"I'll give it consideration."

"If you want to have a job after next Tuesday you'll do more than that. You know the numbers. If Duran sweeps its all over but the coronation."

Macias nodded slowly. He did not question that she was right. He had his doubts about her motives and her methods.

"I'll have to tell my boss where I got this. You know that, don't you? We could lose our jobs anyway."

Merrill didn't hesitate. She had fire in her eyes.

"No one gets in this game to play it safe. If we're going down it's better to go down fighting. My guess is: If it works our jobs are secure. Maybe we get a promotion. God knows we should. Somebody has to show some guts in this race. If it doesn't work, we're finished anyway."

Macias raised his glass. Merrill raised hers.

"To Cervantes and his immortal hero: Don Quixote!"

Merrill laughed, tipped her glass and drank. She stood and walked out, leaving a last comment behind: "It's not as hopeless as you think."

Americans for Fair Trade ran the ad in question only once in a small market in Vermont. Americans for America First answered with a barrage of attack ads against Shelby Duran. The Duran campaign countered with their own ad, ending with the tag line: Duran: The Candidate Republicans Most Fear.

Too little and too late for Black, the last minute barrage helped Duvall edge out a win in Georgia to go with his home state of Massachusetts but it did little for the senator from Ohio. Duran retained a commanding lead but the contest would go on. While Black would drop out of the race within a few days, Molinari, who had staked everything he had in Florida, would require another week or two to reach the same conclusion. The Democratic race was down to two and the outcome all but certain.

On the Republican side Wynn won by large margins in Massachusetts, Georgia, Tennessee, Idaho, Vermont and Virginia. Rivera managed to take Oklahoma and his own state of Texas. Alonzo won Florida by the margin of a razor's edge but could not make a move anywhere else. By all objective accounts, the race was over. Only the dream of a brokered convention could deny the New York billionaire his prize: The Republican nomination to the presidency of the United States of America.

41

WHITE QUEEN TO KING'S BISHOP FOUR

Check

A week before the Democratic National Convention would officially nominate Secretary of State Shelby Duran as the party's nominee for president, Winfred Holmes requested her presence in his office for a serious discussion regarding the content of her acceptance speech. Duran had spent much of the last two weeks working on the speech with her team of writers. She glanced at the latest version on Holmes' desk and read his thoughts.

"I know what you're going to say and you know I don't agree with you so why don't we leave at that?"

"Because," replied a reflective Holmes leaning back in his chair and folding his hands in his lap, "it's far too important."

They'd explored this territory extensively, so much so that Duran felt certain that everything that could be said had been. She knew he would push and he knew she would push back. As far as she was concerned her decision had already been made.

"Alright. We'll go through it again but I won't change my mind."

"You will," he stated calmly.

She fought back an impulse to storm out of the room. She loved the man who sat smugly before her but he could be infuriating. Like her father he possessed the ability to trigger her defensive instinct.

"How's that?"

"Because deep down, in the place of your heart and soul where you really do want to be president, the place that pushed you across the line of denial and made you a candidate for the highest office in the land, that propelled you forward to where you stand today, on the precipice of completing your mission, you *know* I'm right."

She looked around the room, noted the decanter of brandy and asked if he wouldn't mind pouring them both one. He assented with a grin.

"You don't like the speech," she summarized.

"I do. It's brilliant. I wouldn't change a single word."

She sipped her brandy and waited for the inevitable qualification. He waited with her until she felt obliged to offer him a prompt.

"But?"

"I would add a single paragraph."

He unfolded a sheet of paper and handed to her. It read:

"My opponent in this contest for the presidency has made a lot of noise concerning immigration, so much so that he whips his followers into a fury, but what would he do? Build a wall, reaching deep into the earth and high into the heavens, erecting a monument to intolerance that some future generation will be obliged to tear down? My opponent makes a lot of noise about terrorists here at home and abroad but what would he do? Revive the security state, sacrificing the fundamental rights to privacy and freedom of expression that belong to all Americans by right of citizenship? What would he do? Commit our soldiers to multiple foreign wars that have no end, revisiting the failed policies of the past? My opponent makes a lot of noise with regard to Cuba but what would he do? Bring back the embargo, ban trade and travel, cut off relations, reverse the progress we have made over the last eight years? My opponent makes a lot of noise but what does it all amount to if not: Sound and fury, signifying nothing!"

She read it through and read it again, a smile creeping into her expression. She agreed of course with the sentiment. What she objected to was the strategy of going negative at the national convention.

"Do you like it?" he inquired.

"I do. More importantly I agree with it. I can't say I wouldn't change a word but I like it. I'd feel comfortable saying it."

He waited for the inevitable qualification.

"But?"

"As you well know, I want to reserve the acceptance speech to establish a clear and positive vision for the nation, unencumbered by common politics. You know this."

Holmes gathered his most serious demeanor, an expression that made others lean forward in anticipation of a profound message of the utmost importance.

"I do but I am obliged to say this: You will have one chance at this. Never again will you be guaranteed an audience of a hundred million people, maybe more, certainly not before your inaugural address. Danny Wynn is out there pretending he's someone he's not. If you let him, he'll slide to the center and the electorate won't notice. If you call him on it now, we may see the spectacle of a nominee being booed at his own convention. You cannot squander this opportunity out of an abstract sense of moral transcendence that will be utterly lost on 95% of the people."

Duran matched his expression with her own.

"It's important to *me*."

Holmes took a breath and sipped his brandy.

"I'm asking you to sacrifice what is important to you for what is important to every sentient being on this planet. Read it aloud! I know you'll agree."

She did and she liked the sound of it. As with so many decisions of this magnitude that did not require immediate rendering, she would take it to bed, let it float through her dreams, and awaken with a fresh perspective.

"I only want you to consider it, Madam Secretary. *Really* consider it."

"I will. I promise."

They tilted their glasses and drank. Though his candidate would leave his office far from certain, he knew he had won the day.

42

BLACK KING TO QUEEN'S CASTLE SEVEN

Watching televised coverage of the Democratic National Convention from a hotel suite on the campaign trail, Wynn railed and vented like an aggrieved madman. He answered every charge, innuendo and criticism with a booming counterpoint, inevitably before his detractors had completed a thought. His staff had long given up trying to calm or appease him. Some feared for his health for good reason. The Republican candidate was considerably older than his public persona and his fiery disposition put him at constant risk of a heart attack. His doctors wanted to medicate him for a mood disorder but the candidate of course refused. If word leaked that Wynn took psychotropic medications his candidacy would be mortally wounded. His doctors countered to no avail that hospitalization for a heart attack would likely have the same effect.

His constant agitation became so pronounced that his staff had to watch a rebroadcast of the event later in the privacy of their own rooms. Otherwise they would have no idea what the speakers, operatives, broadcasters and pundits were saying.

Jack Morris watched the proceedings from another room, leaving the door slightly ajar to monitor his candidate. When Wynn seemed about to implode, Morris had an aide slip him a muscle relaxant on the sly. He'd figured out a dosage that calmed the big man without making him dull and pliant.

Morris upped the dosage in anticipation of Shelby Duran's acceptance speech. He had heard on the grapevine that Duran, after weeks of resistance, had decided to level a direct attack on Wynn. He had known that Winfred Holmes was pushing for an aggressive approach and he was disappointed Duran had finally yielded. It was an effective strategy and one that he would have chosen in Holmes' place. It would force Wynn to nail down his positions on critical issues. If he held to the hard-line right, as the candidate would want to, it would please his base but harm his appeal in the general election. If he moved to the middle before their own convention, he would be accused of pandering and sacrifice the enthusiasm of his most fervent supporters.

Morris knew they would have to compromise, holding ground on some issues while moderating their position on others. He also knew his candidate would have a fit. Like a petulant child he would have to be restrained for his own well being.

The tag line to Duran's attack was a stroke of genius and would become the foundation of a series of attack ads immediately after the convention: Danny Wynn: Sound and Fury, Signifying Nothing.

They would have to answer the attack swiftly. No matter where they went, no matter how choreographed the event, they would face the same questions until they answered them. What is your policy on immigration? What is your policy on military intervention? Do you support reinstating the embargo on Cuba? On and on, their campaign would come to a standstill until they answered the charges definitively.

Morris did not look forward to it but he knew what had to be done. He had already decided: They would move to the middle on immigration policy. There were just too many Hispanic voters to alienate them completely. They would temper the rhetoric on military intervention. Americans were not prepared for another prolonged war with an uncertain endgame. They would hold their ground on trade policy, Cuba, labor rights, deregulation, voting rights, abortion, equal pay and minimum wage. They would offer enough to appease the base.

Only when they had defined their own policies would they be allowed to push back by demanding that Duran do the same on trade policy and Wall Street regulations, issues that would create similar problems for her campaign. If she declared her uncompromised support for fair trade she would sacrifice a significant share of corporate funding. If she compromised on regulation of financial institutions, she would weaken the support of her base.

As Duran took the podium and began her speech, Wynn began his rant in the suite next door. Morris marveled at how well the secretary had mastered the art of oratory. Her words flowed, riding the waves to each applause line. Wynn had his virtues as a speaker. He did not possess the oratorical skills of his rival but he could sound surprisingly sincere. People believed he was honest even when he was not. He had the skill set of a good con man or a real estate salesman. He had worked on his speechmaking but he had a marked tendency to peak too soon. If not held back he would exhaust his audience and lose his momentum.

Morris braced himself when Duran launched her attack. He gently closed his door as she built her case to its tag line. The convention stood and their applause rattled the walls. In the next room he could hear Wynn shouting obscenities, a thump and breaking glass. He would later learn that his candidate had tipped over a lamp and thrown his glass of whiskey at a volunteer.

Morris continued watching Duran's performance with growing admiration. She seemed majestic and presidential. She did not end her appeal on a negative note. She rebuilt her vision of a world at peace and a nation in prosperity, an equitable economy and a government that cared for the poor and indigent, a presidency that served the working people.

As she concluded her address Governor Pat Duvall, her choice as vice president, and his family, her husband and

167

children, joined her on stage. They formed a perfect Democratic portrait of diversity. Morris could not help admiring their work.

"Well done," he said aloud.

He walked into the next room and began the process of calming his candidate and persuading him that their next move, as unpalatable as it might be, was compromise.

43

WHITE CASTLE TO KING ONE

Lawrence McClure felt the pressure and began to question his decision to enter the political fray. Forced to give up control of Gonzo, his labor of love and primary interest, for the length of the campaign, he now felt new pressures. As majority owner in half a dozen technology firms, he noticed fluctuations in stock prices that could not be justified by the marketplace. He concluded that someone or some entity was making a run at his holdings but he had not been able to determine who was behind the attack. He had handled financial manipulations before but now he had a whole new set of enemies.

He felt the need to spend more time handling his business interests, which meant less time bundling contributions for the Duran campaign. The fruits of his labor had been bountiful. Her campaign had been fully funded and a large portion of that funding had come from unprecedented contributions from the high tech sector. McClure had been at the forefront of the effort, enabling Duran to take the high road to the Democratic nomination. He had made a promise that she would be fully funded throughout the campaign and he intended to keep that promise but he now sensed that his personal role, of necessity, might be diminished.

IIe had gathered important allies in his fundraising campaign and no one had proven more valuable than Sophia Cantu, CEO of Oracle Corporation. He would call upon her now to take a greater role, setting up a meeting in his San Jose office. She took the meeting not knowing what would be asked of her but sensing his unease. She knew he had been forced to withdraw from Gonzo. She knew his companies had come under fire. She suspected he would ask Oracle to step in to bolster his holdings and protect them from an unfriendly takeover.

Lawrence greeted her with a hug and offered a glass of wine. It was early evening so she accepted. He had come to feel a great deal of affection for his former rival in technology. He had always respected her both for her toughness and her adherence to a high standard of conduct. She felt the same for him though she did not share his eccentric tendencies.

"I'd like to propose a toast," he said. "To Shelby Duran, the Democratic nominee and next president of the United States!"

They tipped their glasses and drank. They had both been a part of the team that secured Duran the nomination.

"Shelby Duran owes a great deal to you," said Sophia.

"Well, that's what I want to talk to you about."

She took a step back in her mind. She had never known McClure to back away from a challenge but it sounded as though he was about to do just that.

"As you no doubt know I've been under a lot of pressure lately," he said.

"So I've heard."

He also took a step back.

"How much have you heard?"

"Someone's making a run on your companies."

"Any idea who?"

"No."

He realized the conversation was veering off course. He had no intention of talking business this evening but his thoughts wandered and his words followed.

"I don't either. That's the problem. I have a feeling it's related to my political activities. Retribution. Payback is part of the game."

Sensing the conflicting emotions battling within him, she

resisted saying what she thought: We knew that going in. Instead she moved the discussion forward.

"What can I do to help?"

"Well, I'm reluctant to ask."

"Don't be. I wouldn't be here if I weren't willing to take appropriate action. You're a colleague and a friend. If there's something I can do, whatever form it takes, and it's within my reach, I'm ready and willing."

He should have found her eagerness to help encouraging but it had the opposite effect. He would be asking her to take the same risks that had placed him in deep water. If he was preparing to back away, how could he expect her to step in?

"I'm conflicted, Sophia. I made a promise to the Duran campaign that they would be fully funded. I'm not sure I can keep that promise."

"You want me to step into your role?"

"I don't think I can ask you to do that."

"Of course you can. Look, the problem is your interests are diverse. Your enemy is well financed. They can take you on one company at a time. The solution is to consolidate but you can't do that under siege. You're right to pull back."

He nodded, knowing she was right. She was a master of the game. It was why he went to her in the first place. She continued.

"I don't have the same problem. My wealth is largely consolidated. If they take me on they take on Oracle. We'll be watching. We'll uncover the rat behind it and we'll counter attack. I don't care if it's Morgan Stanley, the Koch brothers and Microsoft combined, they will retreat. The risk is greater than the reward."

"I should have hired you ten years ago," he smiled.

"You and everyone else in the industry."

They agreed that she would gradually take on more of his responsibilities in the Duran campaign. If he could stabilize his financial kingdom, he would return to the fight with Sophia as his partner. If he could not he would withdraw.

"I've made reservations at Delancey Street on the Embarcadero in the event you'd like to join me. There's nothing I'd enjoy more."

She allowed him to squirm in the space between his invitation and her response.

"I'd love to on the condition there will be no more talk of business or politics."

For all his accumulated wealth and knowledge he could not imagine what they would find to talk about that would last through the appetizer but he readily accepted.

44

BLACK PAWN TO QUEEN FOUR

Since the collapse of the Black campaign, Sandy Merrill needed a job. Of the two surviving candidates, she was already on the Wynn payroll and they had no need for her particular set of skills within the campaign. Her value rested on her ability to infiltrate the enemy. The trouble of course was that the Duran people didn't exactly trust her. She had been involved in too many questionable transactions.

Merrill decided her best shot was to attack the problem the old fashion way: veiled threats, deception or outright bribery. She made an educated guess that Duran operative Julia Sands had leaked the anti-Wynn ad that triggered an anti-Duran campaign in retaliation. Merrill had carried the message but she received the tip anonymously. Her connections related that Sands had argued the merits of releasing the attack ads. She didn't believe the ads against Duran would have any appreciable effect but the ads against Wynn were exceptional.

It took Sands by surprise when Merrill called after the convention to appeal for employment. She agreed to meet with her in her Washington office. After the affair that resulted in her firing Richard Dawson, she knew Merrill could not be trusted but she also knew she always had an angle. Maybe she had some information that could be useful against Wynn on the road ahead. Moreover, she had exploited Merrill in leaking the anti-Wynn ad in the week before Super Tuesday. She was confident Merrill had no knowledge that she was behind the leak but in politics you could never be certain. Merrill was a good spy. She had ways of uncovering sources that few in the field could rival.

Merrill walked into her office with an air of confidence. She always made you think she knew something others didn't and more than not she did.

"What can I do for you, Ms. Merrill?"

"I need a job. I thought you might be useful in that regard."

Sands poured a cup of coffee and sat back down. She pointedly did not offer Merrill a cup.

"I'm familiar with your work, Ms. Merrill, and I'm certain you are familiar with mine. The Duran campaign prides itself on its ethical conduct, something you're not exactly known for. I'm not sure what your role in the Dawson business was but I know you had your hand in it. Richard was a friend. So why should we trust you enough to put you on our payroll?"

If Merrill was offended she did not show it.

"Because I'm good at what I do and because you need someone like me."

"I don't doubt your skills. The question is: Why should we trust you?"

Undaunted, Merrill continued without pause.

"Check the record. Ask the Black campaign. Everything I did and everything you might think I did served the interests of my candidate. That includes what happened to Richard. He was a friend of mine as well. I liked him but he was working for my candidate's rival. As for ethical conduct, we both know your campaign has not always lived up to the highest standard."

Sands felt her temperature rise. She waited to allow Merrill an opportunity to volunteer her point of reference. Merrill smirked and offered no comment.

"For the record, I don't know what you're talking about."

"Off the record, you do."

Sands wondered if it was a mistake talking to Merrill at all. At this point there was no way but forward.

"No, I don't."

"The word on the street is: You leaked the attack ad targeting Wynn. As far as I'm concerned it was a brilliant move. It cost Wynn a hell of a lot more than his counterattack cost Duran. Still, the DNC had arranged the truce. Vargas wasn't too happy about that."

"If that's the word on the street," replied Sands, "I haven't heard it."

"If it's not it will be."

"Is that a threat?"

At last they were getting down to it. It did not surprise Sands but it stung that Merrill knew what she appeared to know.

"Listen," smiled Merrill, "I play hardball. That's what I do. I want to work for you but if that road isn't available, I may end up working against you."

"I understand," replied Sands. "I do. And I respect what you do. I can only hope you appreciate the position I'm in. Can I take it under advisement?"

"Of course."

Sands contemplated her future in politics. If it became known that she leaked the attack ad, the pressure for her to resign would build until she could no longer hold it back. Sandy Merrill had played her hand well. She either hired her against all instinct or she would likely lose her job. Who knows if anyone would hire her again?

"But don't take too long," Merrill said on her way out the door. "I really need a job."

45

WHITE KNIGHT TO QUEEN FIVE

Julia Sands should have gone straight to Winfred Holmes. In matters spiritual confession is good for the soul. In matters political, however, only a fool goes down without a fight. Sands chose to fight. Within an hour of Merrill's visit she knew and accepted that she would pay for her transgression.

She had taken it upon herself to break the truce negotiated by the chair of the DNC. She had not consulted Holmes in her decision. She moved ahead without guidance, consultation or authorization. That she had acted in her candidate's interest and that subsequent events had supported her action no longer mattered. When it all came to the light of public scrutiny, Vargas would insist and Holmes would have no choice but to relieve her of her duties.

The option of hiring Sandy Merrill and sweeping the affair under the rug was not tenable. She trusted Merrill even less than she had before and then she had not trusted her at all. She made a few calls to people in the field, Richard Dawson, Mario Macias, Cassie James and others, people who had worked with Merrill, and they all came to the same conclusion: Sandy Merrill worked for Danny Wynn.

Merrill was a low-level operative. No one would protect her, least of all the Wynn campaign. The mere rumor that she had served Wynn while working for Senator Black would ruin her. Certain that she would fall soon enough of her accord, Sands took account and decided to aim higher. If she was going down and she surely was she would take someone with her, someone important. No one fit the bill better and no one was more critical to the campaign's success than Jacoby "Jack" Morris, the brain behind the Wynn campaign.

The central question was: Who gave the order to Americans for America First to run the anti-Duran ads after the truce was broken? If she could prove that Morris had advised, consulted or communicated in any way with the front organization for the Koch brothers, he would become the subject of a lengthy and damaging investigation by the Federal Election Commission. It was hard to imagine that Morris would resign but at the least he would be distracted and his every move would come under close scrutiny.

For several days she held Merrill at bay while she gathered information to make her case. She contacted witnesses who would attest that representatives of Americans for America First had met with representatives of the Wynn campaign. Cassie James had taken pictures of James Delacroix, Nolan Gray and Jim Duke entering the Washington headquarters of the Wynn campaign while Morris was in attendance. She had also taken photos of the same AAF representatives at the headquarters of the Republican National Committee, calling the role of the RNC into question.

The most damaging information came from the campaign's secretary, Mrs. Mary Conover, who provided James a handwritten page from the office log. The evening before AAF launched its anti-Duran campaign Morris had hosted a meeting with Duke and RNC chair Ralph Peterson. It was not against the law for them to meet but the timing suggested that the three had coordinated the release of the attack ads and that was illegal.

Armed with Conover's log Sands felt confident enough to call a press conference to accuse Jacoby Morris of illegally coordinating the Wynn campaign with the attack ads produced and aired by Americans for America First. She pointedly held the document back until the accused parties issued their responses.

The major networks, including the cables, picked up the event, rendering the topic impossible to ignore without fanning the fuels of rumor and speculation. As always happens with such stories, it gathered speed like a wildfire on a wind-blown day and would continue to do so until all questions were answered or another more titillating story came along.

The responses came in sequence. Jack Morris issued a blanket denial of all wrongdoing without specifics. Jim Duke refused to comment pending his own inquiry. Ralph Peterson, assured that no record of the meeting in question existed, denied that it ever took place. He felt confident in his denial because Morris had made the assurance. The office security cameras were turned off. The parties entered separately and through the carefully guarded rear entrance. The office secretary was instructed not to record the meeting.

Something had gone awry but before they could seek it out and clean it up, Ralph Peterson stepped in it.

46

BLACK KNIGHT TO QUEEN FIVE

Knight Takes Knight

Ralph Peterson cursed the day he met Jack Morris. Like every moral apologist he valued loyalty above all other virtues. He thrived on loyalty; he built a career on loyalty and expected it in his associations and partnerships in life as in politics. He should have known better than to trust Jack Morris, the notorious double-dealing traitor. He should have known Morris would throw anyone under the clichéd bus at the least provocation if it gave him a strategic advantage.

The moment he issued his denial Julia Sands produced the handwritten page from the office log documenting his lie for the world to see. His days numbered, his fate decreed, he did what anyone in his position would do: he sought revenge. Logically, he should have struck back at the man who betrayed him but he did not. He was still a team player and the Grand Old Party was still his team. It irked him that Morris counted on his loyalty to party but it made little difference. He surveyed the playing field and took aim at Julia Sands.

He knew that Sandy Merrill set this chain of events in motion when she applied for a job with the Duran campaign. He knew she met with Julia Sands and he knew she was a spy for the Wynn campaign. He did not know what kind of leverage she applied in her efforts to secure a position in the enemy camp. He was determined to find out. He contacted Merrill and arranged a clandestine meeting at a country club in Arlington. After the debacle at Wynn's Washington headquarters he no longer had faith in the usual "secure" locations.

Sandy Merrill did not play golf or tennis but she knew how to dress the part: Bright colored skirt, hem mid thigh, white collared shirt, light sweater, broad-brim cap and white designer sneakers. She checked in at the desk and was escorted to a table in the back of the clubhouse where Peterson waited with a spiked Arnold Palmer iced tea.

"I see someone has his shine on today," she winked, ordering lemonade and a Cobb salad.

"Careful," he replied. "I'm still chairman of the RNC."

"Rumor has it you won't be for long."

They consumed a speck of time going over the good old days and family matters. While Peterson knew Merrill, they hadn't sat down one-to-one since the McCain campaign. Back then she was just another operative working for the party they shared. Now that she worked both sides of the aisle they could not be seen together.

"Are you sure this place is secure?"

He glanced around as if the thought hadn't occurred to him.

"The one thing I've learned, my dear, is that no place is secure, certainly not the campaign headquarters of Daniel J. Wynn."

"Is that what this is about? Saving your ass?"

"Too late for that, sweetness." He leaned in so that she could see his bloodshot eyes and smell the alcohol riding his breath. "This is about revenge. Petty vengeance. Something I'm sure you can handle."

"I'm not sure I should take that as a compliment."

"You should. In our line of work vengeance comes at a high premium."

Merrill caught the eye of a woman at another table. She seemed to be paying a little too much attention to their conversation. She looked vaguely familiar but Merrill couldn't place her.

"Take a glance over your left shoulder. Do you recognize the woman in the pretty pink outfit?"

He tried and failed to be subtle, nearly spilling his drink. The woman threw a bill on the table and walked out.

"I'm afraid I don't. Do you?"

"No. But you're right about one thing: No place is secure."

She took another look around and decided it would be prudent to take care of business as quickly as possible.

"What can I do for you, Ralph?"

"I know you met with Julia Sands. Whatever you said spooked her. She took a big risk in going after Morris. She got me instead. If I'm going down I want company. I want Sands. I want to know what you told her."

Merrill glared at him with cold determination.

"Contrary to rumor I'm not just a pretty face. I work for a living and my currency is information. You want information? What can you offer in return?"

Peterson had been drinking too much and thinking too little. He did not have an answer though he was certain he could come up with something.

"What do you want, Sandy? You want money? I've got money. You want dirt? I've got a ton of it. Just tell me what you want."

"I'll tell you the same thing I told Julia Sands: I need a job. I'm a fully qualified political consultant. If you can nail down a position with a year's salary guaranteed and a significant severance provision, I'll tell you what I know."

Peterson jiggled the ice in his Arnold Palmer and waved to a waiter. His drink replenished he returned his focus to the matter at hand.

"A job? I was under the impression you had a job."

Merrill lowered her voice and hoped he would do the same.

"Like you, I can no longer count on my employer."

He laughed and wondered why he hadn't hired her a long time ago.

"While I still hold the chair I have that authority."

Merrill pulled a contract out of her sports bag and pushed it across the table. Peterson paged through it like a realtor handling a mortgage.

"A hundred and twenty grand?"

"And a hundred and twenty severance. Cost of living, Mr. Chairman."

"Sounds reasonable."

She handed him a pen and he signed on the bottom line.

"Now give me what I want."

She told him what she had already surmised and what she subsequently confirmed by Julia Sands' reaction: That Sands had broken the truce between Wynn and Duran by delivering an anti-Wynn ad to Americans for Fair Trade. She didn't have to explain the significance of that transgression.

Peterson pulled himself together and held a press conference the following day. Within twenty-four hours, Julia Sands would hand in her resignation.

47

WHITE PAWN TO QUEEN FIVE

Pawn Takes Knight

Cassidy James knew how to gain entrance to a private country club. She enjoyed a privileged upbringing in Nashville prior to her college years. A simple Google search and a telephone call yielded the name of a club member not in attendance. She walked in like she owned the place, using her best debutante voice and tossed the name of the club member over her shoulder as she sashayed to a table in the clubhouse.

She didn't hear a great deal, only what sounded like a negotiation and the names of Jack Morris and Julia Sands. She managed to snap a picture before she had to cut her visit short when it appeared that Sandy Merrill recognized her. Ralph Peterson was so drunk and would not have recognized his mother in an empty elevator.

It wasn't much but she reported what she had witnessed to Julia Sands shortly after the clandestine meeting. Taken with what she had already learned and documented it added to an already compelling case that Peterson had not only engaged in suspect if not illegal conduct but lied about it as well. Still, Sands did not seem pleased. She listened to the report and her brow furrowed.

"I have to tell you something, Cass, something I'm not particularly proud of."

Cassie did not like the sound of it. Of all the people she had met and worked with during the course of the campaign, she admired Julia most of all. When she began in the chilling wind and snow of New Hampshire, Shelby Duran had been her role model. Now it was Julia Sands.

"Please, I don't want to hear it."

Julia recoiled as if she'd been struck by a stiff punch to her gut.

"It's not a matter of choice. I have to tell you because I'm going to ask you to do something, something that may come with a heavy price."

Cassie absorbed the implications and braced herself.

"I'm listening."

"We have all the information we need to sink Ralph Peterson before he can do any further damage to the Duran campaign. I know. Maybe that shouldn't be my objective but it is. We're in a war. The Wynn people are nothing if not merciless. We have to be the same."

Cassie felt as though she'd been asleep and awakened in a different movie. The characters were the same but all the particulars had changed. She struggled to understand her mentor's words and how they related to her.

Standing and pacing the room like a cornered beast, Julia pressed on.

"They've got me, Cass. They know that I was the one who broke the truce before Super Tuesday. I delivered the attack ad against Wynn to Sandy Merrill. She delivered it to Americans for Fair Trade. I covered my tracks. I don't know how she found out but she did. She used it to try to get a job with the campaign. I can't have that. That's why she went to Peterson."

She took a breath and realized how confusing it must be to her protégé.

"I'm sorry, Cass. They've got me dead to rights. I acted against the orders of the DNC without consulting Winfred Holmes or anyone else. I did what I thought was best for the campaign but I knew the risk. If they found me out, I was done. Well, they've found me out and I'm done."

184

Cassie rolled her eyes, an expression that revealed her youth.

"It can't be that simple. You've got to fight back."

"I am fighting back and this is how it's done. Listen, Cass, it's important that you understand this: It's all about time and news cycles. Every minute the media spends talking about me and my problems is a minute lost to the campaign. Every time some talking head or beat writer or blogger begins a story with 'Duran staffer accused of wrongdoing' the campaign suffers. It creates a negative impression of the candidate. She can't talk about income inequality or Middle East policy. She has to tackle questions about the latest scandal and no matter how she answers, no matter what the facts are, the impact will be negative. The same goes for the other side. The fact is I did what I'm accused of doing. My job now is to move the cycle along. When I resign the story dies."

"So we go after Peterson."

"That's right."

"We put them in the spotlight."

"Yes. The fact is: It's not that easy to replace the chair of the RNC. It's taken years for Peterson to build his organization. If we take him out, it will hurt their campaign and it will send a message: You go after one of ours, there will be a price to pay."

At last Cassie understood. This was down-and-dirty hardball politics, the kind of backstabbing you read about in novels or see on cable television and hope to God it isn't based in fact. Too often it is.

"Where do I come in?"

Julia leaned back and recovered her balance. She didn't like what she was about to ask of her young friend but it had to be done.

"This is the hard part. I can't do what needs to be done. I've lost my credibility. If I make accusations now they write it off as the ravings of an angry discredited operator."

185

She let it settle in Cassie's mind.

"You need me to make the case."

"That's right. It's a strong case. Airtight. You helped make it. That's why you're the logical choice."

"I'll do it."

"Before you agree, you need to know they'll come after you. When they do you'll have to bow out. You can't become the next distraction."

Julia saw her struggling within and wondered if she was asking too much. Would she have been prepared for such a sacrifice at her age?

"So this is the end of my political career."

"No. Believe me, no one will forget what you did for this campaign. You'll go home, take some classes and bide your time. When the next cycle comes around, I guarantee you a job. I'll call you myself."

It took the edge off.

They prepared for an interview Julia had arranged at MSNBC on Friday evening. It allowed enough facts to be verified over the weekend and the story rehashed the following week. Cassie began with Peterson's lie about attending the meeting with Jack Morris and Jim Duke. She documented a series of meetings strongly suggesting Peterson had illegally coordinated the actions of the Wynn campaign with the Duke brothers' 501 organization all along. His latest meeting with Sandy Merrill led to a whole new set of questions. Why would he meet with an operative from the opposing party unless he had been involved in the ad war between Americans for America First and Americans for Fair Trade?

Ralph Peterson fought back with his accusation against Julia Sands for releasing the anti-Wynn ad that triggered the war. The general public decided in public opinion polls that anyone and everyone connected with the story was dirty. As a result, Julia Sands and Ralph Peterson tendered their resignations.

Against all odds, Cassandra James held on. In the muddled mess of charges and counter charges, she was perceived as a mere pawn in the affair and so escaped retribution. She moved down to Miami where she signed on to work in the office of Chauncey Davis.

48

BLACK QUEEN TO QUEEN SIX

Jack Morris was pissed. As they prepared for the first debate, his candidate was slipping and it was not the big man's fault. Wynn had given a strong speech at the national convention despite the necessity of going soft on immigration and tempering his hard line on foreign policy. In many ways it was Wynn's finest moment. He managed to seem strong and reasonable, knowledgeable and tough while negotiating the nation's most challenging problems – problems that he possessed little knowledge of and even less understanding.

No, Wynn had done his job well. And yet their numbers began to slide within a few days of the convention. The mess of scandals and the difficulty of appealing to minority voters eroded his support and made him seem compromised.

This was his fault and he knew it. Winfred Holmes was outplaying him. Holmes had managed to stay on the sidelines while he was mired in the cesspool of dirty politics. It had clouded his judgment and kept him on the defensive. He needed desperately to reverse the momentum and go on the attack. He needed a bold strike at the heart of the enemy camp. He needed to drag Holmes into the mud as Holmes had done to him.

He booked a one-on-one with a softball interviewer on Freedom Central, the flagship news station of Freedom Network. Rudolf McCall, the network's owner, was a personal friend and fully committed to Wynn being the next president.

The interview opened with a vague question about the campaign's recent difficulties culminating in the resignation of Ralph Peterson. Morris shrugged and waded into the mire.

"You know, Jeff, this whole mess is founded on a fundamental misconception. Everyone thinks we run a dirty campaign. Nothing could be further from the truth. Daniel Wynn is a standup guy. He knows what he believes and he sticks to it. The Democrats can't compete with that so they do everything they can to muddy the waters."

Jeff Spiegel, the Freedom interviewer, had been prepped so he knew where to go and dutifully went there.

"Who do you think is behind this scandal?"

"What scandal?"

"Well, this mess as you put it."

"First of all, there's nothing illegal or inappropriate in folks on the same team getting together to talk. That's number one. Second, everyone in the business knows this whole mess was orchestrated by Winfred Holmes."

"Shelby Duran's campaign manager."

"That's right, Jeff. Holmes is famous for this kind of thing. Some would say infamous. He knew we had all the momentum after the convention. The people were responding to Daniel Wynn's message of individual responsibility and freedom. Our numbers were up and contributions were pouring in so Holmes changed the subject. He sent his spies out to cook up some sort of so-called scandal out of thin air. Underneath it all there was nothing there but he got the bobble heads on MSNBC and CNN chattering, speculating, accusing people, day after day, night after night until a lot folks thought: There must be something going on. Why would they spend so much time on fluff and nonsense?"

"Like the Chelsea Scandal," smiled Spiegel.

Morris glared at him. Under no circumstances was he or anyone else on Freedom News to utter the words: Chelsea Scandal. Fortunately, it was a recorded interview so they could cut it later. Spiegel's smile soured so Morris knew he realized his offense.

"Let's move on."

"Yes. Can you explain why Ralph Peterson resigned as chairman of the RNC?"

"It's unfortunate. If it were up to me he'd still have his job. But it wasn't up to me and it wasn't up to Danny Wynn. Dan wanted him to weather the storm and come back fighting. He doesn't know the meaning of the word quit. So Ralph took one for the team and I applaud him for it. He knew just as Winfred Holmes knew that he had become the story. It was a distraction. When you become the story and you're not the candidate, you're hurting the campaign. That's exactly why Holmes arranged this whole mess and to some extent it worked."

"So what does the Wynn campaign do next?"

"We move on. We've got more important things to worry about than some fabricated so-called scandal. The real scandal is the man behind the curtain, the man pulling the strings, the man trying to muddy the waters so the people can't see the simple truth and that truth is: Daniel J. Wynn is the candidate with a vision, the candidate with the ideas and the strength of character to turn this country around. If Winfred Holmes wants to wallow in the mud let him; we're moving on."

Satisfied he had set the bait, Morris sat back and waited. If Holmes took it he would be swept into the void of infinite distraction like some sinkhole from hell.

190

49

WHITE CASTLE TO QUEEN FOUR

Holmes knew he was being baited. He knew Jack Morris as an unscrupulous but highly skilled adversary. He had a dossier on Morris that could pass as a small encyclopedia. Karl Rove exempted, Morris was the dirtiest political operative since the days of Boss Tweed and Tammany Hall. Morris accusing Holmes of dirty politics was like Pete Rose accusing Ken Griffey Jr. of gambling on baseball. It was like Dick Nixon accusing George McGovern of attempting to defraud American democracy.

Walking into the trap was never an option but neither would he leave the charges unanswered. He needed a surrogate, someone who was smart, quick, knowledgeable and good with the media. Julia Sands should have been the obvious choice but she was no longer available. He could go with Chuck Harrison, the campaign spokesperson, but he preferred someone more removed from the candidate. He puzzled over it, fearing that he could lose the moment, knowing that the wrong choice might do more harm than good.

As if on cue, Lawrence McClure called to express his outrage at Morris' attack. He had his own problems to deal with but he offered to help in any way he could. Holmes took it for what it was worth. In any crisis, tragedy or misfortune, a lot of people will offer help. Only a few actually mean it. They talked for a while on topics ranging from the campaign to baseball. McClure's Giants and Holmes' Nationals were once again in a showdown for the National League championship.

When it seemed the conversation had reached its logical end, McClure said: "I know you think I'm just being polite but when I say I'd like to help I really mean it. I honestly don't know how long I can continue with the campaign. If there's any chance I could do something that would make a difference, I'd jump at it."

Up to this point Holmes had not given any thought to using someone outside the political circle. McClure was a moneyman but he had the qualifications. He was smart and knowledgeable. He was quick minded and surprisingly adept at handling the media. As a business leader his words would carry more weight than the usual suspects. The more he thought about it the more it made sense.

"Can you give me a couple of days?"

"When?"

"Now. As soon as you can. It's something I'd rather not talk about over the phone."

McClure hesitated, more curious than questioning. He considered the possibilities and what needed to be done to cover for his unscheduled absence during an ongoing crisis. His staff could handle it. They'd done it a dozen times without fail. It was the least he could do for Shelby Duran before stepping down.

"I'll fly out tonight."

"Good. Text me when you get here."

He picked him up at the airport in the late evening, going over the proposed plan on the drive to his apartment. Despite a vague sense of discomfort, a fish out of water sort of thing, McClure agreed to do his best. They stayed up to the early hours going over Holmes' dossier on Jack Morris, a sizable task that continued the next day until at length the master politico pronounced him ready.

They scheduled an interview with Christopher Bay of MSNBC with the stated purpose of delivering a refutation to the unfounded accusations of Jacoby Morris. Bay was an enthusiastic Duran supporter and well versed in the dirty tricks of Jack Morris. He set the stage with a succinct history of those dirty tricks and a brief summary of Morris' charges against Winfred Holmes. He welcomed a nervous Lawrence McClure to his show.

Bay (almost laughing): So...I understand you're a little upset over the allegations of dirty politics.

McClure: That would be an understatement. To put it bluntly: Morris is one of the dirtiest political operators in American history. Winfred Holmes is respected on both sides of the aisle as one of the most brilliant and upright political strategists in the modern era. For Morris to accuse Holmes of dirty politics is the pot calling the kettle black.

Bay: Truer words were never spoken. And it's not just Democrats that have a problem with Jack Morris.

McClure (smiling): That's true. Mary Jo Perez of the Pierce campaign accused Morris of running the sleaziest campaign since Karl Rove against John McCain in the 2000 primaries.

Bay: That was the campaign where they accused McCain of bearing an illegitimate child by a black prostitute.

McClure: Not only that. They called his wife a drug addict, suggested he was mentally unstable and actually implied that McCain was homosexual.

Bay: All this on the sly of course. They wouldn't say any of it to his face.

McClure: You couldn't get away with that sort of crap today, where everything a campaign does is recorded and disseminated almost simultaneously. Morris is famous for the same sort of on-the-sly character assassinations in congressional campaigns dating back to the nineties. Books have been written about his dirty tactics.

Bay: I think "infamous" is the appropriate word. Even his own pick for vice president, Sam Sampson, lambasted Morris for breaking Reagan's eleventh commandment against Republicans attacking Republicans. He did this at the first debate, the absolute first opportunity, against the explicit orders of the RNC.

McClure: Unbelievable.

Bay: My sentiment exactly.

McClure settled in and enjoyed a lively exchange. When it was done, he felt he had performed his job well. There would be a price to pay. He understood that possibility. But for now he felt like celebrating. He enjoyed an excellent French meal at Jean-Georges on Central Park West, took in some jazz at The Iridium on Broadway, before retreating to his room at The Hilton. He awakened late in the morning, refreshed and invigorated. He caught an early flight back to the West Coast ready to resume the fight against his business adversaries.

50

BLACK PAWN TO QUEEN FOUR

Pawn Takes Castle

While Lawrence McClure was away in Washington and New York, Jolene Dixon worked her charms in San Jose. Within a few days she identified her mark, a shy guy by the name of Wilson Summers who worked as an accountant in the inner circle of McClure's financial empire. He was brilliant with a spreadsheet and had the memory of a super-computer but like so many on the tech scene his social development arrested about the third grade of elementary school.

Summers knew the company was in trouble. In fact McClure's interests were less a single entity than a loose confederation of companies, some of which made significant profits and others that operated at a loss. He had warned McClure on numerous occasions that he needed to consolidate to protect his interests from unwanted suitors. His boss ignored his advice and now faced the very real possibility that he would lose control.

They had been unable to determine the predator behind the assault. Whoever or whatever it was they possessed vast resources and employed a complex web of front companies and investment firms to purchase shares. Counter measures could hold them back but for how long no one knew. If they succeeded in taking over the more profitable of McClure's companies there would be a massive shake-up. His position, his interest in the company and his retirement fund would be in jeopardy.

He had to consider his options and was doing so over a Guinness stout in a local pub when a stunningly attractive woman approached him to buy her a drink. He naturally figured she was a prostitute and declined. She laughed.

"I'm not out to take your money, Mr. Summers. I'm here to protect your interests."

"You have my attention."

She winked and led him to a booth where they could have some measure of privacy. At this point he was only curious. Did she know he was looking for alternatives or did she assume as much? Who did she work for and what did she want him to do?

"Your boss is in a world of trouble, Mr. Summers. It's only natural that you might be looking for a safe way out. I can do more than that. The people I represent have enormous resources. They can offer you a new job at twice the salary, secure you retirement with a sizeable bonus and buy out your shares in McClure Enterprises at a premium."

Her level of knowledge regarding his personal predicament impressed him almost as much as she did. Her green eyes, the lilt in her voice and the shape of her lips interrupted the logic centers of his brain. He could not get a grip. He felt himself getting dizzy and struggled to find his speech faculty.

"Who are you?" he managed.

"That's not important. If you'd like to know whom I represent tell me you're interested. We'll proceed from there."

Impaired or not, he could think of no reason why he would not be interested. Still, it would not be wise to react too quickly so he waited.

"I am," he said finally.

"You're what?"

"Interested."

"In me or the proposition?" she smiled.

He blushed and resisted the urge to say: Both. He knew better. This woman was not anywhere near his league.

"So who do you work for?"

She took a moment to allow him to think she was calculating whether or not she should trust him with this information.

"You've heard of the Koch brothers?"

"Who hasn't? Four and five on the Forbes list."

"Three and four, latest edition."

"Yes, I've heard of them."

"Would you have any objection to working for them?"

"Philosophically? No."

"You're not political?"

"I didn't say I'd vote for them."

"Well, I can assure you it would be in your economic interest."

"How would I secure such a position?"

"Down to the heart of it. I like that. What's the point of dancing around it?"

She pulled a printout from her purse and placed it on the table before him.

"We've acquired a list of Mr. McClure's email and phone communications with fellow CEO's and CFO's in the industry. If you can provide three or four instances where Mr. McClure's corresponding stock or bond purchases came within twelve hours of those communications, you will have secured your position along with all its substantial benefits."

Summers looked at the list. It contained thirty to forty entries. The information they wanted could be sufficient evidence of insider trading for the Security and Exchange Commission to open an inquiry. With all the other problems on McClure's desk, it could be a debilitating blow.

"I'm wondering if the reward is proportionate to the harm."

"Would you like more money, Mr. Summers?"

"I didn't say that."

"I wouldn't worry about Mr. McClure. He won't be eating at McDonald's any time soon. If he plays his cards right, he should emerge from this as wealthy as he is today."

"I'm not so sure."

"You should be focused on your own future but the choice is yours."

She stood and gave him a kiss on the cheek.

"I'll be here tomorrow at the same time. If you decide to play you'll be here. If not, this meeting never happened."

He watched her sashay out and felt a little pride in the fact that the scattering of patrons witnessed them together. He knew he would take the deal and she probably knew it as well. McClure had been good to him but his instinct for self-preservation exceeded any sense of loyalty. He chose to believe his boss would be fine.

He went to work the next day with one goal in mind: Scouring the list of stock purchases for dates and times that corresponded to the list of communications. He found what he was looking for and began making arrangements for relocation before he reported to the pub at the appointed time. Jolene Dixon smiled.

Lawrence McClure arrived at the office expecting to find the same low-level anxiety driven crisis mode that had prevailed over the last month or so. He'd left instructions to call him only in an emergency. No one had called.

His secretary handed him a 9x12 manila envelope as he walked in, noting that a well-dressed woman had delivered it personally. From the mouth of his secretary, "well dressed" translated to extremely attractive. It aroused his curiosity enough that he set aside his normal routine of going through emails and snail mail as they arrived.

He opened the envelope at once and discovered there a fresh new world of crisis. It contained a letter addressed to the Securities and Exchange Commission purporting to be from an employer who wished to remain anonymous. It referred to possible violations of rules and regulations regarding insider trading. Attached were two documents, each several pages long, with certain items highlighted. One document listed communications by phone or email; the other chronicled stock purchases.

He felt sick. On top of everything else, this could be the tipping point. He felt like a medieval lord of the manor holding his castle against impossible odds, the only question remaining: when to surrender.

There was a business card stapled to the letter. It had a number and said: Call me.

Jolene Dixon appeared at his office door within thirty minutes of his call. As his secretary had noted, she was very well dressed.

"Don't look so glum," she said. "I'm here to solve all your problems."

"You can do that?"

"I can or rather the people I work for can."

This was the moment that confirmed his hypothesis. All his problems began with his involvement in the Duran campaign. It stood to reason that those problems would disappear once his political activities ceased.

"I don't imagine you'd care to tell me who you work for."

"No sir, I don't imagine I do."

"But you can make it all go away."

"Yes sir."

The instinct to fight gave way to resignation. He knew this ultimatum would come. It was only a matter of time. Now that it had he almost welcomed it. He felt grateful he had been able to serve the campaign this long. He had done his part. Now it was time to move on.

"Your conditions?"

"Cease your political activities. No more bundling, no more contributions and no more interviews on political subjects. If you comply, this letter will never be sent and the mysterious raider buying stock in your companies will gradually withdraw. You can resume business as usual."

He extended his hand without further delay: Done.

51

WHITE CASTLE TO KING SEVEN

Check

McClure phoned Sophia Cantu to inform her of his decision and to apologize. Not only was he resigning as the campaign's primary bundler; he could no longer contribute. She said she understood but they both knew the explanation was inadequate. No matter what had happened, no matter how great the financial impact, McClure remained a very wealthy individual. That he could not contribute at all meant he was being squeezed: extortion, bribery or some other form of nefarious threat.

She decided to let it go for the moment and embraced the importance of her new role. McClure was out not only as a bundler, a change she expected, but also as a major contributor. It didn't matter why or how. Somehow she had to pick up the slack.

The first presidential debate between Duran and Wynn was less than a week away. The candidates were essentially in lockdown, making few public appearances as they made preparations for the critical event. She had urged the campaign to make a strong statement on intellectual property rights, an issue the general public cared little about but one that the tech community considered essential. With huge amounts of money flowing from the Koch brothers and the industrial sector combined with the loss of McClure's contributions they were facing an enormous deficit if they could not boost contributions from the high tech sector.

Sensing that the campaign did not fully appreciate the potential crisis, she requested an emergency meeting with Duran and Holmes in Washington. Duran approved a meeting with only three days to go before the debate. It took place in Duran's office at her national headquarters.

"I appreciate your making time to see me, Madam Secretary. I know these are very busy times."

"Nonsense," replied Duran. "I'm so sick of debate preparations I'd welcome a weekend with my accountant."

"Hopefully this won't be that trying."

"I wouldn't be too confident," intervened Holmes.

Neither Holmes nor Duran had ever met Sophia Cantu in person. She was small in stature, stylish in dress with sharp features and piercing dark eyes. They knew she was exceptionally bright and highly regarded in the business world; they were not so certain about her political acumen and they intended to put her to the test.

"It's my understanding you wish to make a case for including intellectual property rights in the debate. I'd like you to know I'm sympathetic to your position. Fred however has a different point of view. So I wanted to get the two of you together to see if we could find common ground. I've heard from Fred but I've only heard your side of the issue second hand."

"Well, my side begins with the acknowledgement that we've lost a significant source of contributions in Lawrence McClure. I know you're aware but I'm not sure you fully appreciate the position that puts us in. We're under a great deal of pressure to compensate for the loss. I've talked to our contributors and they all say the same thing: It's not enough that you've stood up for intellectual rights in the past. They need to know it will be a high priority under your presidency. The best opportunity to do that is to make a strong statement in the first debate when your audience will be greater than it ever has been."

Duran nodded as she spoke, giving the impression that

she was in full agreement. She was in fact and she had been pressing her advisors to make just such a statement. She looked to Holmes for his rebuttal.

"I agree with your analysis but there's this: If we make a definitive statement on intellectual property rights, we have to do the same on trade policy. They're inextricably linked like ham and cheese. If we go there we'll be walking a tightrope."

He inhaled before proceeding, as if some significant part of him did not want to say aloud what he was about to say.

"Shelby Duran is not a proponent of free trade. You can be forgiven if you haven't figured that out. We've kept it under wraps. We've stayed in the gray area. We've muddied the waters and we've done so by design. Once the secretary comes out definitively against free trade we run the risk of losing Wall Street. Not only that but some of your colleagues in high tech may pull back as well. So my question to you is: If she makes the statement you want her to make, can you assure us that the gains will be greater than the loss?"

Sophia felt their eyes bearing down on her. They clearly didn't expect her to have an answer to the conundrum. They were wrong. She had given it a great deal of thought.

"I believe I can. Not only that but I believe we can mitigate whatever losses there might be. Let's face it: any interest that is solely dependent on a free trade policy is already in the Republican camp. The contributions they give to Duran are a hedge against a Republican loss. You're not likely to lose those contributions, especially if you win the debate. You'll enhance your chances of winning the debate if you open up a discussion of trade policy. Why? Because Wynn doesn't expect you to go there and even if he did he's not knowledgeable enough to carry the argument. Why do you think he hasn't pressed the issue? Morris knows what's at stake but he's held his candidate back. Why? He can't trust Wynn to make a coherent argument."

203

Holmes looked to the secretary and Duran smiled.

"She makes a compelling argument," said Duran.

Holmes shook his head in resignation. There was merit in what she said and virtue in how she said it. He had wondered why Wynn had held back on trade policy. It only made sense if he was ill prepared to engage it.

"I still think it's a gamble," he said. "But I can't hold back the tide forever. You've wanted to make the case. Now you'll get your chance. We have three days. We can start working it this evening."

Duran stood to shake Sophia's hand, her smile bright enough to light the city of Manhattan on a moonless night.

"You're the first person I know to go head-to-head with Winfred Holmes and emerge with it still attached."

Holmes shrugged.

"She's right about one thing: you'll win the argument. I only hope she's right about mitigating the consequences."

Hosted by CNN in Atlanta, Georgia, the first debate centered on economic policy. Duran answered each question succinctly and forcefully, once again demonstrating the breadth and depth of her knowledge. Wynn held to the conservative line with equivalent force and absolute confidence, punctuating his arguments with humor and slogans.

Wynn defended right to work laws. Duran countered: "They ought to call them the right to low wages because that's exactly how they affect the workers."

Duran proposed raising taxes on the ultra rich and closing corporate loopholes to finance public works and a raise in the minimum wage. Wynn answered: "The same old Democrat ideas. Tax the rich! Tax the rich! They forget that these so-called rich people are the ones who hire the workforce! I believe in a free market. The government ought to get out of the way and allow the market to work."

On and on the debate followed a predicable pattern

without stumble or gaff until Duran pivoted from a question concerning protectionism to address intellectual property rights.

"The importance of this issue cannot be overstated. The theft of technologies developed in America by Americans by the Chinese, India and South Korea among others, costs billions in lost revenue each year. Our technological innovations are at the center of our economy and must be protected at all costs."

When Wynn replied that he also believed in protecting intellectual property, Duran answered: "I'm not sure my opponent fully understands this issue. Free trade policies, which Mr. Wynn purports to support without qualification, have enabled intellectual property theft. We cannot protect our technologies without trade restrictions and penalties."

Wynn repeated that he supported free trade "as long as it's fair" and he did not believe that intellectual property rights "whatever that is" had anything to do with it. After two attempts at follow-up his responses lost all focus and the moderator moved on.

Wynn demanded that Duran give a clear and concise statement on where she stood on the matter of free trade. Duran complied.

"It may come as a surprise to my esteemed opponent in this debate but the fact is: There is no such thing as free trade. If there were, trade agreements would require no more than the following sixteen words: Trade between the signatory nations shall not be impeded by conditions or consequences of any kind. There does not exist in the world today any such agreement. Instead we have agreements masquerading as free trade that contain sixteen thousand or more pages of conditions. Too often the interests of the working people are not considered in these agreements."

Wynn seemed dumfounded but unencumbered.

"Everyone knows what free trade means. It's been the foundation of our trade policy for decades. Even Bill Clinton believed in free trade!"

Because the general viewing audience did not understand the intricacies of trade or its profound implications, the exchange was not as decisive as it might have been. Nevertheless a consensus formed that Duran won the debate by seeming more knowledgeable and therefore more presidential. Duran's poll numbers surged and her contributions followed. Wynn would never raise the question of trade policy again.

Even Winfred Holmes had to admit: Sophia Cantu was right.

52

PLAYERS

Strings and Shadows

For a long while Willy and Solana gazed at the board constructed of exquisite black and white marble, its pieces carved in pure ebony and 40,000-year-old Wooly Mammoth ivory dating to 1849 by Jacques of London. The pieces were placed to reveal the current state of the match that would (if all went well) determine the most powerful elected leader in the world.

"It's ironic, isn't it?" opined Solana.

"What's that, my dear?"

"That we should manipulate the very individuals who are praised as the most masterful and brilliant manipulators this modern world of scientific polling and instantaneous communications can produce."

"It is indeed," reflected Willy. "If they only knew."

Solana's gaze did not waver from the board, her mind locked on the keys to her next move, a move that could well determine the game's outcome.

"We should tell them."

Willy's laughter cut short when he realized Solana had not joined him. Not even a smile betrayed her sincerity. Was she being serious? Though they had agreed no one would know while they still lived, he'd lately begun to wonder. Among the qualities he admired in her was her unpredictability. It served her well in a game that placed high value on skillful deceit.

"Perhaps we should."

Solana's eyebrows rose perceptibly though she did not look up at him.

"Would we be perceived as villains?"

"We would. People do not take kindly to manipulation of their most cherished institutions. We Americans in particular like to think we believe in democracy."

"I wonder," replied Solana. "No one admires royalty more than Americans. They can hardly get enough of it. We English often suspect you are suffering from a bad case of aristocrat envy. Princess Diana, Downton Abbey, the royal baby, it's an American obsession."

"We are an obsessive culture to be sure but I can assure you the ordinary American would not approve of the kind of subterfuge and interference that we have honed to an art form."

At last she broke her concentration and strolled toward the liquor cabinet.

"More wine, my dear?"

"Please."

They huddled together on the sofa, sipping wine and enjoying the view, their suite at the pinnacle of the Hotel Imperial overlooking a Viennese skyline. They had attended the Opera after supper and were now content to settle in for the night.

"How do we stand?" he inquired.

"How do you mean?" she replied.

"The match. What else? Whom do you consider having the advantage?"

"There is no advantage. At least none that I perceive."

"You wouldn't tell me if there was of course."

"Of course not."

While Solana was content to absorb the ambience of a truly aristocratic surroundings with its marble floors, Elizabethan carpets, classical art and plush velvet curtains, she could tell that something was eating at her lover.

"You might as well tell me," she said.

"I was just wondering: We both have our shadows, our agents of influence, our hired manipulators. In keeping with the spirit of chess, what are their limits?"

"What do you mean?"

"I mean: In chess we don't have to persuade our knights and bishops to make a specific move, we simply move. In reality chess we allow our shadows a great deal of leeway, so my question is: What distinguishes a shadow from a pawn? And shouldn't there be a distinction between the two?"

Solana contemplated the problem though she did not recognize it as a problem except in the peculiar workings of Willy's mind.

"We do what we must to produce the desired result."

She sensed her answer did little to satisfy his concern.

"Is there something more specific you wish to question?"

As he was inclined to do, Willy hemmed and hawed before saying what he meant to say all along.

"I was thinking of Mary Conover, Wynn's secretary."

"What of her?"

"I mean, she did more than influence or persuade. She enabled Julia Sands to eliminate Ralph Peterson."

"Do you think she exceeded her role as a shadow?"

"I'm not saying she did. I'm saying it's a question that should be asked: What are the limits of our shadow agents?"

"Must we have limits?"

"I think we should."

Solana recounted the moves each of them had taken in the course of the match before arriving at an example that would counter his argument.

"Did you not use the accountant in much the same way?"

She referred to Wilson Summers, the accountant in McClure Enterprises who produced incriminating evidence that helped take down McClure.

"Fair enough. I suppose I did."

"Then we have no problem."

"I suppose not but…"

She placed her finger on his lips and kissed him gently.

"Hush now. We play the game as it presents itself to us. We do what we must. There is nothing more nor less to it."

He conceded the point and yielded to her romantic overture. He tried in vain to concentrate the whole of his desire, the fulcrum of all his senses on her lips, her breasts, and the shape of her hips as they moved in harmony with his own. They had arrived at a critical juncture in the match. Well ahead on points, pawn to a castle, he nevertheless felt the pressure of her powerful and relentless attack. He wanted nothing more than to return her aggression, to answer blow for blow, move for move, to attack and consume her as she attacked and consumed him. Even as he felt his body yield to her desire he wanted nothing more than to control her as she controlled him.

There remained plenty of time. There were endless possibilities and countless moves still on the board. She was nowhere near mate. He vowed that he would find a way to turn it around and resume his offense. He held the advantage if only he could turn the momentum around. He would have his day yet.

53

BLACK KING TO QUEEN'S KNIGHT SIX

Wynn refused to believe he lost the debate until Jack Morris showed him the numbers. He'd lost two points in the polls. The race remained within the margin of error but the momentum had swung in Duran's favor. Beneath the numbers, the public perceived Duran as more presidential and more knowledgeable on the issues. The one significant advantage Wynn maintained was that the public perceived him as the stronger of the two candidates.

The polling numbers did not alarm Morris. In the ebb and flow of a long campaign the numbers were bound to swing back and forth. What did alarm him was the trend in contributions. He had expected a Wall Street pivot to his candidate after Duran's strong statement on trade policy, not to mention her attack on right to work laws. She had taken the role of a labor candidate and yet she had not paid a price in corporate funding. He deduced that the so-called smart money was betting on a Duran victory. No matter how antagonistic to the corporate cause it was better to invest in a winner than a loser.

He had to change that dynamic to regain the financial advantage they needed and were counting on. The best way to accomplish his objective was to exploit his candidate's strength. At one time it would have seemed ill advised and counter-intuitive but at this juncture he believed his candidate had to pivot to the one area where his perceived strength matters most: foreign policy.

Up to now it had been assumed that the former Secretary of State would dominate any discussion of foreign policy issues. Indeed, the next debate would focus on foreign policy, a fact that fueled the perception that Duran had the fast track to the White House. Wynn had to challenge that notion. Naturally, he resisted the idea. He wanted to double down on trade and free market economics.

"You tell me Duran kicked my butt on trade policy so now you want me to take her on in foreign policy? That's her backyard! Have you lost your mind? That's where she lives! She's a goddamn bonafide foreign policy expert! She was the Secretary of State for Christ sake! She'll have three counterpoints to every point I make. She'll run me around in circles! You told me this yourself not three weeks ago! What's changed? Did Shelby Duran suddenly get dumber or did I get smarter? I don't think so!"

Morris knew better than to break his candidate's ravings. He simply let it runs its course.

"Is that it? Are you done?"

Wynn shrugged. He was the kind of candidate who thought you were a genius when things went well. When things went sour as they inevitably would he was the first to point the finger of blame.

"Alright then. You want to know what's changed? Everything has changed. You've lost the momentum. The fat cats on Wall Street look at you and they see a loser. So how we do we turn this thing around? Well, I took it to the staff and one of them came up with this: We use your strength to attack Duran's strength. Reverse the polemic. Turn her strength into a weakness. Suddenly we look like a winner and the money flows back in our direction."

Wynn tried not to look too pleased. He didn't have to try too hard.

"Sounds good, Jack. The question is: How do we make that happen? You said it yourself: You can't make me a Rhodes scholar overnight."

"We don't have to, Danny boy. You know what people like about you?"

"What's that?"

"You're strong. You're tough. You're willing to fight and take no prisoners. Spin it one way and it's a liability but when it comes to our enemies it's exactly what people are looking for. Someone who carries a big stick and isn't afraid to use it."

Wynn began to see the light. Every other the day the news was filled with reports of another terrorist attack, a brutal beheading in Syria, a massacre in Africa or a suicide bombing in Afghanistan. As far as he was concerned the president had been soft on terrorists. He promised to hunt them down, degrade and destroy, but what did he actually do? Drone strikes and an occasional bombing campaign were enough to hold back the tide but the terrorists kept coming. His administration would be different. Under his leadership the greatest military force in the world would do everything necessary to ensure that the enemy never came back. This was a fight he wanted to engage.

"Alright then," he said. "I'm on board. What's the next step?"

"We announce a major speech on the Wynn foreign policy three weeks from today. We take the hard line. With any luck at all there will be another terrorist attack or some horrific brutality in the news. We exploit it."

"Not that we want a terrorist attack."

"Of course not. But it's inevitable, isn't it? It's all a matter of timing."

They put their speechwriters to work, scheduled an event with the Project for a New American Century and began preparations. He gradually introduced foreign policy issues, Israeli security, Iranian nuclear intentions, the advance of the Islamic State and the events of the day into his campaign stump speech. He always took the hard line. He would not advocate war or occupation but would not hesitate to put boots on the ground if the military deemed it necessary to the objective of destroying the enemy.

As if on cue, two weeks into the transition, an Islamic terrorist group released footage of a mass killing where men and women in blindfolds were lined up and shot in the head. Wynn clamored for revenge while Duran issued a condemnation and advocated a measured response.

The polls began to turn. People loved "Wynn the Terrible" and the rightwing media ate it up. Daniel J. Wynn was once again at the top of his game.

54

WHITE QUEEN TO QUEEN FOUR

Queen Takes Pawn: Check

If Jack Morris thought his latest tactic would lead the Duran campaign to back off he was wrong. Winfred Holmes was in attack mode and Shelby Duran was more than willing to engage on foreign policy.

Wynn was beating the drums of vengeance for political advantage, a strategy that had been tried before and led ultimately to decades of pointless war. As a diplomat as to any thinking person, it was an unconscionably reckless strategy for any candidate for the presidency. Either Wynn was pandering to the basest instincts of humankind or he meant it, which was immeasurably worse.

She took her case to the people. In town hall meetings and rallies across the land she reminded voters that the same bull-headed, knee-jerk approach to a terrorist attack led to the ill-fated wars in Afghanistan and Iraq. She reminded them of the cost of those wars: hundreds of thousands of lives, hundreds of thousands wounded, loss of limbs, mental disorders, an unprecedented suicide rate among soldiers who had served, trillions of dollars wasted, all to produce a region infinitely more unstable than it had been.

What do we say to the families of those who suffered and suffer still from the nation's colossal strategic errors if we learned nothing from our mistakes?

Holmes left the battle for the hearts and minds of the electorate to the able hands of his candidate while he took aim at the enemy camp. In studying the events that led to the withdrawal of Lawrence McClure from the campaign, a costly blow, he identified the agent who delivered the blow as Jolene Dixon. He recognized the name. She had been observed and reported as a likely spy for an unknown Republican candidate in a Washington bar the previous summer. Her name emerged again in connection with Gonzo reporter Cato Mackay on the campaign trail in North Carolina, an exchange that resulted in the withdrawal of Lawrence McClure from Gonzo operations. That was in January. She next appeared in San Jose to deliver the knockout blow against McClure. That was in October, well after both nominations had been secured.

Holmes deduced that Jolene Dixon had worked for Daniel J. Wynn all along. He dug deeper and determined that she had worked briefly for the New York billionaire several years back. That placed her in Wynn's employ when the infamous yet still unresolved Chelsea scandal was conceived, planned and executed. It seemed logical to conclude that the woman with the striking green eyes was somehow involved. It was her kind of work.

Dixon was not loyal in any real sense to Wynn. She had worked for a variety of businessmen and candidates on both sides of the aisle in between appearances on the stage, mostly off Broadway productions in lower Manhattan. She was an actress, by some accounts a very talented actress, but she had not been able to pay the bills on acting alone.

Spies being spies they often have a problem with their tax returns. It is the nature of their work that they cannot reveal the names of their employers. The employers sometimes use shill organizations to hide their identities. More often they pay their spies under the table. He dug a little deeper and determined that the Wynn campaign had not reported payments to Ms. Dixon, a minor problem for them perhaps but a more considerable problem for her.

He had all he needed to make his case. He took a cab to

Jolene Dixon's Washington apartment, paid for without doubt by the Wynn campaign. He'd had his man Nick Dunn follow her for the past three days so he knew she was inside. He buzzed her apartment and looked directly into the security camera.

Jolene suppressed a gasp and buzzed him in without comment. She turned on the recording app in her cell phone and tossed some scattered clothing in her bedroom while he made his way to her dwelling on the third floor and knocked three times. She answered with a golden smile.

"Mr. Holmes, I presume?"

He stood hat in hand and took stock of the woman. Despite her casual dress, sweats and a sports shirt, she was every bit as attractive as reports indicated. Motioning him inside they sat in her crowded living room, newspapers, magazines and what appeared to be movie or play scripts strewn about.

"For a woman of modest means, Ms. Dixon, you've done a great deal of harm. It speaks well of your talent and perhaps my own neglect."

She demurred, wondering if it was possible that the legendary Winfred Holmes was offering her a job. She would not wonder long.

"It is expensive maintaining two apartments, one in New York, another in Washington, traveling all over the country, staying in hotels, dining in restaurants, on and on. How do you manage it, Ms. Dixon?"

"I rely on the kindness of strangers, Mr. Holmes."

She batted her brows in the Blanche Dubois tradition and he witnessed the seductive pull of her enchanting green eyes.

"You claim to know who I am, Ms. Dixon. If you've done your homework you know I will not be seduced, deceived or trapped in a compromising conversation."

He pointed to her cell phone on the kitchen counter. She turned the recording app off and returned to the living room. Holmes walked to the counter and turned the device off.

"I'm here as a courtesy to inform you that your career in politics is over and to offer you a choice. Do you remember the choice you gave Mr. McClure?"

"I do."

"I doubt that the IRS would be as impressed as I am with your Blanche Dubois impression. Would you like to test the theory?"

"I would not."

He returned to his seat on the sofa, hat still in hand.

"I know you've worked for Mr. Wynn a very long time. You were with him during that nasty business in Chelsea. Pushing an old woman out on the street. That seems beneath even your standards, Ms. Dixon."

Accepting that her charms did not apply to the situation at hand and sensing that this would not end well, she felt her impatience rising to the surface.

"What do you want, Mr. Holmes?"

"Only the truth, Ms. Dixon. A chance for you to atone for your sins."

He handed her a card with the name and number of Gonzo reporter Cato Mackay.

"I believe you know Mr. Mackay. He's staying at the Watergate, room 216. He'll be expecting your call."

She knew exactly what he meant for her to do. He didn't have to spell it out. She'd often been in the room when Danny Wynn plotted his schemes with his staff and advisors, the schemes that would ferment into the Chelsea Scandal. She would say what she witnessed, that the real estate magnate was an active participant, and in exchange she would not have to explain her finances to the IRS. Fair enough.

Holmes turned back at the door, fixing his gaze on her beautiful green eyes.

"You're very talented, Ms. Dixon. You have Hollywood eyes. I have no doubt you'll be a great success once you leave this nasty business behind and focus all of your

218

attention and all of your skills on your art."

He left her with a warm feeling. She would do his bidding and enjoy every minute of it. The big man wouldn't like it but who cared? She owed him nothing. If she played her cards right, she could parlay the publicity of political scandal into a bright future in the public spotlight. In the pursuit of celebrity there's no such thing as bad publicity.

55

BLACK KING TO QUEEN'S CASTLE FIVE

King Takes Knight

Daniel J. Wynn loved the infighting of the political game as much as his campaign manager did. Maybe more. When he read the story that reopened the floodgates of the Chelsea Scandal, his first instinct was to destroy Jolene Dixon. He paced his hotel room and ranted like a mad grizzly that stuck his snout where it didn't belong.

Morris shrugged.

"It might make you feel better but it would do nothing for the campaign and the blowback could take you down."

Wynn lowered his deadpan gaze to where Morris sat, reading the back pages of the newspaper where real news usually emerged. The big man knew better than to challenge his strategist. At this stage of the campaign Morris had established his superiority in these matters beyond all doubt. He assumed the superior mind had an idea and waited for him speak.

"Well?" said Wynn.

"Well what?"

"Have you got something?"

Morris carefully folded his paper and sipped his coffee.

"Yeah, I've got something. Nothing."

"You're not serious."

"Nothing is a hell of lot better than what you've got."

As much as Wynn respected Morris and yielded as a matter of course to his political strategy, he didn't like the sense of humility he so often suffered in the man's presence. It made his temperature rise and he felt the need for release.

"First rule of politics: They hit you, you hit back twice as hard."

"Where'd you get that? The playground bully's guide to winning friends and influencing people?"

"New York politics 101."

As Morris gave him his undivided attention, he felt his urge to argue fade like the dream of an overmatched basketball team in the fourth quarter of a blowout.

"You like rules? I'll give you three: One, you don't waste time and resources on someone who's already out of the game. Two, never risk more than you stand to gain. Three, never take aim at a private when a lieutenant is in your site."

"What do you mean?"

"The Molinari people have been trying to contact us. What do you think that's about?"

"Who the fuck cares? He's a loser."

"He's a loser with something to offer. Naturally, he wants something in return. Up to now we haven't been ready or willing to listen. I'd say the time is right to hear him out."

"What do you think he wants?"

"It's obvious. He's bored being governor. He wants to go national. He wants a spot in the next president's cabinet and he knows he stands a better chance with you than he does with Duran. So let's see what he's got to offer."

Wynn's wheels turned like an old school watch, conjuring possibilities, each more enticing than the last. The idea of using a Democrat to attack a Democratic candidate appealed to him.

"You think he's got some dirt on Duran?"

"My guess is he's got something on Vargas. Everyone knows she wasn't exactly neutral in the primary season. The word is she played dirty with Warner and Molinari. If Molinari goes on record she becomes a liability. If we press the issue, keep it alive, and we will, she'll have no choice but to step down."

Wynn tried in vain not to let his disappointment show. He was hoping for something bloodier, if not Duran then maybe Winfred Holmes.

"Do you really think it makes a difference?"

Morris looked at him like an elementary school principal scolding a wayward child who insisted on questioning the rules.

"I don't expect you to understand how it works, Danny boy. Just take my word for it: It hurt our campaign when Peterson went down. We lost his connections, his network and his influence. It'll hurt them just as much."

Wynn nodded and demurred.

"Alright. I'll call Molinari. What do I offer him?"

"Don't offer a thing. Tell him you've been thinking about him on your team. Mention the Justice Department. Then sit back and let him talk."

Wynn went into his office and made the call. He found Molinari all too eager to strike a blow for the team. His staff had been working on it since the New Hampshire primary. They had acquired some emails implicating Dorothea Vargas in leaking the story about Molinari's offshore tax havens. The story went nowhere but it virtually eliminated any chance that Molinari would win the Democratic nomination. He had evidence she had sabotaged not only his campaign but Bethany Warner's as well.

He proposed writing a commentary for the Wall Street Journal and making himself available for interviews on any cable television stations that would have him. By the time he made the rounds on the Sunday morning news programs Dorothea Vargas knew her fate was carved in granite, a scarlet letter of bias tattooed to her forehead. She issued a blanket denial, painted Molinari as a bitter loser and tendered her resignation.

56

WHITE PAWN TO QUEEN'S KNIGHT FOUR

Check

The second presidential debate on foreign policy failed to produce a measurable effect on public opinion polls. Both sides solidified their base support. Duran maintained a reasoned, diplomatic approach to the world's conflicts while Wynn held to the hard line without openly advocating war on multiple fronts.

The difference became most clear in an exchange of policies concerning the Israeli conflict with the Palestinians. Wynn predictably defended Israel's actions against charges of war crimes by the International Criminal Court. He argued that Israel had the right to attack its enemies, whether Islamic terrorists, Hamas or Hezbollah, Iran or any other agent, preemptively and decisively. He insisted that Israel could not and should not be held accountable for civilian casualties or disproportionate retribution: "That's the only thing these terrorists understand! You take one of ours, we take ten, twenty, a hundred or a thousand of yours!" He argued that America would stand with Israel without any conditions or qualifications.

Duran countered: If disproportionate retribution were the answer, the conflict would have been settled decades ago. "Tragically, we are no closer to a peaceful resolution of this conflict than we were the day Israel was created as a nation." She reflected that in her years as Secretary of State she came to realize that the hard line was never meant to end the crisis but rather to win elections. She came to question whether the current Israeli government or indeed the leadership of the Palestinians had any real interest in peace. Too often their political interests were served by continuing the conflict. One side or the other had sabotaged every initiative during the Marquez administration. As for war crimes she had no doubt that a serious inquiry was justified but she held little hope that the International Criminal Court could satisfy either side in the quest for justice.

She had ventured further toward neutrality in the Middle East and in the Israeli-Palestinian conflict than any major party candidate before her. She had openly criticized the Israeli government and she had done so against the advice of Winfred Holmes.

The Wynn campaign sensed an opening. In the critical electoral state of Florida the Jewish vote was pivotal. Wynn hit the trail in the traditional Democratic strongholds of Tampa, West Palm Beach and Miami-Dade County. He skirted social security and Medicare with a promise not to propose cuts to anyone currently receiving benefits and zeroed in on America's unwavering and absolute support of Israel and the threat Duran posed to that longstanding policy.

Holmes pleaded with Duran to moderate her position but she held firm. She would not misrepresent her policies and she would not be handcuffed on the Israeli-Palestinian conflict since that was a significant part of the problem. If Israel knew going in that every American president would take their side regardless of their behavior, there would never be a just peace. Someone had to break the mold. Someone had to take a chance.

Holmes accepted that she would not yield and so began to calculate a road to the White House without Florida. It was possible. It was significantly more difficult but it was still possible.

Chauncey Davis was acutely aware that Wynn was

making inroads in south Florida and he didn't like it. Like Holmes he hoped Duran would strengthen her support of Israel but unlike Holmes he was not willing to concede Florida. The race was still tight. They had lost some support among Jewish voters but they were persuadable. Some respected Duran for not pandering and some suspected Wynn of doing just that.

Davis watched Wynn pledging his undying allegiance to Israel and frankly did not believe him. He sent his people out to make contact with the candidate's former rivals in the Republican Party. If anyone had dirt on him, they did. No one in the GOP seemed to like Wynn; they only tolerated him. As contestants in hardball politics they respected him but they did not like him.

He assigned Jorge Ramos, one of his more charming operatives, to the Pierce campaign. Of all the former rivals Ellis Pierce was considered most likely to bear a grudge. Moreover, as the former governor of the Sunshine State, anything he had might be particularly useful.

After several days of floating inquiries, Ramos received a call from Pierce's campaign manager, Mary Jo Perez. She requested a meeting over dinner at Scotty's Landing, a beachfront restaurant in Coconut Grove. Ramos was a little surprised she chose such a public place for a clandestine meeting but he readily agreed. When he arrived ten minutes early he found Perez already seated at an outdoor table enjoying a tall glass of beer.

"I love this place. The conch fritters are tasty, the coconut shrimp is excellent and the view is outstanding this time of day. In my experience there are few places in the world where you can taste the sea so distinctly."

The sun was setting over Biscayne Bay, painting a sky in surreal colors with billowing clouds and swaying palms. She consumed it as he sat and ordered a Guinness stout to accompany an order of coconut shrimp and fries. Ms. Perez seemed in a wistful mood so he chose not to push it. If she had anything she would offer it in her own time.

They talked about the weather, the latest storm gathering in the Atlantic, the instability of world affairs, Islamic terrorism and the uncertain future they would leave to their children, when Perez came to the point.

"Excepting terrorists and serial killers, there's no one in this world I despise more than Jack Morris and Daniel J. Wynn."

Startled at the abruptness and severity of her declaration, Ramos cleared his throat and gulped a mouthful of stout.

"I take it Ellis Pierce feels the same way."

"He does indeed."

She seemed lost in the view, her thoughts wandering to personal spaces where no one could visit, before she returned to her purpose.

"You see Mr. Ramos, like Shelby Duran, Ellis Pierce is a fundamentally decent human being. You may disagree with his policies but beneath it all there is a clear sense of decency. He wants to do what he believes is right. Danny Wynn is a different kind of animal. He pretends to be honest and open but he'll say anything and do anything to get elected, which makes him the perfect candidate for Jack Morris."

She reached in her purse, pulled out a small container and placed it on the table. It looked like it might contain a necklace or a pair of earrings.

"It's a flash drive," she said. "It contains a series of anti Semitic comments, some of them directed at the Israeli prime minister. I suspect it's exactly what you need to shore up your support in south Florida."

Ramos suppressed an urge to grab it and run. It was exactly what they needed. Instead he took it in his hands and gazed curiously at Ms. Perez.

"Why didn't you use it in the primaries?"

"We ran the numbers. The only place it helped us was here in Florida and we didn't think we needed help here.

You'd be amazed, in some places in this grand old union it actually helped Wynn."

"Does Pierce know you're doing this?"

"No but it serves his interests. If Duran wins, he can run again in four years. If Wynn wins, it's at least eight years. By that time, the window will have closed."

Ramos finished his beer, expressed thanks, and rushed back to his apartment to view the evidence. He was truly amazed at the level of hypocrisy and bigotry the recordings revealed. Some were audio only. Others were video. They dated from his early years in real estate to no more than a few months ago. On one recording he referred to the Israeli prime minister as a "gutless kike" for not dropping a nuclear bomb on Iran. On another, as he prepared for a fundraiser in Miami, he said: "Grab your wallets, boys, time to hustle up some guilt money from the old Jews in retirement city."

He shared the tape with Chauncey Davis who promptly made a copy and sent it to a small radio station in South Beach. Within a few days it was all over the news. Danny Wynn would of course deny it, protest that it was taken out of context and, finally, apologize. It was too late. Duran's problem with the Jewish vote in south Florida faded with the setting sun.

57

BLACK KING TO QUEEN'S CASTLE FOUR

Danny Wynn's anti Semitic statements did not surprise Jack Morris. The crude language and the blatant bigotry his comments revealed did not surprise him. He was a little tired however of his candidate's incessant, idiotic, and self-destructive behavior. The fact that these bigoted statements were not limited to his days in Manhattan business ventures but continued to recent weeks suggested a dim view of his candidate's intellectual capacity. Morris confronted his candidate on the day the recordings were aired.

"Are you stupid?"

Wynn wore that sheepish, sleepy-eyed look that generally meant he had no explanation for what had occurred. Bad things just happened as a matter of course without any real link to his actions.

"Hey, I grew up in the Bronx," he shrugged. "What do you want me to say? That's the way we talk. It doesn't mean anything."

"It doesn't mean anything? You just gave away the state of Florida and it doesn't mean anything? Do you know the last Republican who won the White House after losing Florida?"

"Not offhand."

"Calvin Coolidge in 1928."

"Well, at least it can be done."

Morris looked at his candidate as an elementary teacher would look at a slow student before referring him to special education.

"That was before Lyndon Johnson gave away the South.

You can't be that dim."

"What are you saying? We've lost the election? We might as well throw in the towel? It's all over but the fat lady singing? What?"

Morris shook his head in utter dismay.

"I'm saying you've made it a hell of a lot harder than it should have been."

"What do we do now?"

Morris sat down and tossed his legs up on a coffee table, folding his hands across his stomach, waiting for his equilibrium to be restored.

"First, we go on an apology tour. We book every local TV and radio station from St. Augustine to Miami Beach and you apologize, sincerely and profusely. You explain that you grew up in a time and place where mindless bigotry was commonplace. You explain that old habits of speech die hard but it doesn't reflect how you feel. Then you double down on your undying allegiance to Israel. You advocate doubling our economic and military aid to Israel. You apologize to the prime minister for your undo criticism. You explain that your criticism was based on the assumption that Israel was empowered to act independent of American support but you now understand that any reluctance on Israel's part was due to our government's obstruction. You do all this and then you do it again and again until everyone is sick to death of hearing it. Then you do it again."

Wynn looked sick. Nothing went against his nature more than apologizing. But he wanted to be president and if this was the price he had to pay, he'd gladly pay it.

"Do you think it'll work?"

"I honestly don't know. But I think it's the only way forward."

It wasn't entirely true. Morris had envisioned a variety of scenarios that could lead to victory even without Florida but the last thing he wanted to do was to give the big man an out. The best path to the White House still ran through Florida.

He wanted Wynn to believe it was the only way. Otherwise there wasn't priest's chance in Hades he could pull it off.

They began the apology tour the next day, three to four interviews a day, and continued at a relentless pace. Wynn seemed to get better at contrition as he went along. By the end of the first week he was almost believable. The prime minister of Israel publicly forgave him on behalf of the Israeli people. By the end of the second week he seemed sincere and the numbers began to change. The race for Florida's platinum electoral votes was back on.

58

WHITE QUEEN TO QUEEN'S BISHOP THREE

Shelby Duran wanted to challenge her Republican opponent to a debate specifically on the Israeli-Palestinian question. She wanted to face him head on, point for point, on the same stage for the nation to see. Winfred Holmes advocated a different approach.

"They're focusing all their resources on one issue in the one part of the country where it matters because they have no choice. They need Florida like a baby needs mother's milk. We don't. It would be a mistake to follow their lead."

"Are we conceding Florida?"

"Absolutely not. There's plenty of time. We'll attack Wynn's Israeli pandering at the next debate. Then we'll go back to Florida and win it. In the meantime, most of the electorate isn't invested in Israel or Palestine. What they think about every day is wages, jobs, the cost of housing and childcare, clean air and water, on and on. They want to know that things will be better for their children. They want unions that will protect their interests. They want an affordable higher education. They want practical trade schools that teach employable skills. We need to be talking to them. That doesn't mean we don't care about foreign policy. We take all questions and we answer them candidly and honestly but for now it is not our focus."

Duran knew he was right. During her time on the campaign trail she had discovered in herself a strong instinct to fight back. It had always been a part of her character but she had learned to subdue it. She had had to as an ambassador. Now she found that urge to counter every blow on every issue sometimes led her astray.

"We go back to domestic issues: minimum wage, the right to organize, job training, lowering health costs, strengthening social security."

"That's right."

"I like it. When do we begin?"

"We rework the stump speech over the next few days, then we hit the trail in Philadelphia, Allentown, Trenton and Pittsburgh."

Duran smiled. Pennsylvania had proven surprisingly strong for Danny Wynn. Polls had him up by double digits. Holmes wanted to take it back.

"You want to hit him where he's strong."

"I thought you might like that. It only makes sense. Pennsylvania is not some knee-jerk conservative state. Wynn has built his lead by playing to the working people. Now that he's stuck on Israel and spending all his time in Florida, his numbers are slipping. Look at the map. If we take Pennsylvania's twenty electoral votes, we're on our way. Then we hit the road to Wisconsin, Minnesota, Arizona, Colorado and Nevada. If all goes well, Florida is icing on the cake."

"We'll need to work in immigrant rights and voter suppression."

"Save immigrant rights for the west. Voting rights play everywhere."

Duran reflected on how her relationship with Holmes had evolved. She trusted him. The polls showed they were in a dogfight. Some had Duran winning, others Wynn, but at no time did she doubt that they would find a way. She had that much confidence in the genius of her campaign manager. She had entered the race trusting him but she feared that her idealism, her natural resistance to pandering and duplicity would be in constant conflict with his political pragmatism. He had warned her that compromise would be required but she found that it was less compromise than understanding. It was more like her job as Secretary of State than she would have thought. She could hold constant in her beliefs and convictions as long as she was diplomatic in expressing them.

"Pull the staff together. Let's get this show on the road."

"The staff is working on it as we speak."

Duran shook her head. "You knew I'd go along?"

"Why wouldn't you? It's the best strategy."

That was Fred, constant and matter of fact, a master of strategy, a friend as well as her most critical ally. She wondered what she would do without him.

59

BLACK QUEEN TO QUEEN FIVE

Queen Takes Pawn

Jack Morris never forgave a debt and never forgot a grudge. His advice to Wynn not withstanding, he kept a book on those who betrayed him or otherwise did damage to his cause. When time and opportunity presented themselves, he would have his revenge.

Cassidy James was in his book. She had played a critical role in the events leading to Ralph Peterson's resignation and escaped unharmed. He fired his secretary for having produced the log that ended up in James' hands but he was forced to give her a generous severance when she threatened to sue. After all, she had only refused to follow an order to cover up illegal meetings. He could not be certain she had delivered it to James. Any number of people, including security, could have done the deed. In any case, a lawsuit would bring unwanted attention and become a major distraction to the campaign. He let it go and made a mental note at the time that he would take her down if and when he had the chance.

Cassidy James was not a high priority target but now he saw an opening. He could use her, if he played it right, to mislead the enemy camp, set them back, and in the process render her untrustworthy to her own people. The Duran campaign had announced its itinerary, revealing their intentions to barnstorm Pennsylvania. Once again, Holmes had managed to surprise him. It could not go unanswered.

He fought back the impulse to abandon the apology tour and head for Philadelphia. That's what Holmes expected and wanted: To disrupt their campaign and muddy the waters. Follow their lead and they'd find themselves driving in circles, spinning out of control.

That's when it hit him: Give him what he wants and then pull it out from under him. Nothing like a little subterfuge to turn the game around. A little juke before going hard to the basket. It only works if the defender takes the bait and he always takes the bait if the move is what he expects. Without bothering to discuss the matter with his candidate he called their Miami headquarters to inform them of a change in schedule. Instead of St. Augustine they would be heading to Philadelphia. He ordered the staff to keep it in house. He called their people in Philly and left the same message.

Morris knew that Ms. James worked out of the Duran headquarters in Miami. He knew where she stayed, where she liked to eat and where she liked to have a drink at the end of an exhausting day. Cassie James was largely a creature of habit. Every Thursday evening around sunset she liked to get away from the political crowd. She found a place she liked called Scotty's Landing, where the food was fine, the view was excellent and the operatives were nowhere in sight.

Sitting at her usual table outside, enjoying coconut shrimp with a tall glass of micro brew, she was more than a little surprised when a smiling Jed Parson ambled up to say hello and ask if he might join her. She knew Parson well enough to know he could not be trusted. She knew he was a spy and a double-dealer but if anyone knew whom he worked for they weren't talking. She nevertheless invited him to sit and enjoy the view. What harm could it do?

"Beautiful, isn't it?" he opined.

"That's why I come here, to get away from all the bullshit," she said.

"Does it work?"

Cass delivered a crooked grin and took a drink of beer.

"It has for the last five weeks."

Parson ordered a stout and an order of fish and chips.

"You don't believe in coincidence?"

"Of course I believe in coincidence. I just don't believe this is one of them."

As he wondered how to proceed she sifted through her memories to find what she actually knew about him. At length she arrived: He had come up with the smoking gun in the Danny Diamond development scandal that turned out to be a dud.

"Don't you work for Wynn?"

He seemed surprised by the question. He depended on the assumption that he worked for anyone who was willing to pay.

"I'm a free agent. I was duped in that scandal business."

"Well, that inspires nothing but confidence."

He was grateful that his stout arrived, sporting a liberal head. He drank and decided his best way forward was straight ahead.

"Look, I knew you were going to be here."

"Who told you?"

"That's not important. The point is: I have something for you. You don't have to take my word for it. You can confirm it with a couple of calls."

"What do you want in return?"

"Not a thing. That's how I get work. I give you something. If it's useful you'll remember. When something comes up, you give me a call."

She could think of no rational reason not hear him out.

"What have you got?"

"A change of schedule for the Wynn campaign."

Parson was a fidgety sort of man. He played with his napkin, swizzled his beer and toyed with his food like a cat with a disabled mouse. She didn't trust him any more than she would a common hustler. Still, she could find no reason not to hear him out.

236

"He's heading to Philly on Friday."

"Same day Duran booked Independence Hall."

"That's right...and I don't believe in coincidence either."

Parson finished his beer and half his meal. He left with a wink and a nod.

"Check it out."

Cass resented the disruption of her routine but she knew she would be unable to sleep until she followed up. She called Wynn headquarters in Miami and asked about preparations for a Friday rally in Tampa. After some delay she was advised to put it on hold. She got a similar response in Philadelphia. That was confirmation enough.

She slept on it and called Chauncey Davis in the morning to deliver the news: a last minute change in the Wynn campaign schedule. Davis was skeptical.

"Where did you get this?"

"Jed Parson."

"He's a Wynn stooge."

"I confirmed it with the headquarters in Miami and Philly."

"They told you he was going to Philly?"

"No, they told me to put it on hold."

"They didn't deny it?"

"No."

Davis waited as if deciding what to do with this information. He still didn't trust it and he began to wonder if Cass had been played. For all her virtues she was young and relatively naïve. He needed his own confirmation but time was short. If it were true, Duran would have to know. You couldn't criticize your opponent for pandering to one community in Florida if he was standing outside the door. If it weren't true it would be a distraction. He had no choice but to pass it on with his own reservations.

His own follow-up left him even more doubtful. The press had no clue. His people inside reported "something fishy" going on. The day passed without an official announcement. As far as he could tell, they hadn't booked a hall in Philadelphia and hadn't made any of the arrangements that needed to be made.

He came to the conclusion that Cassie James had been duped. She should have known. She should have nailed it down before it went any further. She should have informed him before sleeping on it. From here on out, she would be assigned precinct work, answering phones and canvassing voters. Her days as an operative were over.

60

WHITE CASTLE TO QUEEN'S CASTLE SEVEN

Ironically, Americans for America First loved the new Israeli campaign. A policy that seemed to place the interests of Israel above our own not only played to the Christian conservative base, it played to certain money interests as well. Both major parties traditionally bow to the lobbying power of the American Israel Public Affairs Committee (AIPAC). Both parties traditionally profess strong support of the Israeli government and the Israeli people. Consequently, support for Israel is generally not a pivotal issue. The American Jewish community tends to be liberal and its vote tends to lean strongly to the Democratic Party.

That political reality was threatened first when Duran took a far less biased stance on the Israel-Palestine conflict than any candidate in the modern era and again when Wynn took the strongest pro-Israel stance in modern memory.

Nolan Gray of Americans for America First was on a run. He received a generous bonus for every up tick in contributions and the money poured in like floodwater topping a levee. He went from one AIPAC source of funding to another, New York, Miami, Los Angeles, San Francisco, feeding the ultimate fear of an anti-Israeli president. Like a hustler building a con or a comedian building a laugh, he pushed the envelope. He took the fundamental truth that Duran believed the current Israeli government an impediment to peace and over the course of a few presentations transformed it into an indictment of Israel on war crimes, full recognition of Palestine in the United Nations, withdrawal of military and economic assistance, and a demand that Israel surrender its arsenal of nuclear weapons.

As a prominent member of the Jewish business community, Sophia Cantu had friends and family in the audience for Mr. Gray's invitation-only San Francisco performance. Obtaining a recording of the event, she was outraged and determined to not only set the record straight but to expose Nolan Gray as a fraud and a liar. She called Winfred Holmes to explain what was going on and to request a comprehensive policy statement from Duran on the Israeli-Palestinian conflict. Holmes explained that they were holding off on foreign policy until the next debate only a few weeks away.

"Look Fred, we're bleeding out here. Money we were counting on is now going to Wynn. Money is like clean water: When it's gone, it's gone. You can't get it back. The community is running scared and Wynn is capitalizing on their fear. Without a specific policy statement, Nolan Gray can say anything he wants. We can't counter it. If this doesn't stop you're looking at a deficit that could cripple the campaign."

The silence on the other end of the line told her he had not appreciated the seriousness of the situation.

"The truth is," said Holmes, "I'm not sure a policy statement would stop the bleeding."

Sophia took a moment to fully absorb the message he was communicating. Was it possible that Duran's positions mirrored what Gray was telling the Jewish community? If so she had to wonder if she could continue supporting her candidacy.

"What do you mean?"

"She wants to be the first American president to be elected without being handcuffed to unconditional support of Israel."

"We're not asking for unconditional support."

"Aren't you?"

"No, you can't believe that."

"It doesn't matter what I believe. I have a candidate who is determined not to deceive the electorate. I have a candidate who simply will not pander to any interest. I've spent many hours telling her where she has to compromise and she's spent as many hours drawing the lines she will not cross."

"Let's start with this: Will Duran uphold America's commitment to Israel's right to exist in peace and security?"

"Of course. But she's also committed to Palestine's right to exist as a people and as a nation."

"Does she support the indictment of the Israeli government for war crimes?"

"She believes that an objective review of the facts would likely reveal that both sides are guilty of war crimes. Israel is certainly guilty of disproportionate response."

Sophia did not expect the conversation to move in this direction. She did not disagree with what Holmes was saying but until now all presidential candidates had yielded to Israeli interests. Even the mildest criticisms of Israeli policy were met with accusations of anti-Semitism and demands for an apology.

"You're confident you speak for Shelby on this?"

"She's right here. I'll put you on speaker but I need you to guarantee this is not being recorded."

"Do you have to ask?"

"Sadly, I do. I sense some conflict in this discussion."

"Fair enough. You have my guarantee."

Duran had indeed listened to their conversation. Holmes had accurately reflected her thinking. She knew it would be problematic but had not expected to deal with it so soon. She was still preparing a major speech on foreign policy.

"What can I do for you, Sophia?"

"You can assure me that America's alliance with Israel will not be weakened by a Duran presidency."

"I can assure you that my policies are designed to promote the interests of both Israel and the region. I cannot assure you that the current government of Israel will be happy with them."

Sophia began to wonder how far she should take this discussion. There are times it is best not to know. She decided at this point she needed to know all of it.

"I can assure you the prime minister will not be pleased with an investigation of war crimes or an official recognition of Palestine. Mr. Gray has said you will also propose a significant drawback on military and economic aid. Is he correct?"

"Mr. Gray is wrong. We both know the president couldn't cut aid to Israel. Congress controls the budget. It is not something I would propose."

"Thank God for that. One last point: Mr. Gray claims you will propose disarmament of Israel's nuclear arsenal."

"That plane cleared the runway and we're not about to shoot it down. Mr. Gray is bullshitting. Is that clear enough?"

"Thank you, Madam Secretary. You've given me something to work with."

"Is it enough?"

"I honestly don't know."

She feared it was not enough but it would help. It would at least slow the bleeding if not close the wound.

"I have a question for you, Ms. Cantu, and I want you to be honest with me, friend to friend. The whole world is in constant crisis, three steps away from catastrophe, and at the heart of it all the Middle East is on fire. It's only a matter of time before the jihad comes to Israel. We both know that. The best option I can think of that could change the dynamic is peace between Palestine and Israel: a two-state solution."

"I agree. That would be game changing."

"But it can't happen as long as Israel pursues its current policies, expanding the settlements, sabotaging negotiations, refusing to make even a modest concession in the interest of peace. For Israel's sake, as well as for the entire region and the stability of the world, we have to find a way forward. The next American president has to make that clear."

"I understand."

"Do you? Because if I've lost your support, I've lost Florida and if I've lost Florida I may have lost the White House."

Sophia condensed her thoughts to a certainty. She sensed the seriousness of Duran's inquiry. If she could no longer support her candidacy without reservation now was the time to speak out. The alternative, a Wynn administration, was unthinkable.

"I understand, Madam Secretary. I stand behind you one hundred percent."

61

BLACK BISHOP TO QUEEN'S KNIGHT SEVEN

The more she thought about it, the more Sophia appreciated what Duran was trying to do. No one she knew in the Jewish community truly believed that the current leadership of Israel was committed to peace. Even those who supported the prime minister would admit as much. He was a knee-jerk response to fear and while that fear was fully justified, a mindless pursuit of never ending retribution and revenge would only lead to greater violence, greater unrest and an eventual cataclysmic confrontation with Israel's Arab neighbors.

The more she thought about it the more she realized that she could win back majority support or better in the Jewish community.

Her next step was a matter of timing. It was one thing to catch a campaign operative like Nolan Gray in a lie; it was another to catch the candidate. On this she was torn: She could clean up the shit now and stop the bleeding or she could wait for the candidate to step in it. Knowing Danny Wynn, he was inclined to do just that.

She slipped the story of what Gray was saying to AIPAC contributors behind closed doors to Gonzo reporter Cato Mackay and waited to see what followed. She would give it no more than two or three days. After that she would act on her own.

At a core level Nolan Gray knew he had gone too far. Like an addict on crack cocaine he could not hold himself back. He tried but his audience was as hungry as he was. They wanted more; they always wanted more. So he gave them what they wanted: red meat, blood on the tracks, and he braced for the consequences.

It was inevitable that a message delivered in confidence, behind the walls of secrecy where no one could peek, would eventually slip through the cracks into the open air. He knew it. He accepted it. But he could only play it out and enjoy the ride.

Cato Mackay caught Wynn off guard at a campaign rally in Key Biscayne. Before Jack Morris could rein him in, Wynn took the bait.

"Mr. Wynn, I've heard reports that a spokesperson for Americans for America First is raising funds by telling members of AIPAC that Duran supports major cuts in aid to Israel and full nuclear disarmament. Are those claims true and do you stand by them?"

With Morris glaring and signaling "cut it off" Wynn waved his hand as if to say: I've got this one. Then he waded into the fray.

"First, Americans for America First is a fine organization but they do not represent this campaign any more than you do. We have no connection except for our desire for a new and better nation. Do I believe Duran would propose cuts in military aid to Israel? Yes I do. Do I believe she wants to take away Israel's nuclear arms? Why wouldn't she? She's made her position clear. If you elect Duran president you might as well be electing the leader of Hamas!"

By this time Morris had made his way to the podium where Wynn was holding court. He placed his hand on the candidate's shoulder, moved in and whispered, "Shut the fuck up!" Wynn threw up his hands and followed Morris to a waiting car. He had no clue as to how he had fucked up this time. It was always something.

Safely inside the moving vehicle, Morris wondered how many more of these incidents he would have to endure.

"I suppose you want to know why I'm upset."

Wynn shrugged and nodded.

"We're playing the hard line on Israel. That's exactly what I was doing."

"You sanctioned a blatant and deliberate attempt to misrepresent your opponent and you put it all on camera. For your information, presidential candidates don't do that. Dogcatchers, mayors and apparently New York City business operators can get away with that shit but presidential candidates can't."

They rode along in silence, Morris staring out the tinted windows and Wynn seemingly studying his hands. Wynn couldn't stand silence.

"How bad is it?"

Morris had been calculating that equation all along and planning damage control. He did not appreciate the interruption.

"Let's see: First you're recorded making anti-Semitic remarks, then you go on record misrepresenting your opponent on Israeli policy, and then, as if it's never enough, you link her to a terrorist group! Hamas? For Christ sake do you even know who Hamas is? It's not good."

Wynn returned to an uncomfortable ride of silence. He wasn't worried. Morris always exaggerated the harm. He'd deal with it. He always did. In the end, Danny Wynn would be taking the oath, Jack Morris would be his chief of staff and all this would be forgiven. There's nothing like success to take the sting out of a minor error.

Nolan Gray watched it all unfold on the television screen of his room in the Biltmore Hotel in Los Angeles. He gave it a wry grin, a sarcastic commentary and an enduring sense of incredulity. He broke open the courtesy liquor cabinet and drank little bottles of booze on the company dime to celebrate his last days on the trail.

To paraphrase someone he never knew and never could identify: It's not if you win or lose, it's how you end the game. He would end his game by driving off a cliff and taking all the blame with him. He would accept all responsibility for misrepresenting Duran's Israel policy not only to AIPAC contributors but to the Wynn campaign as well.

"I made it all up. My bad!"

He laughed and downed a little bottle of whiskey. He would be a pariah for a while until they realized that he had delivered Wynn from the brink, sparing him the blow that should have cost him Florida and therefore the election. Thanks to Nolan Gray he would live to fight another day.

62

WHITE CASTLE TO QUEEN'S KNIGHT SEVEN

Castle Takes Bishop

Mr. Gray got up late, very late, having ignored the barrage of phone calls and emails from people no doubt wanting to berate him for planting a dagger in Wynn's back. He took his time preparing himself for an angry world, shaving and grooming, looking dapper for the bombardment awaiting him.

He didn't need to call a press conference. A swarm of reporters greeted him in the lobby. He sat down, calm, collected, and held court.

"There comes a time in every campaign when you hit the wall. I hit mine about a week ago. I was tired, exhausted, I had nothing left. Duran seemed to me a big supporter of the Palestinian cause so I decided to extrapolate. So it turns out she doesn't want to take away Israel's nuclear arms? Fine. So it turns out she doesn't favor cutting aid to Israel. So be it. I made it up. I made it all up and passed it along. I told the Wynn people I had it on good authority. I lied. I made a mistake. So crucify me. Hell, I'll make it easy on you. I quit!"

He walked out of the Biltmore Hotel into a bright sunny LA day, breathed it all in and caught a cab to the airport.

It unfolded as he knew it would. For three solid days the media skewered him relentlessly and repeatedly. All the networks and news outlets clamored for an interview. He declined. He took a long, lazy vacation in Maui. Sitting on a beach, absorbing the sun, admiring the view and entertaining the ladies, he watched the story fade.

In the end even the talking heads realized the whole episode was a break for Wynn. Nolan Gray, the new bogeyman, the consummate practitioner of deceptive politics, had taken all the attention away from the GOP candidate and his colossal blunder.

Behind closed doors Dick Morris raised his glass to Mr. Gray, the man who saved Daniel J. Wynn's campaign. Wynn would never know it but he did and he would remember. He owed him one. Big time.

Sophia Cantu wondered if she might have played her hand better. She had the big man in her sights and let him get away. She didn't have time to dwell on it. If she had she would have realized there was little else she could have done. It is difficult to anticipate self-sacrifice in politics; it is such a rare occurrence. The important thing now was to keep the pressure on the enemy. Having been spared a disaster, they remained on the defensive. Contributions had stabilized and Florida was still in play.

63

BLACK QUEEN TO QUEEN'S BISHOP FOUR

Two days after the third debate the race remained too close to call. Duran made a strong case for a balanced approach in the Middle East. Wynn countered with strength. Duran delivered effective argumentation on a wide range of issues but Wynn beat expectations and in the game of modern politics that is enough.

It seemed entirely possible that for the first time since Bush v. Gore, one candidate could win the majority vote while the other claimed the prize. After the debate it was no longer a battle of ideas, no longer a struggle for hearts and minds, it was a geographic battle of states and electoral college votes to the finish line. The battleground states included the usual suspects, Florida and Ohio, but they also included Arizona, Colorado, Nevada, Wisconsin and Pennsylvania.

Jack Morris was happy with where they stood. If the election were held today he'd take his chances. But the election was still five months away and he was not happy with how it was going. By this time in the process he expected to have a great deal more money to spend than his opponent. That had not come to fruition. He expected to have Florida and Pennsylvania securely in the Wynn column. Instead, they were forced to expend too much time and resources defending their ground while the Duran campaign was constantly on the offensive. Something had to give. He needed a way to turn the momentum, to enable his candidate to go on an offensive, to take the battle to enemy ground.

His mentor in the political game taught him one essential

truism: There are two ways to win an election. One is to boost your vote total; the other is to suppress your opponent's. Everyone engages in the first but those who ignore the second are losers of the first order. Voter suppression may have an unsavory ring to it but it has been going on since the first election when one Roman senator said to another: I have two front row seats to the Coliseum Friday night for a senator who doesn't show up to Friday afternoon's vote.

Voter suppression is simple politics. Have you ever wondered why elections are held on Tuesdays instead of Saturdays or Sundays? Have you ever wondered why jurors are chosen from the voter rolls instead of the much broader DMV lists? There are a hundred and one ways to suppress the vote and all of them operate in full view every presidential election: long voter lines, limited hours, restricted registration, last minute changes in polling places, on and on.

Disenfranchisement is a more complicated proposition. It involves taking a list of registered voters and editing it in such a way that you eliminate those voters who are most likely to vote against you. If done crudely there are both political and legal ramifications. If done artfully it is the most effective means of altering the result of a close election. The most famous or infamous example of effective disenfranchisement is Florida in the year 2000. Arguably, the Great Disenfranchisement altered the course of human events for at least a century. Though he was not in charge at the time, Morris had a hand in that game-changing event and he was proud of his roll in it.

As he took stock of the current campaign, Morris decided he needed to wage war on two fronts. He would take his candidate to the west: Arizona, New Mexico, Colorado, Nevada and Oregon. He would engage each state with a barrage of television and radio ads, signaling his independent Super Pac and 501 allies to do the same. The numbers showed all those states were within their reach and Duran was counting on them. At the very least, they would force Duran to expend her resources defending her territory.

In the meantime he would send his best operative, Charles Rogan, on a mission to visit the secretaries of state in Pennsylvania, Ohio, Wisconsin and Florida. Rogan would carry a simple message: the Wynn campaign needed their full cooperation in voter suppression. He would tell them each there would be serious consequences for those who performed their responsibility well and those who did not.

Rogan smiled when he received the assignment. He'd been on the sidelines far too long and was looking forward to getting down and dirty. It was his specialty. He was given authority to offer positions in the party and in the new administration contingent on Wynn's election. Saving Florida for last, his first stop was Harrisburg, Pennsylvania, where he scheduled a meeting with Secretary of State Caroline Aiken.

"I assume you know why I'm here," he opened.

In her sixties, Aiken was a Republican stalwart in a state that swung back and forth according to the political wind; she had likely advanced as far as she hoped to in her lifetime. If she aspired to the governorship or a cabinet post she kept it to herself. Her apparent lack of ambition in a field of cutthroats made her uniquely trustworthy to her colleagues but to Rogan she was a hard sell. He didn't know what to offer.

"Enlighten me," she replied.

"Your state is far too close for comfort this close to the election. We were counting on a ten-point margin at least."

"If our candidate stopped tripping on his own feet and paid a little more attention to the folks that count, he'd have his margin."

"I'll tell Mr. Wynn you said hello."

She smiled and they both relaxed. They were after all on the same team.

"The fact is we don't have enough time and resources to

cover all the states that are still in play. We need to know Pennsylvania is behind him."

"You want a sure thing?"

"That's correct."

"There are no guarantees in politics. You know that."

"Let's just say: We'd like a high degree of certainty."

She fiddled with the papers on her desk in a play for time, indicating to Rogan that she had a certain outcome in mind.

"Let's just say this: If I can deliver Pennsylvania, what could I expect in return?"

Rogan tilted his head to one side and waited to catch her eyes. This was the part he most enjoyed, getting down and dirty.

"What would you like, Madam Secretary."

"My son has political aspirations, Mr. Rogan. You didn't know that, did you?"

"I'm afraid I didn't."

"Neither does Daniel Wynn apparently. He's running for the assembly. I'd like our party nominee's endorsement. I'd also like the party's support for congress in the next cycle."

"Is it close?"

"The assembly race? He'll win."

"Well, I think I can guarantee full party support, now and in the next cycle. As for Wynn's endorsement, it's a little dicey at this point. We don't want to call attention to what we're doing here."

"I understand your concern but I'm the one taking most of the risk. Wynn goes to the White House and I face a federal indictment."

"Not if Wynn's in charge."

Aiken gave it due consideration. There was always the possibility that the candidate could lose the election with or without Pennsylvania.

"Can I count on Wynn's endorsement in the next cycle?"

"Absolutely. Do we have a deal?"

"All the preparations have been made. We only need to

follow the numbers and make the necessary adjustments."

Translation: She would do whatever they needed – close precincts, challenge voters, under-staff key Democratic districts or change polling places – to ensure the outcome. As a last resort, they could flip a few votes. Whatever it took to guarantee a Wynn victory. Rogan stood and extended his hand.

"Great. I think we're done here."

"Not quite, Mr. Rogan. I'll need to hear it from Morris."

She was far shrewder and more knowledgeable than he would have thought. She knew who held the real power: not Wynn and certainly not Rogan but Jack Morris, the man behind the curtain.

"I'll have him call you."

She stood and took his hand.

"Great. I think we're done here."

64

WHITE QUEEN TO KING'S BISHOP SIX

Queen Takes Knight

Holmes had a feeling something was amiss when Wynn went west without shoring up his support in the east and Midwest. The Duran campaign was hitting the battleground states hard, pounding economic issues, protecting unions, raising the minimum wage, providing affordable housing and childcare, and bringing well-paid manufacturing jobs back home. The daily numbers showed they were having an impact. It seemed illogical that Wynn would yield so much ground this close to the election.

After a few days, letting it float around in his thoughts, hearing an offhand discussion of the 2000 election and the events in Florida, it hit him like a jackhammer surprise: Morris was playing the disenfranchisement card. He had hoped to avoid the issue this time around. Along with gerrymandering and unlimited corporate contributions, disenfranchising voters for political advantage was one of the greatest threats to modern American democracy.

He placed a call to Moses Dunn and asked him to check and see if anyone from the Wynn camp had made a visit to Tallahassee, Harrisburg, Madison or Columbus. The capitals of their respective states, there was really no reason to visit any of them except that the secretaries of state resided there. If you wanted to put the fix in, you would have to deal with the officials who ran the elections.

Two hours later Dunn called back to report that Charles

Rogan had been to Harrisburg and was in Madison, Wisconsin as they spoke.

"I made a few calls," said Dunn. "Rogan met with Secretary of State Caroline Aiken for half an hour. Right after the meeting she called her son Charles who just happens to be running for state assembly."

Holmes thanked him and did some digging. He checked recent allocations of funding by the Republican National Committee and there it was: Five thousand dollars to the assembly campaign of Chuck Aiken. It was not a large sum of money but it was highly unusual for the RNC to contribute to an assembly race while a presidential election was in high gear. Moreover, the race was not even close. It seemed clear that a quid pro quo had gone down in Harrisburg: party support for the secretary of state's son in exchange for the fix.

He passed the information along to Gonzo reporter Cato Mackay. The story would write itself but Mackay went the extra mile. He caught up with Rogan at the state house in Columbus, Ohio, just before his scheduled meeting with the Ohio Secretary of State. He stated the facts in succinct sequence and asked if he'd like to confirm or deny them. Rogan smirked, offered "no comment" and turned around to get in a cab and go straight back to the airport. The gig was up. If Morris wanted a fix he'd have to take care of it himself.

65

BLACK KING TO QUEEN'S CASTLE THREE

King Takes Pawn

The story followed the usual path from the worldwide web to the mainstream media where it became the rage of the day. At first the Wynn campaign denied it and then they denied any knowledge of it. Charles Rogan was acting on his own: Rogan Gone Rogue.

With Rogan's downfall Morris knew they'd have to do it the hard way. The thing about disenfranchisement is: it doesn't work if everyone and his second cousin are looking for it. They would have to cut short the western swing and head back to the battleground.

Meantime Wynn was his typical livid self. He would not let it go. Someone had to pay the price of betrayal. That's how he saw it. While all the world knew they were trying to cheat the system, Wynn perceived it as a dirty trick that someone called them on it.

"Who is this asshole?" he bellowed in reference to Cato Mackay, the Gonzo reporter who broke the story. The staffers in the room knew better than to answer him. If you dared to engage him he would find a way to turn it on you.

"How is he allowed to print this bullshit?"

Morris shrugged. His candidate was not exactly in the loop but he wasn't so naïve as to think the story was concocted out of thin air.

"His ass is mine! Do you hear me? I want him blackballed! Anyone in this campaign so much as utters a syllable to this guy and he's done! We don't let him on the bus, we don't let him in the hall and we don't allow him at a press conference! Is that understood?"

Morris had no particular feelings about this petty matter but it occurred to him that Wynn could have his revenge and it could serve the campaign at the same time. When in the midst of a crisis or a scandal the first move is to change the subject.

"Hold off on that, Danny boy. I've got a better idea."

Wynn slowed his stomp to a standstill and listened.

"We make sure he's at the next press conference. Put him right up in front."

Wynn nodded though uncertain where this was going.

"I want you to undress him with all the cameras rolling. You know that thing you do: Sit down and shut up! Expose him as a stooge for the Duran campaign. Ask him where he got his information. Tell him directly he's no longer welcome in Wynn territory and have his ass thrown out of the room. The press will eat it up."

Aside from appeasing Wynn's need for fresh blood, it would eat up two or three days of media frenzy at the end of which everyone would have forgotten about the disenfranchisement scandal. If it cost the reputation of a young web reporter so much the better. He was just a pawn, a foot soldier that wandered into the path of a freight train.

Collateral damage.

66

WHITE QUEEN TO QUEEN'S CASTLE SIX

Queen Takes Pawn: Check

Jed Parson couldn't help but notice that the casualties of war in this presidential campaign were severe. On the Wynn side of the ledger, operatives Charles Rogan, Nolan Gray, Rowan Darby, Jolene Dixon and Sandy Merrill were all out of the game. On the other side the losses were equally severe. He felt like the last man standing.

With the field of experienced operatives depleted, he was not surprised to get a call from Jack Morris. His specialty was misinformation. If he couldn't find what the campaign needed he invented it. As long as it could not be traced back to him it would serve the purpose and leave him unscathed. Even if the charge didn't stick it made an impact. The Duran camp would lose time denying and disproving the charge. By having to assume a defensive posture they would create the illusion of guilt.

Morris needed something to boost their slim lead in Pennsylvania. Pennsylvania encompasses a large swath of the central Appalachian Mountains and that is coal country. The campaign had searched its archives for something Duran had said condemning the coal industry. It stood to reason that she should have taken a hard stand against the dirtiest fossil fuel on earth but they had come up empty. It seemed she had guarded her position on coal in anticipation of this election and the growing importance of the Keystone State.

Morris wanted Parson to work his magic, come up with

something believable enough to work its way through the media and start a dozen rumors in every coal-mining town in the Appalachians. Parson could do it in his sleep.

"It's going to cost you, Jack."

"No problem. Name your price, double it and send the bill to Americans for America First. I don't want my name or Wynn's name anywhere near this."

"Understood."

Winfred Holmes had also noted the dearth of seasoned operatives. He had his tech crew following the activities of those who remained, including Jed Parson. When the daily report showed Parson searching for Duran statements on the coal industry, it didn't take a lot to figure it out. Holmes had already made the search. Duran certainly did not favor coal but she had made no statements condemning the fuel or the industry. The closest she got to criticizing coal was: "In a perfect world we would have no need for fossil fuels; unfortunately, that world has not yet arrived."

In a world where irony is all but lost, if anyone had asked Duran about the future of coal she would likely have replied: Coal has no future; the future belongs to renewable energy. The fact is: no one asked. So having neglected to do it the honest way, they proceeded to do it on the sly.

Parson was just about to release his hit piece when Moses Dunn arrived at his Washington apartment building with a message from Winfred Holmes.

"We know what you're doing and how you're doing it. We can trace every step of the process right back to your door. So as a courtesy we're offering you a choice. Go ahead and release it and we'll immediately expose the fraud and who created it. Or don't and we'll let it die a natural death."

Parson couldn't decide whether he should play dumb or knowledgeable. He would be lying if he said he was not impressed. No one had cracked his security measures up to now.

"You'll have to let me in on the secret, Mr. Dunn."

"If that's how you want to play it fine. We know you're about to put out a hit piece concerning Shelby Duran on the issue of coal. Is that specific enough for you?"

Parson could feel himself going pale.

"Let's assume, for the sake of argument, that you're right. How many laws did you break tracing it to the source?"

"You're claiming the right to commit fraud in anonymity? We'll take our chances in court."

Dunn started to walk out but Parson asked him to wait.

"Again, assuming you're right about all this, if I was asked to put out this piece and I fail to deliver, I'm done."

"If you don't put it out, Mr. Parson, you're done for this cycle. If you do put it out, you'll be done for good. It's completely up to you."

Dunn walked out. The hit piece would never be aired and Jed Parson would be sidelined for the remainder of the campaign.

67

BLACK KING TO QUEEN'S KNIGHT FOUR

King Takes Pawn

Lorena Moreno took on the important job of building a grassroots organization in south Florida to register minority voters and get out the vote on Election Day. She traveled from precinct to precinct, raising awareness, using the catch phrase: The Fat Cats Don't Want You to Vote!

"The fat cats don't want anyone to vote if your skin is a tint darker than the sand on Miami Beach!"

She'd raise her open palms as the crowd guffawed and laughed.

"What? It's true! You know it's true!"

The fat cats inevitably morphed into the big man as in: "The big man don't want you to vote...or you or you! So what you going to do?"

Rising in one voice, the crowd yelled: Vote!

So what do you do? Vote!

So what do you do? Vote!

She was having a marked effect, gathering new voters sworn to the cause by the dozens, by the hundreds and by the thousands. Minorities flocked to her rallies, striking fear in the hearts of Florida's law enforcement community as well as its political establishment.

The Wynn campaign noticed and started a rumor that Moreno was registering illegal aliens. She should have ignored it. Of course they would respond in the typical GOP way. But when confronted with the accusation, in a fit of temper, she was caught on camera saying, "I don't care if they're fresh off the boat, as long as they vote Duran!"

Wynn picked it up and incorporated the remark into his campaign stump speech.

"There's a woman in Florida, what's her name? That's right: Lorena Moreno. She keeps talking about a big man who doesn't want you to vote. Frankly, I don't know who she's talking about. Certainly not me. I want everyone to vote...as long as you're a citizen of the United States of America!"

His audience consumed it like manna from the gods. He could riff on Lorena Moreno for five, ten minutes if the spirit moved him.

Lorena watched his act on her favorite news program, turned off her phone and watched an old movie on Turner Classics. In the morning she reported to work, answered all questions and tendered her resignation.

68

PLAYERS

The Last Debate

Two months shy of Election Day, the fourth and final presidential debate in Phoenix, Arizona was dedicated to the pivotal issue of immigration policy. Both sides were committed to their established positions: Duran supported amnesty for all law abiding immigrants who had established residency for at least five years. She wanted to free the families of legal immigrants from fear of deportation. Wynn supported a colossal wall, a strict border policy with green cards only for highly skilled labor. He once advocated mass deportation but softened his stance as the election drew near. He would not entertain any notion of work permits for those already here until the border was fully secure. Translation: Never.

In the calculus of presidential politics Duran was betting that shifting demographics would play in her favor while Wynn gambled that there were still enough white conservative immigrant haters to carry the day.

Solana and Willie sojourned at the Royal Palms for a few days of golf and relaxation before the big event. Solana did not share Willie's enthusiasm for the game but she was competent enough to enjoy the round. Willie believed that golf was the chess of sport, a sentiment that Solana found amusing but did not contest. They were entering what Solana termed the acceleration stage of their match. From this point forward they would play under the increased pressure of knowing that they had to reach a conclusion before Election Day.

She sensed that Willie had renewed confidence in his strategy. She was no less confident. It was a classic match of points versus position, in which she continued to control the board with a relentless attack yet he held a castle to bishop advantage. If he could get both of his castles engaged in the battle he could exploit that advantage. She had to maintain her aggression to preempt his attack.

The evening before the debate they sat in the courtyard during sunset, enjoying Mexican cuisine and Margaritas. Barring a major gaffe neither of them expected the debate to have anything more than a temporary effect on the polls. Both sides were increasingly entrenched and the numbers remained within the margin of error. In a tight race so many random factors, the weather, an October surprise or a terrorist event, could alter the outcome of the election. There was a distinct possibility that the match and the election could have different results and that alarmed them. It would nullify the experiment and render the experience virtually meaningless.

"We must do everything we can to ensure that does not happen," said Solana.

"I absolutely agree," replied Willie.

They resolved to finish the match a week in advance of Election Day and take appropriate actions to ensure the result. They both had people in place in the battleground states. There were any number of actions they could take from voter challenges, misinformation, altering the electronic vote counting software and ballot stuffing to ballot nullification. Each came with its own set of risks but the binding validity of the match had to be protected. They very much hoped it would be unnecessary but it would not be left to chance.

They attended the debate and politely applauded their candidate's performances. The evening went according to script and without obvious mishap, leaving little to sway the electorate. Secretary Duran was sincere, thoughtful and knowledgeable. Daniel Wynn was Daniel Wynn, forceful and irreverent. As the candidates finished their summary remarks, played to an audience of millions, little did they suspect that the only audience that mattered was the attractive couple in the elite section of the balcony reserved for very important people.

69

WHITE PAWN TO QUEEN'S BISHOP THREE

Pawn Gambit: Check

Jose Velasquez had a simple assignment: to heckle and bait Daniel J. Wynn into a display of his vaunted temper. He studied the candidate's rallies and press conferences on video recording. He knew where the security guards and secret service agents were posted. He knew the triggers that tended to ignite the man: references to his hair, challenges to his intellect, implications of racism, and accusations of falsehood. Subtleties were lost on the big man. You had to be loud and persistent to gain his attention but if you were too aggressive the agents would close in on you and security would escort you out.

The Wynn campaign had returned to Florida for a barnstorming tour of the coastal communities, beginning with Ft. Lauderdale. Velasquez obtained a press pass through a Spanish-speaking radio station in Miami. That got him in the door. He positioned himself for maximum distance from security and waited for the candidate. Wynn would make his standard boilerplate stump speech and then he would take questions. The hall in the community convention center had room for about 2,000 spectators, nearly all of them avid supporters of the GOP. It was more or less a staged event, carefully screened and orchestrated by the candidate's operatives. Even the questions were pre-screened. Wynn did not intend to make news; he simply wanted to be on the news.

Velasquez knew he would have one shot and one shot only. Once he made his move he would be blacklisted by the Wynn campaign. He would go back to working at the local level, walking the precincts, getting the vote out. This was his one chance to make an impact.

70

BLACK KING TO QUEEN'S BISHOP THREE

Wynn strolled in with a smile and a wave. Confident and full of energy, he had found his stride and sensed his momentum building. He took the podium to a warm round of applause. Velasquez waited for his first reference to Lorena Moreno or voting rights or immigration to make his first move.

"I hear there's some woman in Miami," Wynn said.

"Fat cats don't want you to vote," said Velasquez.

He spoke at a low volume, turning a few heads. Wynn's perceptible reaction told him he had gained the candidate's attention. Wynn went on.

"What's her name?"

"Lorena Moreno!" someone answered.

"That's right. This woman claims the fat cats don't want you to vote."

"You *don't* want me to vote!" said Velasquez a little louder than before. The agents and security guards were on the move.

"Excuse me?" said Wynn. He raised his hands, suggesting his people let the man speak. He was geared for an encounter.

"I said: You don't want *me* to vote," repeated Velasquez.

The crowd hissed and booed but Wynn protested.

"What's your name, sir?"

"Jose Velasquez."

Wynn rolled his eyes. "Jose? Jose! Do you have a green card, Jose?"

"I'm a citizen the same as you. I don't need a green

card."

"Well, good for you. Why are you here, Jose?"

"I'm here to cover your campaign."

"No you're not."

"Are you saying I'm lying?"

"I'm saying we all know why you're here, Jose. You're a troublemaker! You had it in your little mind that you could ambush a candidate for president of the United States. Well, it's not going to work because no one wants to hear it, Jose! No one wants to hear what Jose has to say on immigration policy or anything else! Am I right?"

The crowd cheered him on.

"Lots of people want to hear it!" replied Velasquez. "Lots of people want to hear how you intend to deport millions of law-abiding immigrants who only..."

"No, they don't! And don't give me that bull crap about law-abiding immigrants! They broke the law when they crossed our border illegally! They're criminals, Jose! They broke the law!"

"They were only trying..."

"Yeah, yeah, they only wanted a better life for their families! We've heard it all before, Jose! Why don't they try improving their own country so they don't have to come to ours!"

"These are hard working people..."

"That's enough! Now I've given you your say. I've given you your fifteen minutes! Now sit down and shut up! Let the grown ups talk."

Wynn nodded and the security detail escorted Velasquez out of the hall. He'd accomplished his mission. He'd forced Wynn to lose his temper. The GOP base would eat it up, the rightwing media would rejoice, but the everyday voter trying to decide who would be the next president had been given cause for pause. Did they really want this man to hold the most powerful office on earth? Did they really want his finger on the nuclear trigger?

71

WHITE QUEEN TO QUEEN'S CASTLE ONE

Check

Winfred Holmes had a singular purpose: to maintain a constant and intense attack mode. Every hour and every day Daniel J. Wynn consumed defending his policies, his person or his character brought them closer to a Duran presidency. He used the raw footage of Wynn's latest display of temper to craft a new ad reminiscent of the infamous Daisy ad that Lyndon Johnson used to crush Barry Goldwater in the 1964 presidential campaign.

The ad featured a very young girl in an open field counting the pedals of a daisy. When she reaches the number nine a countdown begins, culminating in a blackout and a mushroom cloud. A voice says: "Vote Lyndon Johnson for President. The stakes are too high."

Though the Johnson campaign aired the ad only once, its impact was among the most profound in political history. Goldwater was a hawk and a man known for his temper, not unlike Daniel J. Wynn. Holmes knew better than to duplicate the imagery but he exploited the same theme by using a series of images of tragic international events, wars and terrorist attacks, giving way to images of Wynn displaying his anger. The last image was fresh: His dismissal of Jose at a recent campaign event. The message: "It's a dangerous world. Who do you trust with the world's most powerful weapons?"

The image of Wynn's anger faded and an image of

Shelby Duran came into focus as she spoke: "The world has become as complicated as it is dangerous. War must never be a knee-jerk reaction but only a last resort."

BLACK KING TO QUEEN TWO

Wynn resisted the idea that he had to defend himself for as long as he could hold out. There was no doubt that he was at his best on the attack.

"Damn it, Morris! I'm a Republican. My people don't want a pansy president! They want a commander in chief who's ready and willing to kick some terrorist ass! They want a leader who will stand up to our enemies! They don't want an apologist!"

Morris shook his head. He didn't like it any more than Wynn did but the numbers told a different story. The daisy ad had an impact. Far too many people were afraid of a Wynn presidency. Far too many described him as angry. He had no choice but to re-image himself and he did not have a lot of time to accomplish it. Morris booked his candidate on a series of interviews at Fox, CNN and NBC.

"I'm not going over it again, Wynn. If you want to be president you're going on these programs with one objective: Be calm and thoughtful. Do you think you can do that?"

"Of course I can! I'm not an idiot! The point is: I don't have time to do interviews right now. I need to be out on the trail!"

"I'm not the one who decided to go after some Mexican reporter! I'm not the one who can't tell he's being baited! You did that! Now it's up to you to repair the damage."

Wynn and Morris both knew it was not a viable argument. Wynn would do as he was told. He just liked to go through what had become a ritual of resistance to preserve an illusion of independence.

WHITE QUEEN TO QUEEN'S KNIGHT TWO

Check

Despite his coaching and constant reminders, Morris knew the risk. In his drive to appear calmer and more even-tempered, Wynn might alter the content of his message. Worse, he might contradict his own policies. In an interview with John Garrity on Fox News, he did exactly that: Asked about a hypothetical uprising of Hamas in Lebanon, Wynn advocated a temperate approach.

"We should slow things down, talk to them, see if we can't find a diplomatic solution."

Wynn registered the shock in Garrity's expression and quickly added: "Now if we can't that's a whole different story."

"You're not seriously suggesting we should negotiate with terrorists?"

"Of course not."

"Hamas is a terrorist organization."

"And we would not negotiate with Hamas. Absolutely not! But there are other ways of handling these things. Believe me. There are backchannels that we might be able to use."

He walked it back as best he could but the damage was done. In a hotel suite in Denver, Colorado, Winfred Holmes smiled. The ad would write itself: Footage of Wynn taking the hard line: "America never negotiates with terrorists!" Excerpts of the recent interview: "We should talk to them, see if we can't find a diplomatic solution." An exasperated John Garrity: "You're not seriously suggesting we should negotiate with terrorists?"

The tag line: "In an uncertain world, the American president must be certain. Shelby Duran for President."

BLACK KING TO QUEEN ONE

It felt like déjà vu all over again, a revolving nightmare like some twisted political version of the Bill Murray movie Groundhog Day. Wynn had to assume a defensive posture to rebuild his standing with Israel and to restore the foundation of his foreign policy: America does not negotiate with terrorists. America never wavers in its support for its closest ally in the Middle East. Under a Wynn presidency, America stands strong!

"From here on out," said Morris, "you stick to your guns. We can handle Wynn being Wynn. So what if you misspeak or make a mistake? When you become president you'll be surrounded by advisors and diplomats to temper your instincts. America needs a strong leader. Give 'em one."

"Thank God!" said a relieved Wynn. He was tired of the nice guy act. Playing calm and easy literally put a strain on him. He was like a fast moving training: putting the breaks on derailed him.

Morris didn't know how long it would last but he had to put his candidate back in his natural mode for as long as could manage it. He knew there would be more events and more crises that required immediate adjustment.

Seven weeks in the game of politics is forever. Anything can happen. If you expect to win – and Morris always expected to win – you had to stay ahead of the game. His immediate mission was to find a way to reverse polarity and apply the pressure to Duran.

Meantime, he would see to it that the Daniel J. Wynn campaign was prepared for any and all contingencies.

WHITE BISHOP TO KING'S BISHOP ONE

Chauncey Davis spent much of his time in the trenches of Florida politics. Half the operatives in the state and throughout the south had fought with or against Jack Morris and most of them consider him the dirtiest man in politics. Davis collected stories, some of them verifiable, others common knowledge or pure fabrication, that could damage him with the voters who would decide the election.

Morris grew up in a suburb of Little Rock, Arkansas, at a time when anti-Semitic sentiment was as prevalent and powerful as any other form of bigotry. He exploited bigotry and racism as often as any operative in American history after the Civil War. He developed the strategy as an art form and it served him well. He used rumors of illegitimate black children born of prostitutes to defeat opponents. He used rumors of name changes to hide Jewish ancestry. He exploited racial hatred of Mexican Americans in Texas and Arizona.

One of the most damning incidents occurred only a few years ago in Missouri where Morris started a whisper campaign suggesting that a Democratic candidate for governor was secretly Jewish. That candidate committed suicide. It was shocking in multiple ways: First, that the candidate would consider such an accusation so shameful that he would consider suicide and second, that the electorate would even care.

No one was surprised that he had tried to play the disenfranchisement card in the current campaign. If anything they were surprised he was caught. Of course he was not indicted. Neither the FEC nor the Justice Department could prove he gave the order but everyone in the business knew it was his work.

Davis had enough to write a book. He ran it by Winfred Holmes and to his surprise Holmes gave the go-ahead. He had known the Missouri Democrat who took his own life. He knew well how dirty his nemesis had played the game and gotten away with it for so long. Normally, he would have resisted going after the campaign manager but not this time. Everyone in the game assumed Morris had a book on his adversaries that protected him. Holmes took account and decided it was long past time to test that theory.

He suggested a reporter from the St. Louis Post-Dispatch who had covered the suicide case. He had also known the deceased and would be more than interested in writing the story.

76

BLACK CASTLE TO QUEEN TWO

Jim Duke of Americans for America First read the expose on the dirty politics of Jack Morris and was determined to strike back. He didn't know what Morris planned to do. They were under too much scrutiny to make contact in the waning days of the campaign. Being the target of the attack might put restraints on what Morris could do. Duke operated under no such restraint.

One of the primary tenets of politics was: Keep it Simple. When Bill Clinton made his case for a new economic approach, it fell on deaf ears until his operative James Carville coined the phrase: It's the economy, stupid. The people could understand the stupid economy. It didn't matter if your attack was grounded in the truth. If you forced your adversary to make a complex argument in his defense the public would perceive evasion and deception. If you want to win, you keep it simple.

Duke would use Winfred Holmes central role in the Stairway Scandal, an event that nearly toppled the Marquez administration and resulted in systemic reform of the intelligence community, to paint him as an enemy of homeland security.

In a complex story of international intrigue history would attest that Holmes and Duran played essential roles in preserving the heart of American democracy. Duke would reflect his own interpretation. He pulled quotations from the archives where intelligence personnel condemned the actions of Duran, Holmes and Marquez for placing the country at risk. Using still photographs of Holmes shrouded in shadows, interspersed with footage of 9-11 and other terrorist attacks, Duke released his attack ad.

The former Secretary of Homeland Security said: "At a time when terrorists are attacking our friends abroad and planning attacks at home we cannot afford an administration that puts the rights of terrorists above the safety of the American people."

A spokesman for the CIA said: "We as a nation are at risk today because of the actions of one unscrupulous political operator: Winfred Holmes."

As the gruesome work of terror played out on the screen a voice in ominous tones repeated: "This is the work of Winfred Holmes."

The ad concluded: "Winfred Holmes, the man behind Shelby Duran. Can we afford to take that risk?"

77

WHITE CASTLE TO QUEEN SEVEN

Rook Gambit

As CEO of Oracle, Sophia Cantu had access to the world's most advanced technology. As the election drew near and she witnessed a nefarious attack on the integrity of Winfred Holmes, one of the few fundamentally decent individuals she'd encountered in business or politics, by a man who didn't know the meaning of ethical boundaries, she was determined to employ it.

As a representative of Koch Industries she knew Jim Duke was as dirty as the coal they harvested from the Appalachians. She asked a team of hackers to look into his finances, his communications, his purchases and his web searches, anything that might be used against him or the Wynn campaign. As anyone who followed the Edward Snowden case knows, you can learn a great deal by following an individual's communications combined with bank or credit card usage. It took several passes before she saw the pattern and realized the story it told.

Duke had allowed the use of his organization's funds to hire a contractor infamous for developing lists to be used in disenfranchisement. The lists employed name similarity to prisoners and ex-cons to deny predominantly black and other minority voters the right to vote. The lists were useless unless the local precincts applied them to their voting rolls. Normally, the order would come down from the secretary of state but after the controversy involving a Wynn agent visiting secretaries of state in key states, the Florida secretary had not given the order. That meant that the Wynn campaign would have to take their case to the precincts.

In order to hide his tracks, Morris went to Americans for America First for personnel to carry out the program and media mogul Rudolf McCall to finance it. Ironically, his effort to hide his tracks revealed a whole new set of tracks that incriminated not only himself but his co-conspirators as well.

The question that Sophia Cantu had to answer was this: How could she best exploit this information? If she simply came forward she would have to explain how she obtained it. The story would immediately become clouded and the enemy would hunker down, mount a legal challenge and tie it up in the courts until well after the election. If however she accused Duke of an offense for which he was clearly innocent it might induce him to open the books to prove it. It would also trigger a chain of cover-up activity that could take down Jack Morris.

Having made a false accusation, she would have to withdraw from the campaign. So be it. They were close enough to the goal line that fundraising was no longer a priority. The problem was: once she withdrew she could not monitor the reaction without exposing Oracle to a costly investigation. She needed a partner in this venture. She needed someone savvy enough to do the job and bold enough to take the risk.

She called Chauncey Davis and arranged a meeting in Miami. Flying out the same day with a team of tech experts, she briefed Davis on her plan. She would draw Duke out by accusing him of using campaign funds for personal benefit. He would deny the charges and she would challenge him to open his books. Being innocent he would accept the challenge. Morris and McCall would scramble to cover their tracks. The tech team would track and record their actions. It would be up to Davis to expose them.

Would it work? They could only hope that Duke's instinct to counter-attack would lead him to act on impulse. It was a gamble. Cantu would lose her role in the campaign either way. By bringing Davis in on the scheme, he would be at risk as well. But if it worked, they could take down Jack Morris and neutralize Rudolf McCall. By any reckoning it was a risk worth taking.

78

BLACK CASTLE TO QUEEN SEVEN

Rook Takes Rook

Jim Duke smiled when he read the article posted on Politico. When he saw Sophia Cantu take her accusations to MSNBC, his eyes narrowed and his grin twisted with sarcasm: "Your ass is mine!" He was a wealthy man, richly compensated for his service to the Koch brothers. He had no need to skim or misuse campaign funds for his own benefit. Of course, that hadn't stopped at least a dozen others he could think of offhand but in this particular case, he was an innocent man.

He had his staff draft and disseminate a statement of protest and called MSNBC while Cantu was still on camera with Christopher Bay. Once his identity was verified, Bay took his call live and allowed the two to interact in a heated exchange.

Bay: We have Jim Duke on the line. Mr. Duke, can you hear me?

Duke: Yes.

Bay: Have you heard Ms. Cantu's accusation?

Duke: I have and I categorically deny it. I don't know where Ms. Cantu gets her information but I can assure you there's absolutely no truth to it.

Bay: You're saying you've never used funds from Americans for America First for your own personal benefit?

Duke: That's exactly what I'm saying. I find it offensive

and I demand a retraction and an apology.

Bay: Ms. Cantu, would you like to respond?

Cantu: I have the information right here. Mr. Duke, as Director of Americans for America First, you hired at least two private contractors, Data and Information Processing Services and Equity Management Limited, using AAF funds.

Duke: Those companies provided services to Americans for America First.

Cantu: Those companies specialize in setting up complex financial networks to hide questionable transactions and establish off shore accounts to avoid paying taxes.

Duke: Where did you get this information?

Cantu: That's not your concern. We happen to know that you reduced your tax liability in the same timeframe by employing exactly those strategies. Do you deny it?

Duke: What I do with my private finances is my business! I can tell you this: I never used AAF money for any purpose not related to Americans for America First.

Cantu: If what you're saying is true there's an easy way to prove it. Open the books and let the public see the expenditures!

Duke: As a 501 organization, we have a right and an obligation to protect our contributors.

Cantu: I'm not asking you to reveal your contributors. I'm asking you to reveal your expenditures. If nothing's there you have my word: I'll apologize and withdraw from this campaign.

Duke: I have your word?

Cantu: That's right.

Duke: Ms. Cantu, you have a deal. My people will contact your office to arrange the details. I look forward to your apology.

Jim Duke clicked off feeling larger than a titan. He felt he'd won a major victory and he was pleased it played out in the spotlight of national media coverage. That it took place on MSNBC, the bastion of liberal media, made it even more gratifying. Within minutes, however, he received a call from Rudolf McCall of the Freedom Network that reduced him to a blubbering fool. How could he promise to open the books? Did he have any idea the risk he was taking? Did he even know what was in the books? Before he cut off he informed him that he would be calling Jack Morris to formulate a damage control strategy.

Duke had the impression that he would be expected to fall on his own sword and it did not sit well. Until the exchange with McCall it had not occurred to him that anything incriminating or embarrassing loomed on the expenditure side of the AAF ledger. Now he wondered. His certainty that he had not done anything wrong or at least anything for which he could be prosecuted disintegrated like an ice sculpture on a warm day. He knew that neither McCall nor Morris nor the Koch brothers would hesitate to sacrifice him if it meant protecting themselves.

He did what most men do when surrounded by adversaries more powerful than himself: he vacillated. His staff went about their business preparing the relevant documents for release. He sat in his office examining them page after page, line by line. He soon discovered the source of concern. While everything technically went through his office and required his approval, some allocations went over his head. One of them was for personnel from Data and Information Processing Services. They were assigned to the Wynn campaign under the authority of Jack Morris. The other was for Equity Management Limited, a transfer account from Rudolf McCall to the same campaign, also under the authority of Jack Morris.

The Koch brothers sent word that he should take no action until he received instructions from them. A day later they sent a team to handle "final preparations" of the documents in question. He knew without asking what they were tasked to do: Edit out the names of Morris and McCall along with any references to the Wynn campaign or the Freedom Network. He wondered what in hell they expected him to say about the entries. Surely they understood he would have to offer some explanation. What were they hired to do? What was their assignment?

He called Morris who refused to take his call. He called McCall and received the same response. He called the Koch brothers and was told through a staffer he could say whatever the hell he wanted as long as he left them out of it.

So this is how it was: They were all cutting him loose and expecting him to take the fall like a good little soldier. Every man for himself. Survival mode. He called Data and Information Processing Services. They told him they were working the precincts in Florida and could offer no further information. He called Equity Management. They told him they were handling the financing for DIPS. He asked where the money originated. They said it came through Americans for America First.

He asked both companies to issue a statement that neither had performed any services at his request and they complied. With those statements in hand he released the documents on line and waited for a response. Within the hour he accepted an invitation from MSNBC to appear on the Christopher Bay show with Sophia Cantu.

Bay: Some of you may recall a rather heated exchange on this program between my guest, Sophia Cantu, a fundraiser for the Duran campaign, and Jim Duke, director of the conservative 501 group Americans for America First. In that exchange Ms. Cantu accused Mr. Duke of using money from AAF for his own personal benefit. Mr. Duke called in and emphatically denied that charge. Ms. Cantu challenged Mr. Duke to open the books and if she was wrong promised to withdraw from the campaign. Mr. Duke accepted the challenge. Let the record show that upon first examination it appears that the documents do not support Ms. Cantu's accusation. Tonight we welcome both Ms. Cantu and Mr. Duke to our program. How are you, Mr. Duke?

Duke: I'm well. Thank you for giving me the opportunity to clear my name and set the record straight.

Bay: You're welcome. Ms. Cantu, I want to thank you for returning to the program under these circumstances. It can't be very pleasant for you.

Cantu: I can assure you it isn't but I am prepared to honor my word. It appears I was wrong, I was misinformed, and I owe my sincere apologies to Mr. Duke.

Bay: Mr. Duke, do you accept Ms. Cantu's apology?

Duke: I do. We all make mistakes. I can only hope Ms. Cantu will be more careful in the future before she makes public accusations of wrongdoing.

Bay: Ms. Cantu, you promised to resign you position with the Duran campaign in the event you were proven wrong. Are you prepared to keep that promise?

Cantu: I have every intention of keeping my promise. We do however have a few questions regarding these documents. For example, what services did Equity Management and Data and Information Processing provide?

Duke (fidgeting): I can only tell you what I know and what the companies told me: Data and Information Processing is working the precincts in Florida. Equity Management is providing financing for the program.

Bay (eyes wide): Precinct work? What? Do you mean they're running a get-out-the-vote program?

Duke: As far as I know.

Bay: Let me get this straight: You authorized this program. You signed for them. But you don't know exactly what they're doing?

Duke: Look, what's important is that these companies did not perform any services at my request or for my benefit. I have signed statements...

Bay (discombobulated): Wait, wait, wait. Something doesn't add up here. These are your hires, this is your program, but you don't know exactly what they're doing?

Duke (flustered): That's all I can tell you.

Bay: Did you make these hires?

Duke: They passed through my office.

Bay: Did you sign for them?

Duke: Not specifically, no.

Bay (dumfounded): Maybe we're talking to the wrong person. Is there anyone at Americans for America First who can explain these expenditures?

Duke: I don't think so. If I were you, I'd ask the people at DIPS and Equity Management. Maybe you'll have better luck than I did.

It was an astounding interview. Jim Duke had opted to turn on those who left him holding the proverbial bag. In its wake Sophia Cantu did in fact withdraw from the campaign as the media began a frenzied investigation into what would come to be called the DIPS Scandal.

79

WHITE BISHOP TO QUEEN'S BISHOP FOUR

Bishop Captures Queen

Chauncey Davis was fully prepared to help the investigation along. His team had tracked every move, every communication and every decision since Sophia Cantu's public accusation aimed at Jim Duke. They knew that McCall contacted Duke. They knew that Duke reached out for help to Morris, McCall and the Koch brothers. They knew that Duke was thrown under the bus, discarded like milk well beyond its expiration date. They knew that Duke would not go down without a fight.

More importantly, they knew that a team from the Wynn campaign had altered the accounts of Americans for America First. All things electronic are accessible. They had a copy of the original and documentation imbedded in code of the time and date of its alteration.

Morris was the target and Davis had him in his sights. They leaked the original documents with references to Morris and McCall to several websites including WikiLeaks and Politico. When stories were published citing the documents as speculative and unconfirmed, they followed up with communication logs and telephone records. That was enough for several websites to run with it but it was not enough for the mainstream media. They needed more. They needed a source. They needed someone to interview whose credibility they could judge. They needed someone to sit down with, have a cup of coffee and observe. How many ways are there to figure out a person is lying? They needed someone to write about, talk about, a protagonist or antagonist, a hero or anti-hero. They needed a sacrificial lamb.

At some fundamental level he knew it would come to this. Politics is a game of chess. You have to give in order to take. He called a reporter at the Times and arranged a meeting to lay out his case.

80

BLACK PAWN TO QUEEN'S BISHOP FOUR

Pawn Takes Bishop

When the story broke and the frenzied reporting began Morris knew he had arrived at his personal endgame. He took some consolation in the fact that it required a brilliant and costly series of moves and ultimately the betrayal of an ally to take him out. He didn't hold a grudge against Jim Duke. He and McCall had cut him loose. Duke had only responded as he would have done in another time and place.

Chauncey Davis was done. He had a man following his every move ever since Sophia Cantu came to visit him. Damned shame he hadn't figured out what he was up to in time to alter the result. Only after the story broke did the pieces fall into place. Davis would soon find himself under investigation for illegal espionage. Whether he was indicted or not, convicted or not, sentenced to jail or not, his part in the campaign was done.

Morris almost looked forward to his last session with the big man. No, he did look forward to it. He could see the exasperation and despair on the big man's face, his "all is lost" or "woe is me" look. Wynn as the lamenting Hamlet: "How all occasions do inform against me!" Yes, at some level he would very much enjoy it. He summoned Wynn to his office.

"I've got good news and bad news," he opened.

"For Christ sake cut the crap, Morris! I've read the paper! This is a goddamned crisis and you're giving me puzzles?"

"Take it easy, big man. The sky's not falling. You'll live to fight another day."

"Well that's reassuring."

"The good news is: You can still win this thing. The bad news is: You've got to cut me loose to do it."

"Cut you loose?"

"That's right."

"Not an option."

"It's the only option. The fact is I'm guilty as hell. The voters don't take kindly to disenfranchisement and neither can you if you want to win."

"Cut the crap, Jack. We both know I don't have a pig's chance in a slaughterhouse without you."

"Cute, Wynn. Two weeks ago I'd have agreed with you. Today I have to tell you that it's the opposite of true. The best and probably the only chance you have now is to go on camera and explain how you had to let your closest advisor go, how you just can't sanction any actions that would deny any citizen the right to vote. Democracy is too important, more important than any campaign or any one person. You know the act. It writes itself. You can take a hard line if you want but that's what you have to do."

Wynn went silent. He sat down and took a breath. He knew his campaign manager was right. If it was anyone but Morris he wouldn't have hesitated.

"Tell me, Jack, how did you let this happen?"

"That's a tough one, Daniel. I dropped my guard, got caught watching the wrong target, took my eye off the game. The short answer is: I got outplayed. But I guarantee you it'll cost them. It already has. You've still got a few moves left, my friend. My final revenge will be watching you deliver your inaugural address."

Wynn rose and shook the hand of his mastermind.

"I'll never forget what you've done for me, Jack."

"Just take it home, big man. Keep it simple and don't do

anything stupid. If you can stick to that, you'll be living in the White House come January."

81

WHITE QUEEN TO KING'S CASTLE EIGHT

Queen Takes Castle

Winfred Holmes accepted Chauncey Davis' resignation with profound gratitude and regret. He promised to provide for his legal defense should it come to that. He had reason to believe the case would not be pursued once Davis had withdrawn from the campaign. In any case he could not afford to be distracted until the election was over.

With Davis out, it fell to Holmes to the finish the job Sophia Cantu had begun. The elimination of Jack Morris struck a blow that could not be underestimated but the same evidence that indicted Morris also indicted Rudolf McCall of Freedom Network. He could not be allowed to escape a similar fate.

He knew McCall. Everyone in the game knew McCall. Despite his rightwing conservative philosophy and the most biased news network in modern history, McCall had been known to strike a deal with politicians on the opposite side of the divide, most notably the Clintons. First and foremost, McCall was a businessman and his eye was always on the bottom line.

Holmes called to request a meeting and McCall readily accepted. He then flew to New York and rendezvoused in the restaurant of McCall's favorite hotel. McCall's table in the rear was separated from the general public and afforded them an assurance of privacy. They began their discussion with a recounting of the campaign and an assessment of how thing's stood. McCall believed that Wynn was still well positioned for victory. Holmes could only smile.

"So much for niceties, Mr. Holmes. I know you didn't fly to New York in the midst of a campaign just to chat."

"And people say you lack insight."

"Can I assume you have a proposition?"

Holmes nodded. "We both know you were involved in the great disenfranchisement scheme that caught your colleague, Mr. Morris, in its web."

"Pure speculation," McCall smirked.

"Your name is on the documents. You provided the financing. Whether you knew what that program was about is an open question."

"I'll take my chances in court."

"How'd that work out for you in the UK?"

"It was your man who committed espionage."

"He uncovered a wrongdoing and paid a price."

Freedom Network had lost a major lawsuit in Britain for tapping the phones of private citizens, including victims of violent crimes and their relatives. It cost McCall a great deal in both money and prestige.

"Let's just say: I would prefer not to go to trial."

"I can't promise you that. I can however promise you that you will go to trial if certain reasonable expectations are not fulfilled."

"I'm listening."

"I would expect a fairly balanced coverage of the candidates in the waning days of this campaign. By that I mean no unsubstantiated hit pieces, no speculative journalism and no October surprises."

McCall took a moment to process the proposal. The conversation was of course being recorded but Holmes probably anticipated that. His words could hardly be interpreted as a threat since he was only asking for fairness.

"It is a little difficult to define those expectations."

"Like pornography, we know it when we see it."

McCall smiled. He enjoyed his interaction with Holmes and trusted him. Though they fought on opposite sides in political warfare, he considered him a worthy and honorable adversary.

"In exchange, you and your people will not bring suit."

"That is correct."

"And the Justice Department, the FEC?"

"I can't and won't influence the actions of government agencies."

They left business behind while they enjoyed a four-course meal and superb bottle of California merlot. As McCall lit an after-dinner cigar, Holmes stood to take his leave. McCall stood and extended his hand.

"I've always liked you, Mr. Holmes. We have a deal."

Holmes nodded and completed a firm handshake.

"Who do you think will win?" he asked.

"If I were a betting man, Mr. McCall, and I am, I would not bet against Shelby Duran."

McCall laughed.

82

BLACK CASTLE TO QUEEN THREE

Jim Duke recognized that these were desperate times. In the wake of his own actions he had witnessed a critical shift in the balance of power. A staffer who couldn't organize a company barbecue no less strategize a winning campaign had replaced Jack Morris. In the waning days of a close election he suddenly felt alone, his only surviving ally of any real significance was Rudolf McCall of Freedom News.

He felt somehow responsible for the demise of Morris, the mastermind and chief strategist from the inception of the Wynn candidacy, possibly because he was. It didn't matter that Morris turned on him. It was his duty to take the fall if that's what the cause required. He had failed at that duty. Surely the Koch brothers were aware of his failure. They would take no action before Election Day because frankly they needed him. But once the campaign ended the hammer of retribution would swing.

His best hope (in fact his only hope) was to take decisive action for a Wynn victory. He still had a few tricks in his bag and no time to vacillate. He had a story ready to go, a sordid tale of illicit international romance and betrayal in which then Secretary of State Shelby Duran had an affair with a German ambassador and passed state secrets that may have made their way to our adversaries in Russia.

As with every good propaganda piece it contained a seed of truth. Prior to her marriage, Duran had dated the German ambassador for a brief period of time. No state secrets or information of substance had been exchanged although speculations of that nature had appeared in that part of the

Internet world that thrives on speculation. The speculations had occasionally made their way to print. Duke used selected quotes from those speculations in preparing the story and the ads that would follow, as if they came from reputable sources. At the least the Duran campaign would waste valuable time disproving the allegation. It would leave a mark of doubt in the minds of voters as they entered the polling place.

He fed the story to his connections in the secondary media of the web and sent a copy to Freedom News. He would wait for the story to be covered by Freedom before he launched the ad campaign.

He waited and waited and waited. On the third day he called Freedom News. Rudolf McCall refused to approve the story and they would not air it without his approval.

WHITE QUEEN TO QUEEN'S CASTLE EIGHT

Holmes observed the manipulations of Jim Duke and was pleased to see that McCall had kept his word. Freedom News would not be a willing conspirator in the waning days of this campaign. It was new ground, uncharted territory, and politicos would spend years speculating on why McCall stood down.

With McCall neutralized and Morris out of the game, it came down to him against Jim Duke. It narrowed the field of possibilities. In the absence of new developments, an October surprise, he liked Duran's chances. There would be no "shenanigans" in Florida or elsewhere. For once in modern history it would come down to the voters.

His remaining task was two-fold: Keep Duke in check while maintaining the attack on Wynn. Duke was smart, experienced and unscrupulous, but he was not in the same league as Morris. He was under a great deal of pressure and now that he came to the realization that he was the last man standing the pressure would only build.

Holmes added to the pressure by debunking Duke's latest hit piece strictly on the back channels of the worldwide web. He had his best operative, Moses Dunn, trailing Duke but he cautioned him to keep his distance. He was not to do anything of questionable ethics or legality. He was simply to observe and report. If Duke stupidly went after Dunn, Holmes would take him down.

Desperate men make desperate moves.

BLACK PAWN TO QUEEN'S BISHOP THREE

For most of a long campaign Darren McGhee had played but a small role as a spy in the Wynn campaign. He gained notoriety as the man who took down Chauncey Davis in the chain of events that forced Jack Morris to resign. Their side knew he had provided evidence of illegal espionage to the Florida attorney general's office. The other side did not.

Duke called upon him now to get as close as he could to the Duran camp, to uncover something, anything that could be used against her in the closing days.

It was long shot. It was the last wager of a gambler after a long night at the tables. McGhee shook his head and promised to do his best.

WHITE QUEEN TO QUEEN'S CASTLE FOUR

Check

Wynn delivered his farewell to Jack Morris address with sincerest remorse. He made the rounds of television interviews, town halls and press conferences, lamenting the loss of his closest advisor and confidant. He conveyed a balance of anger, sorrow and renewed determination. Dirty politics had ripped at the heart of his campaign but he summoned the strength to carry on.

It played well but it was all an act and after a while the act gets old. He had nothing but yes men left to guide him. His repeated attempts to contact Morris were rebuffed. With Morris out of the game his response to the latest crisis in the Middle East was knee jerk, contrasting starkly with Duran's reasoned analysis. He invariably took the hard line: Nobody messes with Wynn.

Holmes took the opportunity to renew the Daisy ad campaign in all the battleground states, featuring the latest Wynn footage. The pressure mounted and Wynn responded like a man lost in a deep forest without a compass. At times it almost seemed he was ready to give up the fight but he marched on like the good soldier he was.

BLACK KING TO KING ONE

Faced with the backlash of his hard line stance on the situation in Syria, Wynn asked himself: What would Morris do? The answer seemed clear: Retreat. He was reaching the end of a hard fought campaign. He was tired. The lines in his face, his whole demeanor, spoke of a man who had been tested. As president he would not be so quick to react. He would consider the options. He would seek the advice of those more knowledgeable than himself. The voters had no reason to fear that he would lead them to war.

But the voters did fear. They wondered if a man could not stand up to the pressures of a campaign, how would he withstand the pressures of the presidency?

WHITE PAWN TO KING'S BISHOP FOUR

Holmes recognized the endgame. They had done all they could to secure a Duran victory. They had proven beyond all doubt that theirs was the better candidate and would become the better president. Now it was time to pull back and let it play out. He pulled the attack ads and went positive. He instructed his operatives to stand down. He told Moses Dunn to go home and be with his family. Barring the unexpected, some dramatic event, an unconscionable gaff or desperate attack, they would simply count the days to the election and let the ballots decide.

BLACK PAWN TO KING'S BISHOP FIVE

Moses Dunn was largely a creature of habit. With his role in the Duran campaign effectively concluded he returned to his duties as a private investigator. Every Friday afternoon before going home he went to the same corner bar and grill for a couple of beers and the company of familiar faces. On this Friday an attractive woman he had never seen before caught his eye with a suggestive glance. As she walked over he knew exactly what was what.

"How can I do you for?" he inquired.

"I thought you might need a little company."

She stood one hand on hip, batted her lashes and waited.

"Got plenty of that, darling."

"Give a girl a break, mister. I'm just looking for a friendly conversation."

"I know exactly what you're looking for, my dear, and it ain't friendly conversation. What I don't know is who sent you: Was it Duke or Wynn or is Morris back in the game?"

Realizing her cover was blown, she acted offended as she turned on her heels and walked out the door.

Dunn held up his glass for a toast: "Must be amateur night around here."

WHITE KING TO QUEEN'S BISHOP ONE

Behind closed doors Shelby Duran had to admit she was tired. The intense support and energy of her followers kept her going. They gathered at her rallies by the hundreds and thousands. They wrote letters to the editors of their local papers. They contributed money and held fundraisers. They volunteered to canvas neighborhoods house-to-house, door-to-door. They painted signs, organized town hall meetings and designed websites. Wherever she appeared they chanted: "We want Shelby!" and "Duran for President!" Their collective enthusiasm gave her strength.

She accepted her campaign manager's solemn advice: Now was not the time to go off script. Now was not the time to make news or make bold statements. Now was the time to keep it simple and straightforward.

Holmes looked out at the crowd in Philadelphia, a diverse population of young and old, black and white, brown, yellow and red, a crowd filled with the hope of a new and better world, a crowd that represented all of America and all of the reasons she wanted the job. As she was taking the stage, he whispered:

"Be presidential, Shelby, and they will make you president."

BLACK CASTLE TO QUEEN TWO

There comes a time in any campaign when you realize you've done all you can. Nothing remains but to wait and see. You hope your enemy will make a mistake and prepare to pounce if she does. If she does not, you just wait.

Jim Duke had reached that final realization but it was not in his nature to simply wait. He studied the polls. How any voter could still be undecided was beyond understanding. In modern presidential campaigns everything that can be said has been said. Every argument has been argued with dizzying repetition. Every nuance had been explored and every bias exploited. The only way you could not have made up your mind at this stage of the game is if you were isolated from the world for the last eighteen months or you just don't give a damn. Why would such a person even bother to vote? And yet a significant percentage of the voters still claimed to be undecided.

The only objectives left to him were voter turnout and winning the inexplicable undecided in the critical states. The polls hovered within the margins in both Pennsylvania and Florida. He decided in the final two weeks of the campaign he would pull most of his ads from the other forty-eight and focus on those two. Wynn would need to win both if he hoped to become the next president. It was still within reach.

WHITE QUEEN TO QUEEN'S CASTLE SEVEN

Holmes liked where they stood. By his calculations they had more than enough electoral college votes to win the White House. They could win even without Florida and Pennsylvania. The Wynn campaign had to win both. Without disenfranchisement or vote flipping or ballot tampering Wynn could not win and neither Jack Morris nor Rudolf McCall could come to his rescue.

Holmes waited and watched. When Americans for America First shifted their ad campaign to the critical states, he countered by doing the same. They had a debunking ad for every attack their adversaries could mount. Moreover, the relentless attacks began to make the Wynn people appear desperate.

He liked where they stood and there was little left to do but wait and watch.

PLAYERS

Resignation

Ten days before the election Solana and Willy gathered at the birthplace of democracy: Athens, Greece. They spent the day absorbing the memories of ancient carved stone: The circle of leading Athenian thinkers, the teachings of Aristotle, the persecution of Socrates and the very seed of democracy: one man, one vote. Yes, they were all white men of great wealth but they planted the seed and the seed grew into a mammoth oak and the oak produced seed that the wind scattered, the rains nourished and a forest grew from fertile soil.

Then a man with an ax cut down a tree to build a house and more men came to build a village. Then came industry to harvest the trees like fruit in a canning plant and the forest was no more.

"Who are we?" asked Solana. "In this metaphor who are we? Are we the seed, the oak, the house builder or the industrialist?"

"We are the Athenian philosophers," replied Willy with a strangely satisfied smile. "We exist on a plain above the forest, beyond the actions of common men."

"The overlords of the Acropolis," said Solana wistfully, as if in a dream, as if transported to the fifth century BC when Pericles oversaw the building of the Parthenon and the temple of Athena. "And yet we are but men and women, blood and flesh. We bleed, we thrive, we suffer, we heal, we find happiness and sorrow, we grow old and we die like any other human being. What right have we to meddle in the affairs of men?"

"What right has any man to be king, a woman to be queen, a prince or a pauper? We are who we were born to be. We have earned the right to play our roles."

"Have we?"

For two days they explored the ancient ruins in a city still crumbling from the intrigues of international finance. Greece and Spain and Ireland were pawns to the players of the monolithic global banking and commerce institutions that thought they could create wealth out of thin air like the alchemists of a former age creating gold from copper and tin.

Pawns to players: It was the way of the world from the very birth of civilization. It was written into the DNA of humankind, indelible, immutable, inevitable as death. Then again, even players inevitably recognize that they too must answer to greater forces: the weather, fate, mortality. In a very real sense, even players are pawns.

In the evening after dining they would sit on the veranda of Solana's villa, enjoying the view and the best red wine Athens could provide. As they exchanged thoughts on endless topics from ancient history to moral dilemmas and contemporary affairs, Willy studied the board. The board revealed the endgame status: He held his castle and four pawns. Solana held her queen and three pawns, a decisive and insurmountable advantage at this late stage.

There comes a time in every match where the last hope is to play for stalemate. One of the most difficult skills to master in the elegant game is the ability to close in for the kill. Some of the best-played matches end without a victor. Willy hoped that this was one of them.

He studied the possibilities. He pursued a thousand different scenarios. All of them led to the same conclusion: Only a careless mistake could spare him defeat. Solana was not a player to make a careless mistake. He fell back into contemplating how he could have allowed this to happen. It would consume months trying to understand the series of moves that cost him his queen and turned the match irrevocably in Solana's favor.

"You cannot change black to white or stop the sun from rising," she said.

He smiled. They both knew how this would end. They were only waiting for the moment. He reached over and tipped his king, the traditional gesture of resignation. No last minute interventions would be required. The polling places and counting process would be closely monitored. Any attempts to alter the vote would be quashed.

Therese Shelby Sinclair Duran would be elected the next president of the United States of America.

William Bates and Solana Rothschild would be married at Notre Dame Cathedral in Paris on Inauguration Day.

No one but they would know that the two events were intrinsically linked.

93

PLAYERS

Deus ex Machina

While the game of chess has near infinite possibilities, the board has only sixty-four squares, sixteen pieces on each side and two players in command according to a fixed set of rules. Applying the game to the real world was always an imprecise art. William and Solana took every precaution and anticipated as many variations and contingencies as humanly possible. When pieces acted against the intent of their masters, they took corrective action. When outside forces threatened the course of their match, they acted in concert with countermeasures.

They had always been able to overcome the problems and complications of lesser players until now. With only nine days to the election, an external force set in motion a series of events with indelible consequences. They turned the election on its head and, more importantly, negated the outcome and viability of the second real-world chess match between Solana Rothschild and William Bates.

They were livid. In retrospect, they could see the signs but they failed to take the threat seriously. They were only able to put the pieces together after the fact. They knew that the Russians had launched a propaganda and cyber war against Shelby Duran who had led the campaign to sanction Russia for its incursions in Ukraine and Crimea. They knew they had hacked the Democratic National Committee and used WikiLeaks to release damaging information and emails.

They knew they were engaged in a false news campaign, exploiting social media for its lack of fact checking.

They knew what the Russians were doing and why but they also knew they were notoriously bad at it. Their false news stories were absurd. No one but the absolute fringe even looked at them. Their email leaks, while effectively distracting the public by claiming valuable media attention, were fundamentally inconsequential. Who cared what Winfred Holmes thought of the intellectual curiosity of the former president's daughter?

What Solana and William did not know was that the Russians held a trump card: They had damning information regarding FBI Director James Collins. Collins had survived a major scandal that rocked the intelligence community four years prior but he left himself vulnerable. Russia swooped in and gathered enough incriminating information that they could effectively force the director to choose: Either go public with a new investigation into Secretary Duran's actions in the Congo which benefited her husband's major investments or they would go public with an entire series of hacked emails and intercepted communications. Collins chose what he considered the easy way out.

The accusations were bogus but the timing was perfect. The media went into frenzy mode trying to uncover fresh evidence of misdeeds by the candidate. Solana and Willy acted quickly with their own misinformation to compel Director Collins to issue a hasty retraction three days before the election but the damage was done.

That the outcome of both the election and their match was altered they had no doubt. Willy graciously conceded but Solana would have none of it. It was like a sporting event in which the league declared after the fact that the game officials made critical errors that would have altered the final score. It mattered to no one – least of all those who won or lost bets on the game. The outcome stood. It could not be negated.

The wedding would have to be postponed. All arrangements in Paris, including hotel reservations and Notre Dame Cathedral, were canceled at great expense. Willy pleaded with her to reconsider but she held firm. If anything her anger only grew in the days following the election. She remained behind the walls of her estate in Cornwall, refusing to answer the phone or engage in any other forms of communication. It took weeks for her to calm down enough to accept Willy's invitation to dinner.

He had her transported by helicopter and limousine to one of their favorite restaurants in London. Over appetizers Willy cautiously broached the subject.

"It is most unfortunate," he confided, "that we could not prevent it before it happened but we knew the risks. We could not possibly control all variables. What would you have me do?"

"You shouldn't have to ask," replied Solana.

The content of her remark and the casual tone employed to deliver it pushed him back a step. Was she actually suggesting that he arrange the assassination of the president? She observed his dissonance before releasing him with a smile.

"There is only one party I hold responsible for this breech, this unpardonable intrusion, this interference in the affairs of privilege. It is not the Director of the FBI, though he certainly deserves some measure of retribution. It is not the unwitting president of the United States. It is the so-called president of the Russian Federation, Vladimir Dmitri Putin, who is responsible for this crime."

Willy was once again surprised though he tried in vain not to show it.

"How can you hold Putin responsible for doing precisely what we intended to do? What is his crime? That he succeeded where we did not?"

Putin is a despicable man. He has murdered political opponents, invaded sovereign nations, inflicted hardships on generations of people in his own country as well as others. We have merely engaged in a civilized game, a match of wits from which neither of us stood to benefit. What we have done bears no resemblance to what this monster has done."

"You hold him personally responsible?"

"I do."

He could see that she was determined and would not yield. He would have no choice but to accept her point of view or watch their bond slowly crumble. He could agree that Putin was a bad actor and a man guilty of many crimes if not this particular one. He was also aware that Putin was the unchallenged leader of the largest nation on earth. He had unfettered access to all the resources of the state. Because there were no real checks on his authority, he was arguably the most powerful leader on earth.

"Very well, my dear. Let us agree that Putin is accountable for this tragedy. The question remains: What can we do about it?"

Solana sipped her wine, an exquisite Chateau Lafite Rothschild from Bordeaux, and calculated her next move.

"I have given this matter a great deal of thought. I am acutely aware of the risks. I am also aware that we have polished our skills and developed the networks and associations required to accomplish our next goal."

He dreaded the next words she would speak but he knew there was no other way – not if he intended to spend the rest of his life at Solana's side...and he did.

"What goal is that, my dear?"

She smiled broadly, raised her glass, and delivered her coup de grace.

"We end the reign of Vladimir Putin once and for always!"

He smiled and raised his glass in kind.

"Let it be so."

ABOUT THE AUTHOR

Jack Random has lived an ordinary and extraordinary life. His roots firmly planted in the fertile central valley of California, he has marched the streets in protest, haunted jazz town bars, read poetry in cafes and town squares, strutted his hour upon the stage, crisscrossed the country by air, rail, highway and thumb, mourned at Wounded Knee, gazed into the eyes of the crow at Grand Canyon, and paid tribute at the grave of Geronimo. He has labored in the fields of plenty, toiled on the assembly line, pursued higher education and attempted to enlighten children in the public schools. He has been a pilgrim and a seeker of truth. He is married to the love of his life. All the while he has chronicled his thoughts and revelations in words: plays, poetry, novels, stories and essays. His first novel *Ghost Dance Insurrection* (Jazzman Series) was originally published by Dry Bones Press (2000).

OTHER BOOKS FROM CROW DOG PRESS

Wasichu: The Killing Spirit – A Novel by Jack Random. A modern day telling of the life of Crazy Horse recalls the history of Native America and its most revered leader.

Number Nine: The Adventures of Jake Jones and Ruby Daulton – A Novel by Jack Random. A woman on the run picks up a hitchhiker and takes us on an adventure that winds its way to New Orleans in the summer of Katrina.

A Patriot Dirge – A Novel by Jack Random. Political genius Roman Mason takes on the political and economic forces that rule our lives.

Jazzman Chronicles: Volumes I–X – Essays by Jack Random. Wide-ranging commentaries from 2000 to 2014.

A Mother's Story – Stories, Art and Reflections by Artis Brown Miller. A mother of eight children reflects on a life of hardship and love.

Pawns to Players: The Stairway Scandal – A Novel by Jack Random. An aristocrat and a billionaire play a chess match to determine the fate of the American government.

The Grand Canyon Zen Golf Tour – A Memoir by Jack Random. Two friends embark on a journey of golf, music, poetry and family in the summer of 1993.

Hard Times: The Wrath of an Angry God – A Novel by Jack Random. Civilization collapses and a father is forced to make a hard choice.

Made in the USA
Middletown, DE
22 January 2023

22853938R00191